# WRAITH

Edie Claire

For Grace, and dancers everywhere.

# chapter one

I squinted into the sun with one eye to see sun-bronzed legs and a dripping wet pair of board shorts. The guy attached to them dropped down onto the sand next to my beach mat and stretched out beside me. Given that I had never seen him before and didn't have a clue who he was, you might think I would be intrigued enough to open both my eyes. But I only needed a peek from the one to know that he was dead.

I closed the eye with a sigh and settled back into the sun. He looked about my own age, too. I hadn't even seen any other high schoolers yet, much less met one, and I'd been scoping out the beach ever since we arrived. If I didn't meet anyone during spring break, I'd be stuck trying to make friends over the summer, which—as any other military brat could tell you—totally sucks. My mom, dad, and I were set to move to Oahu in June, and if I didn't make progress during this house-hunting trip, I'd be a loner from then till September.

*Hawaii.* The irony was too cruel, really. I had wanted to move here since forever. All my life, every time a transfer came up, this was what my fingers had been crossed for. Any time except now, it would have been perfect. Back then I had gotten hauled off to Biloxi, Mississippi. San Antonio, Texas. Bangor, Maine. Only in March of my junior year, when I was happily entrenched in Cheyenne, Wyoming, when I had only one more year of high school left, and when I had the most awesome friends in the entire world to spend it with... only *then* had my dad gotten the order.

But I was determined to make the best of it. The sun was warm, the palm trees were swaying in the brisk ocean wind, and somewhere in the distance roosters were crowing. (The last was a surprise. Who knew there were wild chickens in Hawaii?) I *would* meet some of the locals—just as soon as my parents found a house and we figured out what high school I'd be going to. In the meantime, I would settle for one friendly, helpful person, whether we ended up at the same school or not. The guy lying next to me would have been a great find, if he hadn't drowned a decade ago. Or suffocated in a sand pit. Or whatever.

A thought struck. He couldn't have died that long ago, not with those board shorts. They were the same style all the other surfers on the North Shore were wearing right now.

I opened both eyes, propped up on an elbow, and studied him. He appeared to be resting after a long, exhausting surf session. He lay flat on the sand next to me, elbows out, his hands locked behind him to cradle a head of sea-soaked, dark blond curls. He was lean, built like an athlete. His face...

I turned my eyes away. What was the point in torturing myself? He didn't go to high school here, or anywhere. Even if he did, no guy who looked like he did would give a girl like me a second look, much less show me around the island and introduce me to his friends.

I was able to look elsewhere for exactly four seconds. Then I went back to staring. The guy *was* young— seventeen or eighteen. Nineteen, tops. He was also downright gorgeous, with the face of an angel and a body that looked like it had stepped out of an ad for some seriously cool jeans.

I leaned closer, trying to see what color his eyes were,

but he had them closed against the sun. I wondered if the light had been just as bright—and shining from the same direction—the day that he had been here.

How long ago was that? It must have been recently; maybe even this past winter, when the surf was at its highest. The North Shore's winter waves—monstrous swells that often topped twenty feet high—could be lethal, even for the professionals. And he seemed so... *present.* His body was near solid enough to have fooled me. Unlike the older shadows, the transparency wasn't visible everywhere—it merely floated through him, like ripples. If I hadn't seen the blue sole of one of my discarded flip-flops quite clearly through his left thigh as he lay down, I might not even have suspected.

I watched him doze a moment more, then sighed and lay back down on my mat. "The cute ones are always dead," I muttered.

The feeling came over me like a cold prickle. The feeling that I was being watched. I didn't hear him move. I didn't feel him stirring. I wouldn't anyway, because the shadows can never *move* anything, except whatever equally nonexistent things they happen to be carrying with them. But still, when I opened my eyes to find him leaning over me, staring intently into my face, I was surprised. I was more than surprised. I was totally freaked.

"What did you say?" he asked.

I sucked in a breath and held it. His voice was a beautiful baritone—smooth and deep, even if it did crack just a little at the beginning. He looked at me with a bizarre intensity, as if the words were the most important he had ever said. His eyes, for the record, were amazing— green mixed with a light chestnut brown. At that moment, I would have given anything to believe he was talking to *me.*

He wasn't, of course. He had no idea I was even there. None of the shadows ever did. They appeared, disappeared, and reappeared on their own time and for their own reasons, reenacting moments of their lives which often seemed totally random to me, but which I had always assumed must have some significance to them. Otherwise, what was the point?

"Were you talking to me?" he asked again. His voice had dropped to a whisper, his features tense as he waited, breathlessly, for an answer.

I released my own pent-up breath slowly, then twisted my head, looking carefully to the right and left. Whatever shadow he was talking to had to be here somewhere. Why couldn't I see that one? Could I be lying on top of her?

I rolled over to the far edge of the mat and sat up. There was no one in the space I had left. Not even the faintest hint of a shape. That was odd.

When my gaze went back to him, my heart froze in mid beat. He was still looking at me. Not at me, where I was *then*, but at me, where I was *now*. His eyes had followed me.

I jerked my body quickly to one side, then looked back. Nobody.

He cocked his head at me quizzically for a moment. Then his face erupted into a smile. "You don't think I can see you," he announced, as if explaining to himself. "But I can. And you can see me, too. I knew it!" He leaned closer. "Say something to me. Anything. Please?"

My heart was no longer frozen. It had melted at the first sight of his smile, and was now beating so violently I was sure I'd bust a rib.

"You can hear me?" I said stupidly, blinking at him like a deer in headlights. As much as I wanted it to be true, I hadn't come to live so comfortably with the shadows without understanding the rules. I could see and hear them, but they were oblivious to me. They weren't real, and they weren't my concern. If I hadn't accepted that at an early age, I would never have slept at night. If I accepted this now, I might never sleep again.

"Don't be afraid of me," he said apologetically. His soft whisper sent an odd, prickly feeling up my spine, and my shoulders shuddered. "I'm nothing to be afraid of," he continued, "I swear."

The guy looked almost hurt. Words failed me. I sputtered and stuttered like an idiot. "I'm not afraid of *you*, exactly. I mean, it's not that..."

Another smile lit up his face. He had straight white teeth, perhaps just a trace of dimples. "You have no idea how good it is to be having a real conversation," he said cheerfully. "I don't know how it's possible, and I don't care. Just don't run away from me. Please?"

Was he a mind reader, too? Or had I actually sprung up, my feet poised to flee?

I looked down.

Yep. I had.

I took in a deep breath. I let it out. *In. Out.* There was no reason to freak. If a guy who looked like this one was talking to me in real life, then yes—I would be allowed to freak. If some other shadow had come alive, say one that weighed three hundred pounds and was swinging at me with a spiked club, then flipping out would be a perfectly reasonable reaction. But this guy was no threat to me. He couldn't hurt me. He was just another shadow.

Chill, girl.

"I'm not going to run away," I said, proud that my voice had steadied. With as much casual grace as I could muster, I sat back down on the mat beside him. "You just startled me, that's all. The shadows don't usually...

interact. What makes you different? Do you know?"

His brow furrowed. He shook his head, slowly. "I know absolutely nothing. Except this beach, those waves, and a whole lot of people who have no idea I'm even here." He grinned at me again. "Except you."

The shudder returned. I reminded myself, forcefully, that he was not alive.

"You say you see others like me?" he questioned, settling himself to face me, his torso propped up on one perfectly muscled arm. His outstretched fingers sank through the uneven surface of the sand without stirring it. Down the beach, a female surfer carried a short board toward the water, and as she passed behind him I could still see her in the occasional transparent ripple, first through his shoulder, then his chest. To say this was a distraction to conversation would be an understatement. "How do you know the difference?" he asked.

I gave my head a little shake to regroup. "You're not solid," I explained, feeling distinctly uncomfortable. I didn't talk about the shadows. Ever. To anyone. I hadn't mentioned one thing about them since I was five years old. "You're transparent, at least sometimes. Most of the shadows I see aren't nearly as solid as you are. They're more like wisps—some are barely there at all."

"But they don't talk to you?" he asked. "Do they know that you can see them?"

I allowed myself a deeper look in his eyes. My answers clearly meant a lot to him. He was even more confused than I was.

"They're not..." I searched for the right word. The last thing I wanted to do, given his unenviable situation, was hurt his feelings. "*Present*. They're not here, with me, on this particular day. I'm just seeing things that have happened in the past."

He was silent a moment. "Shadows," he repeated.

"That's right," I answered softly.

He turned to look toward the ocean, then rubbed his face in his hands. "I've never seen anything like that. I only see a bunch of normal, living people. And then there's me."

He didn't speak again, for a long time. I sat in silence beside him, listening to the crashing of the giant waves on the nearby shore, feeling the vibrations of their pounding on the sand. A sudden gust of wind kicked up, lifting my unruly locks of dark brown, curly hair and whipping them awkwardly around my face.

His own curls didn't stir.

He lifted a hand, tentatively, and attempted to restrain a particularly vicious tangle of curls from pummeling my left eye. I watched, my breath held, as his hand passed harmlessly, ineffectively, right through them.

His expression flashed, ever so briefly, of a biting pain. Then, just as quickly, a poor imitation of his smile returned.

"I guess it's for sure then," he said, his tone unnaturally chipper.

"I really am dead."

# chapter two

"There you are! I thought you said you wanted to go to Foodland with me this afternoon."

My mother's familiar, pleasant, perfectly ordinary voice knocked me out of the moment like a wrecking ball. I sprang to my feet and faced her. "What? Oh, right. Is it time already? Sorry—I wasn't paying attention."

I leaned down to roll up my beach mat, convinced, for one steadying second, that my conversation with the surfer had been nothing but a fantastical dream, inspired by a combination of hot sun, crashing waves, and jet lag.

My illusions along those lines were shattered when I saw his foot, which had been standing on the far corner of my mat, lift graciously out of the way. Never mind that it was both an empty gesture and a beat too late, as the mat began to slip through his foot the instant I pulled on it.

I raised my eyes hesitantly. He was watching my mother, his expression curious. She, of course, couldn't see him.

"Do you need to go back to the house first?" she asked. "Or can we go from here? The car's in the beach lot."

I glanced down at my perfectly decent cami and shorts—I never wore a swimsuit if I could help it—and told her I was ready.

"Are you okay?" she asked suddenly, studying me. "You look a little... frazzled."

"I'm fine," I answered too quickly, unable to meet her gaze. I was a rotten liar. Always had been. It didn't usually cause me a problem, because I didn't usually lie. Only about the shadows... and that was necessary for her own good. "I'm just out of sorts. I think I must have fallen asleep or something."

"You were sitting up when I got here," she said skeptically, shoving a lock of identically curly, dark brown hair from her own eyes. We looked a lot alike, my mother and I, except that—aside from being nearly forty years older—she always kept her hair short and the waistband of her jeans high. The last part, I was working on. What was harder to deal with was the fact that she was so blasted perceptive.

I cast another surreptitious glance at the surfer. He smiled back at me. My heart pounded.

"Can we stop at that roadside market up by Turtle Bay, too?" I babbled, employing the tried-and-true tactic of diversion. My mother was a highly intelligent woman, but she was easily distracted, particularly when food was involved. "I want to get some fresh mango. And pineapple too. I bet it's cheaper there."

With my best effort at casualness, I turned away from the beach—and the shadow—and headed toward the parking lot. I tried not to look back. What had I been thinking, talking to one of them like that? Ignoring the shadows was ingrained behavior; it was something I *had* to do. Ever since that horrible time in my childhood, the darkest in my parents' lives, when they honestly believed what multiple psychiatrists told them—that their otherwise happy, healthy little girl was desperately, hopelessly, mentally ill. I was the one who had saved them from that horror. It was easy enough, once I realized that all I had to do was lie.

But I couldn't help looking back.

He wasn't smiling anymore. He was standing on the beach right where I had left him, gazing after my mother and me with an expression I can only describe as melancholy. Yes, melancholy. Like something out of poem. In an instant, the sadness in his eyes seemed to leap the distance between us and stab at my gut like a knife.

My mother wasn't paying attention. She walked on ahead, stretched out her arm and pushed the remote button on her car keys. I knew I should keep on walking myself, but that wasn't possible. Dead or not, real or not, I couldn't just walk off and leave him there, forever, looking like that.

On my next step I twisted around a little. Then I stretched back an arm and waved goodbye.

I unloaded the groceries into the fridge, keeping one eye on the small sliver of beach I could just see out the picture windows in the great room of our condo. I tried to pretend I didn't know what I was looking for, but I was no better at lying to myself than anyone else. The surfer shadow was all I could think about.

It had to stop.

I could *not* let myself go back there, to that horrible place where a terrified five-year-old had been forced to decide whether the rest of the world was crazy—or she was. Against all odds, I had found a way out of that hell, and I was *not* going back. Not for anything. I had succeeded in ignoring the shadows for over a decade now, and I was doing just fine with that plan, thank you very much.

I finished putting away the groceries, grabbed a plastic baggie full of fresh, chilled mango, and headed out onto the deck. My mother had set off to collect my dad from the base and wouldn't be back for a couple hours. Hickham Air Force Base was at Pearl Harbor—a long haul

from the North Shore, perhaps, to a local. But to a family
from Wyoming, it was a donut run. Already I was struck
by the small scale of everything in Oahu. From our rental
on Sunset Beach, we could reach all the North Shore had
to offer in a matter of minutes. I only wished I had access
to a bike, as we had only the one borrowed car among the
three of us.

I settled into a patio chair, popped a juicy slice of
mango into my mouth, and prided myself on the fact that
I had just gone a whole sixty seconds without thinking
about the shadow. There *was* hope. Never mind that I had
been sure, on three occasions, that I had seen him skulking
around the Foodland. But that was ridiculous. The
shadows never changed location; they were always rooted
to particular spots, even if the location was no longer as
they might have remembered. I once saw a farmer plowing
away a good ten feet up in the air over the parking lot of a
shopping plaza that had been dug out of a hillside. The
shadows didn't give a hoot what was going on in the
present.

And I didn't give a hoot about them.

My cell phone buzzed in my pocket, and I dug it out
with a grin. I hadn't been at all sure I could get coverage
on a rock in the middle of the Pacific Ocean, but
technology is a wonderful thing. It was a text, from Kylee.

Hows the beach? Met any hot guys yet? TEXT
ME! Luv u!

My cheeks grew hot; I was thinking about *him* again.
Gritting my teeth with annoyance, I texted back quickly.

No hot guys yet, but the waves are awesome! Miss
u!!!

I sent off the reply with a flourish. I was *not* lying. Whatever I had seen on the beach, it was *not* a guy.

"I take offense at that, you know."

I sprang up so quickly my thighs banged under the iron patio table and lifted it off its feet. The voice had come from directly behind me, but I didn't need to whirl around to know that it was his.

"Are you saying I'm not hot?" he asked innocently, flashing another grin. "Or that I'm not a guy? I could take offense at either."

I forced my breathing to slow. I reached around behind me, grabbed another patio chair, and lowered myself into it before my knees could buckle.

"You *can't be here*," I said weakly. "It's not possible. You're supposed to stay at the beach."

"Really?" he answered, sitting down in the chair I had just left. Strangely, it looked as though he was fitting into its contours, even though his body had no weight to support. Could he *think* himself into a particular appearance?

"Perhaps you'd better teach me the rules, then," he continued. "Because I've been all up and down the North Shore. Never been inside Foodland before, though."

"That *was* you!" I said accusingly.

He smirked.

My heart raced. I felt slightly nauseous.

"Listen," I began, my voice unsteady. I had no idea what I was about to say. I only knew that a gazillion red lights were flashing in my brain, warning me, begging me, reminding me how huge a threat he posed.

I took a breath and started talking, my voice a mere squeak. "I don't know why I can see you, but I do know that I *shouldn't* see you. I can't deal with a talking shadow that follows me around. It's too... weird. And believe me,

I know weird. So please, no offense or anything, but will you do me a huge favor and just *go away*?"

He leaned towards me. In the slanting sunlight of late afternoon, his green eyes had a cast like a cool lagoon. His lashes were long and perfectly curled—way too pretty to belong to a guy. His blond curls looked dry now, and he had somehow changed into a new pair of board shirts and a tight swim shirt that molded perfectly over the muscles of his torso.

"You have mango in your teeth," he responded.

I turned my head away with a groan. Was he *trying* to torture me?

"Look—" he began, his tone placating. "Do you realize I don't even know your name? Why don't we start this over again?" He reached out a hand towards me as if to shake, but realized the error and jerked it back. "Hi there. My name is Zane. And yours?"

I turned to face him again, fairly certain I'd taken care of the mango. Either way, I could hardly feel more mortified than I already did. The alarm bells in my head still sounded, but their dire warnings refused to gel with what either my eyes were seeing or my ears were hearing. How could any... *being* that was so friendly and so beautiful be dangerous? "Kali," I answered flatly, spelling it out for him. I always did that, otherwise people spelled it "Collie," and I preferred not to be confused with a dog.

He smiled.

My heart skipped uncomfortably. I really wished he would stop that.

"That's a beautiful name. It sounds... Hawaiian."

There was a hesitancy in his voice, and the unspoken question touched me. He was trying to be sensitive, of all things. Because aside from having a dark complexion, I didn't look in the least bit Polynesian. My gray-blue eyes were far too light, my hair too curly, my nose too long. "It is," I admitted. "Kali is just a nickname. I was named 'Kalia' after my grandmother. I'm one-quarter Hawaiian, though you'd never know it from the hair and the giant schnoz. For those, I can thank the Greeks on my mother's side."

"Giant schnoz?" he repeated wonderingly. "You'd better watch that self-esteem. You have a beautiful nose. Among other things."

My cheeks flared red once more. How exactly had I gotten derailed from telling him to go away and never talk to me again?

"Zane's a nickname, too," he continued. He started to say something else, but stopped, the merriment in his eyes being replaced by frustration. "It's short for something. Zachary, I think. But I don't seem to know a whole lot about myself."

My brow furrowed. "What do you mean?"

He looked away from me, his eyes searching in the direction of the ocean. Following his gaze, I became aware, suddenly, of the sound of the waves crashing in the distance. They could be heard all the time at the condo, but after a while, just like traffic noise, they blended into the background of one's brain. I preferred to keep on hearing them.

"I told you earlier," he said quietly. "I don't seem to know anything except the beach. It's like I've been here forever, but that can't be right. I know I have a past, I can sense that I still remember things—but somehow, it's like I can't get to those memories anymore."

He sighed with exasperation. "I know I must be dead. I get that. But why can't I remember living? And why am I here?"

I swallowed. The warning lights pulsed at strobe speed

now. Already, whether he meant it to happen or not, he was drawing me back into the very darkness I feared. And I wasn't at all sure I could fight him. I was the worst sucker in the world when it came to people asking for help—Kylee and Tara teased me about it all the time. I was a hopeless bleeding heart.

But I *couldn't* help him, even if I wanted to. Even if the mere thought of trying didn't scare the crap out of me.

"I'm sorry, but I can't answer any of your questions," I said gently. "I don't know anything about it, except what I've already told you. This isn't some hobby that I enjoy. I don't *want* to see shadows; I try not to even think about them. It's the only thing that keeps me sane."

He studied me for a moment, silently. Then he leaned forward, holding my gaze. "But you can *talk* to me," he insisted. "Don't you understand how much that means? Do you have any idea what it's like to be ignored, day in and day out, by every other human being in sight... to be *invisible?*"

The warning lights sputtered; the clanging bells muted. My resolve was crumbling.

"There has to be some reason, Kali," he continued, showing no mercy. "Some reason why I found you, and that you can see me when no one else can. You have to help me."

I waited for it. I was not disappointed.

His voice dropped to a husky whisper. "*Please,* Kali."

I hung my head in my hands. I didn't answer him then. I was too busy composing another text to Kylee in my head. One I knew I could never actually send.

Just agreed to help totally hot dead guy walk into light. What's new with you?

# chapter three

I picked at my fruit salad, nervously banging my fork against the rim of my plate. My father was telling us about his day on the base, barely able to contain his enthusiasm about the new techno-gadgets and people he would soon be working with. Mitch Thompson was the definition of a glass-half-full kind of guy—spending the first half of his life training to become a fighter pilot and the second half convincing himself that it was actually a good thing that he could no longer meet the medical requirements, because flying was for the young and his technical skills were needed more on the ground anyway. My mother was laughing at his description of himself skipping around the base like a kid; we both knew that odds were, it was literally true.

"So Kali, Babe, what were you up to today?"

The fork dropped from my hand with a clatter. Not at my dad's unexpected question, but because somewhere between "Kali" and "Babe," the nearly perfectly solid figure of Zane had inserted itself in the empty chair across the table from my mother.

"Umm..." I responded mindlessly, my stupid cheeks flaring red again. "Not much. I just hung out on the beach, soaked up some sun."

"Did you meet anybody?"

Zane smirked at me, raising his eyebrows.

I forced my eyes back to my father. "No. I didn't see anybody my age. There were more surfers out today, though."

My father clapped his hands in delight. "Fabulous. I've got to get out there myself sometime this week."

"Over my dead body," my mother declared in a deadpan. "You promised. Lessons first. And down in Waikiki, not up here."

My father pretended disappointment. "Those wimpy little waves aren't any fun."

My mother smiled. "Precisely."

"And you remember what *you* promised?" he said slyly, leaning toward her.

"Unfortunately, yes," she responded.

My father winked at me. "After decades of begging and pleading, your mother's finally going to come surf with me, Kali. Make sure you have that video camera rolling!"

My mother rose from the table with her empty plate and headed toward the kitchen, smacking my father on the shoulder as she went. He laughed and dug back into his dinner.

I allowed myself a glance at Zane. He wasn't looking at me; he seemed totally amused by my parents. The Thompsons, who were older than the parents of most kids my age, often had that effect on people. They had married young and wanted children, but had trouble conceiving; my miraculous appearance in my mom's late thirties had really thrown them. Perhaps it was having a kid so late, perhaps it was something in the water—but my parents had always appeared blissfully unaware of their status as boring old married people. They had been together for over thirty years, but still acted like a couple of honeymooners.

I was used to that dynamic, of course. But Zane was looking at them as though they were a zoo exhibit.

"Oh, and I almost forgot," my father continued, catching me staring at an empty chair. "Got a surprise for you. I was talking to a couple of the officers about you—asking about high schools and such. One of them has a son who's also a junior, said he'd be real happy to show you around. We set it up for tomorrow afternoon. How's that for service?"

I opened my mouth, but nothing came out. I *would* like a tour guide, of course, but a blind rendezvous set up by parents had about as much chance of being fun as skating barefoot on asphalt. The guy had probably not even been asked if he wanted to do it.

"Well, what do you say?" my father pressed. "Did I do good, or what?"

I could feel Zane's eyes on me, but didn't dare glance his way. My father was looking extraordinarily pleased with himself, and for more than the obvious reason. It was his considered opinion, ever since I hit sixteen, that I spent way too much time with my girlfriends and needed to get out and date more.

I said my parents weren't normal.

"Sounds great, Dad," I forced out, attempting to hide my face in my plate. Mercifully, my cell phone chose that moment to vibrate in my pocket, and I dug it out like a lifeline. It was from Tara. I didn't need the phone to tell me so; Tara was the only person on the planet under thirty who always texted in complete sentences.

> What do you mean you haven't seen any hot guys yet? The serious surfers will be on the Banzai Pipeline at the south edge of 'Ehukai Beach. You don't have to get wet to watch them!

I rolled my eyes with a smile. I had no idea what pipeline she was talking about, or even what beach. When we found out I was coming to Oahu, Tara had done more research than I had. She was the undisputed queen of information; what she didn't know, she could always find out. She had promised to keep me informed of everything

I needed to make the most of my time while I was out here, and for someone sitting in a double-wide trailer in the middle of Wyoming, she was doing a pretty good job so far.

I only wished I could ask her about dead people.

"Kali," my mother reproached as she returned with dessert, "No texting at the table."

"Sorry," I said lamely, setting the phone down beside me. "It was from Tara. She was telling me that all the serious surfers would be at 'Ehukai Beach, wherever that is."

Zane sat up straight in his chair. "Are you kidding me? Where do you think you were all afternoon?"

My father spoke to me at the same time, creating a dizzying effect. "She means the pipe, of course. It's just down the beach. I told you that."

Zane threw my father an approving look. "What he said."

"Kali," my mother said simultaneously, "would you like some chocolate *haupia* pie?"

"I was surfing the pipe all morning!" Zane insisted. "Didn't you see me?"

"What's *haupia*?" my dad asked.

"Coconut cream," my mother answered. "And yes, I know it's rich, but we're on vacation, and I'm not too fat for my swimsuit yet. Kali?"

"If you were looking for guys your age," Zane continued, talking over my mother, "you *should* have noticed me. You really don't think I'm hot?"

"Yes, you are," I blurted, "it looks delicious."

My mother stopped cutting the pie and stared at me. My father stopped eating his fruit salad and stared at me.

Zane himself looked startled for a second. Then he fell back into his chair in a paroxysm of laughter.

My mind spun. What the *heck* had I just said?

"What I meant—" I spoke up quickly, then faltered. It was an explanation I had no idea how to finish. I wasn't sure how it had happened, but I was pretty sure I had just simultaneously called my mother fat and propositioned a dead guy.

"I mean you're entitled to a little treat," I said with blessed inspiration, keeping my gaze firmly on my mother. "We all are. After all, like you said, we're on vacation!"

I helped myself to a heaping portion of the pie and buried my scarlet face as deeply in it as possible. My parents' conversation turned studiously to the weather.

Out of the corner of my eye, I could see Zane doubled over in his chair, still laughing hysterically.

If he wasn't already dead, I would have killed him.

—⁓—

I stepped out of the shower, threw my hair up in a towel, and dried off. It felt good to get rid of the sand. It also felt good to have a little privacy.

Zane had disappeared from the table shortly after dessert, and had not had the decency to reappear the entire time I had waited for him alone on the deck afterwards. Perhaps that was because he knew why I was waiting for him.

I slipped on my most comfortable sleep shirt, brushed my teeth, and stepped out into the hall. Whatever had happened at dinner tonight, I was never doing it again. Either he agreed to my rules or I would simply ignore him, just as I did all the other, considerably less annoying dead people I saw every day. I *could* do it. And I *would* do it. Period.

I opened the door of my smallish corner bedroom and

walked in, enjoying the omnipresent sound of breaking waves that floated in through the open windows. The condo was a modest two bedroom on one level, nothing fancy. But it had come cheap for the week, thanks to my father's connections; and it was superbly located in a cluster of houses within a stone's throw of Sunset Beach. I had slept with the window open every night, enjoying the sea breezes that rolled in constantly through the slats of the wooden shutters.

I shut the door behind me, and without thinking—and in a move I did not choose to psychoanalyze—clicked the lock. The condo wasn't very old; from the eighties, maybe, which was good. When it came to hotels and motels, the newer the better, because the shadows were fewer. Some buildings replaced older ones, of course, but the rooms never lined up perfectly, and shadows that floated randomly through walls and ceilings had long since ceased to draw my attention. I had once slept like a baby in a hotel room in Atlanta where three bikers packing pistols had played poker all night long. I could only take them so seriously when their feet dangled in the air above the toilet and their heads were on another floor.

I grabbed my book off the nightstand and hopped into bed with a smile. Ocean breeze, crashing waves, soft mattress, and a good book. What more could I ask for?

I was well into a second chapter when I noticed his ankle. He was sitting across the foot of my bed, his back propped up against the wall, his legs actually overlapping mine on top of the covers. He had the gall to flash me a smile.

"I was wondering when you'd notice," he said cheerfully.

My teeth clenched. I wanted to jump out of the bed, but that would hardly accomplish anything. At least here, I was under the covers.

"You are NOT allowed in my room," I growled.

"Why not?" he asked innocently.

"Because you're a guy!"

"Under ordinary circumstances, maybe," he argued. "But as you so painfully keep reminding me, I don't *count* as a guy."

I took in a deep breath. He had a point. Sort of. But I was not going to let him call the shots. He was the one asking for help, here. Either we played by my rules, or we didn't play at all.

"What do you want?" I barked.

He looked back at me for a long moment. I didn't know whether it was calculated or not, but his eyes had an amazing capacity to mesmerize me. It was as if, when he chose to, he could throw open some inner window that showed pure, raw emotion. The kind most people—like me—tried hard to hide.

"I'm sorry about what happened at dinner," he said softly, his expression radiating regret. "I shouldn't have put you in that position—having to pretend in front of your parents. I won't do it again. I promise."

I stared back into his genuine, troubled face and felt the anger quickly drain out of me, replaced by an unexplainable need to apologize to *him*. Luckily, I squelched it. I would not be taken advantage of, no matter how gorgeous his eyes were... or how nonthreatening he looked in the soft cotton tee and sweats he had mysteriously changed into.

"We have to set some rules," I squeaked, forcing my eyes back to his face.

"No problem," he said quickly, smiling at me.

I looked away again. Where the heck was I supposed to look with a guy like him sitting on the end of my bed?

Conversation was a whole lot easier when I was mad at him.

"First off," I began, "you cannot surprise me by popping up all over the place. Particularly in my bedroom!"

He nodded. "I'm assuming the shower's okay, then?"

Perfect. Now I *was* mad at him.

My eyes narrowed. "If I so much as see one half-transparent toe of yours anywhere NEAR any bathroom or bedroom I ever go in, I will NEVER talk to you again. EVER. Got it?"

He considered. "Fair enough. Except for the part about the bedroom. I mean, it is the perfect place to talk privately, isn't it? At least when you're fully clothed. What if we consider it 'by invitation only?'"

I let out a sigh. Tara was right. I sucked at negotiation.

"Fine. Assuming I ever invite you. And the second thing is—"

"I can't be talking to you or distracting you when you're around other people, particularly your parents," he finished. "I already promised that, remember?"

"So you did," I responded.

We stared at each other for a moment. I took a breath. "Assuming you stick to the rules, I'm willing to do what I can to help you. But you have to understand something. I don't know crap about any of this. Seriously, I don't. I know you think I *must*—that I'm secretly hiding some profound truth from you. But I'm not. I'm just an ordinary person who's been cursed with this ability to see weird stuff nobody else sees, and I have no idea why. It's never done me or anybody else any good, that's for sure. So whatever I may do to try to help you with your... issues, I need you to understand that I am totally and completely winging it."

He looked back at me with a curious expression, but his eyes had become unreadable. "You really shouldn't think of it as a curse, Kali," he said quietly. "You should think of it as a gift."

I snorted. "Being constantly aware of dead people is no gift, believe me."

He gave a slight shrug. "It is to me."

I suddenly wished, really hard, that I was wearing something other than a worn lime-green nightshirt with a yellow duck on it that said, for inexplicable reasons, "Summertime Funtime" in big pink letters across the chest. I also realized that my hair was still wrapped up in a towel.

It was too late to worry about either.

"Look, Zane," I began, trying to muster whatever shreds of dignity I had left. "I think that what you are is more like a ghost. And from everything I've ever read or seen on TV talk shows about ghosts, they get stuck on earth for a couple specific reasons. One is that they were murdered, and they want justice."

He shook his head. "Nobody would murder me. I'm too lovable. Next."

I sighed. Lacking in ego, he was not. "Two, they murdered somebody else, or did some horrible thing they want to atone for, or they've been sentenced to some hell-on-earth chain-dragging gig. Like Jacob Marley, you know, in *A Christmas Carol.*"

He lifted his arms innocently. "No chains. No guilt. Next?"

I sighed. "The only other thing I can remember is people who don't realize they're dead, and they get lost somehow on their way to the light."

His eyebrows rose. "That sounds promising. And what light would that be?"

I shrugged. "I don't know. Didn't you see anything? Maybe when... when it first happened?"

He let out a sigh of his own. "I told you, I don't remember anything happening. All I can remember is surfing on this beach. For the most part, I've had a great time doing it, too. It's just been confusing, since I can't remember anything else. And after a while... lonely."

"You don't remember seeing a light?"

"No." He sprang up and began to pace, his voice edged with frustration. "No! I've never seen anything like that. There must be something else. Some point. Some *reason*." He stopped and held my gaze. "I mean... what am I supposed to *do* with myself?"

He looked so distraught, so helpless. Those blasted puppy dog eyes of his were killing me. I almost folded back the covers and got up to move closer to him, but I caught myself in time.

"Listen," I began, an idea forming, "I'll admit I haven't read much about ghosts; in fact, I've avoided the subject, just like I've avoided everything to do with the shadows. But I'm pretty sure I've never heard of a ghost with amnesia. Whatever it is you're supposed to be doing, surely you have to remember your own life in order to do it. Maybe that's where you need to start?"

A smile spread slowly across his face. "See there," he said more hopefully, plopping back down on the edge of my bed. "I knew you could help me."

"I haven't done anything yet," I protested.

"Oh yes, you have," he insisted, his green eyes twinkling. He had propped himself up on one muscular arm and was leaning over my legs at knee level. "I wish I knew how to thank you."

I drew in a ragged breath.

How about you turn real and take me to prom?

"How about leaving me alone now and letting me sleep?" I said instead. "We can work on your memory tomorrow."

He stood up immediately. "Whatever you say, Beautiful. Where shall we meet in the morning? I wouldn't want to drop in uninvited."

"How about breakfast on the deck?" I responded, pretending I hadn't heard what he'd just called me. I had no makeup on, my hair was in a turban, and I was wearing a sack that looked like something out of a seventh grade slumber party. He was only flattering me because he wanted something. Duh.

"Can't wait," he said with a grin. Then, after a blur of action that made his entire body translucent for the smallest whiff of a second, he was gone.

# chapter four

" *Kali!* Kali, wake up! Hurry!"

The voice filtered through the haze of my brain like a fly trying to swim through syrup. That is to say, it didn't get too far. My mind was deeply involved in an endless, ho-hum dream in which Kylee, Tara, and I were driving around Cheyenne in a car with no doors, trying to tell everyone that the spaghetti supper at the high school had been cancelled. Only no one was home, because they had already left to go eat the spaghetti, which meant, clearly, that we were all about to be jailed for stealing their ticket money. The fact that my brain was reluctant to leave this spellbinding tale, and resisted, quite strongly, the voice that kept trying to intrude on it, I can only blame on continued jet lag.

"Kali, please! You have to wake up!"

I knew whose voice it was, but that didn't help anything. My brain seemed pretty sure that Zane was part of another dream, so it was okay, therefore, for me to go on sleeping.

"KALI!" the voice yelled, mere inches from my ear. "Wake up NOW!"

I lifted my head off the pillow with a start. "What the—"

The apology came quickly. "I'm sorry, really I am. I didn't want to yell, but I can't shake you!"

I fought to get my eyes focused. I could barely make out Zane's uneven silhouette leaning over me in the near total darkness. It was still night.

"Are you crazy?" I muttered. "Leave me alone!"

"I can't!" he said desperately. "Please, you've got to get

up and come with me. I can't do anything to stop her, but you can! It's a matter of life and death!"

It was his tone, rather than his words, that at last began to clear the cobwebs. I lifted my head and propped up on my elbows. "What—"

"Just follow me," he ordered. "We can be there in two minutes." He reached out as if to help me up, but his hand passed through the crook of my arm, causing him to groan aloud with aggravation. "Come *on!*"

I forced my body up and out of bed, even as my mind stayed a step behind. I had felt something when his hand passed through me. I wasn't sure what... a curious sensation, like the slightest pinging of vibration. But maybe I was only imagining it. I was almost certainly only imaging that I was grabbing my jacket off the hook on the back of the door, stumbling through the dark condo after Zane's rapidly moving form, and then opening the door to the deck.

"Wake up, Kali!" he demanded as I stepped outside. "Are you with me? You have to be alert for this!"

I paused a moment and blinked. The fleece jacket I had thrown on covered me little better than my sleep shirt, and the two together did nothing to ward off the chill of the brisk ocean wind that suddenly buffeted me from every side. When a burst of sand, spray, and grit pelted me full in the face, I at last jolted completely awake.

"What are we doing out here?" I yelled angrily.

"Good," he said with a nod. "You *are* awake. Now follow me!"

He began to move toward the beach, but I kept my feet planted. What could he possibly want from me? I was crazy to have followed him this far.

He turned around and was back at my side in an instant. "Kali, please! Trust me. I don't have time to explain. She could die. Just run after me and you'll understand soon enough!"

I don't know why I followed him. All I know is that it was close enough to dawn that a few scudding clouds had begun to glow white against the otherwise inky sky, and that there was just enough light on his face—at that angle and that moment—to convince me that the terror in his voice was real.

The pathway from our deck to the actual beach was rough. The condo was jammed into a large cluster of houses at an odd angle, making us "oceanfront" by only the broadest of real estate definitions. After navigating the wooden steps off the deck, we had to cross multiple scrubby yards, gravel walks, and asphalt driveways before my tender feet (still months away from barefoot weather in Wyoming) at last sunk into the relative luxury of the coarse, shell-laden island sand.

Zane kept running.

"It's not much farther," he encouraged, alternating between leading me forward and jogging at my side like an athletic trainer. "You're doing great."

His voice was measured, but the tenseness was still there. I picked up my pace, trying to ignore both the biting coldness that gnawed at my bare legs and the ominous closeness of the ocean itself—which seemed, in the eerie glow of near dawn, to be composed more of shining, frothing, whitecaps than dark and rolling waves. This was only a guess on my part, though, as the only way I could force myself to keep going was to avoid looking directly at the water.

We ran along the shore for a couple hundred yards, the slowness of my progress seeming to drive Zane to a near frenzy. Once or twice he disappeared, again with the same odd blur that dissolved his form to nothingness in an instant. But each time he reappeared within seconds, seeming even more agitated, making me think he was checking on the mysterious *her* that lay ahead of us.

The sand on the dry part of the beach was deep, and with every step it grabbed my feet up to the ankles and sucked me downward, providing a perfect imitation of the supernatural, lead-footed feeling I'd suffered so often in nightmares. Zane tried repeatedly to lead me onto the more densely packed wet sand, but his efforts were in vain. Try as I might, I could not block out the near deafening sound and pulsing vibrations of the sea. I didn't need to look to know that the waves were more numerous, higher, and more violent than any I had yet seen. The air was thick with their salty spray, and my skin was blanketed with moisture even as the wind whipped my minimal clothing around me.

It was the anxiety in Zane's voice that drew me on. I had no idea what he could be afraid of. I only knew that in his case, it wasn't the ocean.

"There! Right there!" he said finally, pointing down the beach ahead of us. "Do you see her?"

I took a breath. Then, for the first time, I looked fully out toward the roiling water.

I could see her. The "she" of Zane's concern was just a toddler. Eighteen months old maybe—no more than two. The child was running, carelessly and fearlessly, right along the water line of the menacing ocean, flirting with its fickle waves. It was a game many children played, chasing the receding wave toward the ocean, then racing back to land ahead of it, squealing with delight should the leading edge of foam catch their ankles. In gentle surf, on a clear day, and with competent adult supervision, it was a timeless, harmless enough amusement.

But in the predawn darkness, for a toddler alone on

the North Shore of Oahu, the game was deadly. Here on
this island, I knew, the ocean contained a raw power
rivaling any on the planet. In high surf, constantly shifting
sands on the beaches gouged precipitous drop-offs and
exposed sharp coral, while just a few feet beyond, the giant
swells of water spurred unpredictable rip currents and
fatally fierce undertows. It was difficult, even for an adult,
to judge how near to shore the next wave would break and
how far out was too far out for safety.

The child didn't have a chance.

Even as I stood rooted to the spot—for one endless
moment struck numb with horror—I could distinctly see
the silhouettes of a set of higher, even more powerful
waves gathering steam on the horizon behind her.

"Run, Kali!" Zane ordered. "There isn't much time!"

My feet began to move. The wet sand was indeed
easier to walk on, and after a few faltering paces, I was
running full tilt. I came within range just as she had chased
a receding wave all the way to its source. The child
watched with amusement as the last of the waterborne
sand sped around her ankles and returned to the sea; she
was less amused when the next wave crashed into a white
froth within feet of her. She attempted, with an admirable
burst of speed, to run up the beach out of its way; but
natural apprehension at last got the best of her, and with a
plaintive wail she lost her balance and fell, face down, into
the rising water.

I was there, close enough to grab her, before the body
of the wave struck. It was not a large wave, barely up to
my knees, but it would have been big enough to cover her
prone form. The child screamed and struggled as I held
her—both out of fear and, perhaps, the indignity of
having her fine game interrupted by the rudeness of a
stranger. I lifted a foot to make my way back out of the

water, barely noticing, above both the child's screams and the roar of the ocean behind, that Zane was again yelling at me.

He was telling me to look behind us, saying something about the next one. But he didn't have to. I knew without looking that a larger—no, a much, *much* larger wave was gathering behind me. I could feel it in the force of the back current that was sucking the remnants of the last wave around my legs. I could hear it in the hellish silence that hung in the air where the crash of another, smaller, wave should already be heard—but was not.

Zane was right beside me, still shouting. I couldn't hear him; I couldn't even look at him, much less at what lay behind us. I did the only thing I could do. I held on tight to the little girl, fixed my eyes on the beach, and ran as far as I could run before it caught me.

I did not get far. I felt a splash of hideous cold on my back, and within an instant my legs were covered to the thigh. I continued slogging forward, holding the child high, as the water continued rising to my waist.

*No higher*, I prayed silently, *no higher*.

The water stopped rising. But I also stopped moving. Going forward was no longer an option. The direction of the water had reversed; the wave was rolling out. And it really, really, wanted both the child and me to go back with it.

Zane was at my shoulder, shouting into my ear. Something about swimming parallel to something, not fighting it. But he didn't understand.

By pure instinct I made the choice to stop where I was. I anchored my feet in the sand, digging in my toes. I braced my legs, forward and back, as best as I could. I kept my eyes closed and my mind focused. All I had to do was stay on my feet.

The pressure against me was enormous. My foothold was iffy. The child continued to struggle, flailing like a wild thing. But I hadn't taken eleven years of dance for nothing. I might be tall and skinny, but my legs were strong, my back was strong, and like any ballerina who danced *en pointe*, I had learned to balance in precarious positions. In the endless seconds that followed I came close to losing it more times than I could count. But I was determined. I was not going backward, I was not floating up, and I was *not* letting go of that baby.

Even if the little demon did take a plug out of my shoulder with her teeth.

The water level dropped. Thigh high. Knee high. I waited no more. I lifted my feet and sprinted up the beach and onto the dry sand.

My feet sank down to the ankles again, and my legs began to wobble, but I kept moving steadily away from the drone of the ocean until the painful crunch of scrubby grass and sticks underfoot told me I was well away from the water's reach. I paused only long enough to catch my breath, still holding the crying child in a death grip.

"Where did she come from?" A thin, squeaky voice said. I think it was mine.

Zane hadn't stirred from my side. He pointed towards a beach house directly in front of me. Six wooden steps led from a stone patio up to a large deck; one of a set of French doors leading into the house hung ominously open, swinging in the wind. I shifted the child's weight to my opposite hip. Her waterlogged diaper weighed half again as much as she did, and with every wriggle she made, another stream of water trickled unpleasantly down my already drenched leg. I renewed my grip on the child and began a slow trudge up the steps. Her cries had reduced to whimpers, but she was still struggling mightily to be put down.

"That was magnificent, Kali," Zane praised as we went. "I can't believe you stayed on your feet. Have you ever surfed before? You'd be fabulous at it."

"I'm a dancer," I said shortly. I reached the house and banged loudly on the door that was still closed.

"Are you all right?" Zane asked. He was studying me with concern, even as he beamed at me.

I banged again, more forcefully this time. Somewhere in the depths of the house, a light turned on.

"You look wiped out," he continued, "but you deserve to. It's not every night you get ripped out of a sound sleep to save a drowning child."

Footsteps pounded down a staircase. More lights flew on. A woman in her early thirties, wearing a cotton nightgown with a silk kimono thrown hastily over one shoulder, looked out the French doors and, upon catching sight of her soaking wet, squirming daughter in my arms, turned pale and swayed on her feet. "Lauren?" came a man's voice from the stairs behind her. "What is it? Who's there?"

The woman half stumbled, half ran towards me, and as she approached the French doors I stepped inside and extended the toddler to her, fearful she would otherwise crash into the glass. Once in her mother's arms, the child calmed a bit, but after only seconds of that woman's overzealous clasping, she began to struggle for freedom again.

"What happ—" the man, who wore nothing but boxer shorts, had caught up with us. He looked from the child to me with wide eyes, clearly imagining and guessing correctly the nightmare that had occurred.

"I found her on the beach," I confirmed, my voice sounding oddly distant. "She was playing in the waves."

For a long moment, neither parent seemed able to speak. The man lifted the struggling child from her mother's grasp, hugged her tight for a moment, then balanced her lightly against his chest with a strong arm. They stared at me with equal measures of relief and wide-eyed horror while the child, content with a lighter degree of restraint, began absently playing with her father's chest hair.

"Is she... hurt?" the mother said finally, her voice a squeak.

"I don't think so," I answered flatly.

"How did she—" the man began, but the woman interrupted him with a stifled cry.

"I *saw* her playing with the doorknob earlier," she admitted, her voice choking on every syllable. "But the door was locked. I know it was. She must have woken up early and climbed out of her crib... how she turned the lock I can't imagine... she just had so much fun playing outside yesterday—" her voice broke off completely, replaced by deep, wracking sobs.

I began to feel uncomfortable. This was a private moment; I wasn't needed anymore.

"I'm glad she's okay," I said awkwardly, stepping back out onto the deck.

"Wait," the man called. I turned to look at him as he stood, clearly overwhelmed, one arm supporting his daughter, the other around his wife. "We didn't... I mean... *thank you.*"

The woman found her voice again. "Thank you," she repeated. "How we can we ever thank you enough?"

I took a step backward. My legs had begun to tremble, I was drenched to the bone, and my teeth were chattering. I just wanted to go home. "You're welcome," I said simply. Before they could say any more I turned and hurried down the stairs.

A sharp stab of pain in my left foot told me I had probably picked up a splinter, but I didn't care. I continued to race back along the beach and across the yards and asphalt and did not slow my steps until I had reached the deck of the condo.

Zane kept pace with me, as always, but because he had fallen uncharacteristically silent I almost forgot that he was there. Only when I stopped at last, hand on my own doorknob, did he step around to catch my attention.

"Are you sure you're all right?" he asked again. The dawning sky was brighter now, and I could see that his concern was genuine. That knowledge filled me with an unexpected warmth, but not enough, unfortunately, to overcome the bone-chilling cold that now permeated every inch of me.

"I'll be fine," I answered, putting as much warmth into my own voice as my frozen body could muster. "I just need a hot shower. And a couple hours more sleep." I opened the door, let myself in, and turned around. "I'll see you tomorrow, Zane." I attempted a smile. "In someplace *other* than my bedroom, if you don't mind."

He grinned broadly, then nodded. "As you wish."

He stayed where he was, and I began to close the door. "Goodnight," I mumbled.

"Sleep tight, Hero," he returned.

The door clicked shut. I did not look back, but made a beeline for my bedroom. I stumbled through the doorway and collapsed face down on the bed, wet clothes and all.

Hero, indeed.

Despite the relative warmth of the room, my skin felt cold and clammy, my every limb was shaking like a jack hammer, and I was pretty sure I was going to be sick.

Zane should be calling himself the hero. If not for him,

I would still be sound asleep, and the little girl would almost certainly have drowned.

But the next time he needed a lifeguard, he really should pick someone who could swim.

## chapter five

Zane was true to his word. I did not see him the next morning until I took my sesame bagel, fresh pineapple, and hot tea out onto the deck. My father was with me, enjoying his toast and coffee, and Zane kept his distance. I only caught sight of him occasionally, leaning against one of the palm trees or sunning himself on a neighbor's roof. He waited patiently, not looking in my direction, but studiously scanning the ocean from a variety of angles. I did notice that he managed to stay within earshot as my father described to me, in typical dramatic fashion, some of the lesser known aspects of the attack on Pearl Harbor that he had learned on his tours of the base.

Unlike me, my father actually did look Hawaiian, taking very little of his appearance from my Minnesota-born grandfather. But because my grandmother Kalia had died when he was a child, leaving him to be raised on the mainland by an Irish Catholic stepmother, he was no more culturally in tune with the locale than I was.

"Are you sure you don't want to ride along with your mother and me?" he asked again when his breakfast was finished. "We won't be at the base all morning. We can drive over to Waikiki after. Or we could take that hike up Diamond Head."

I searched my mind for a suitable excuse. The hike up Diamond Head sounded good; a day's worth of killing time at the base did not. Primarily because Hickham wasn't just any base.

"No thanks, Dad," I said simply. "I'd really rather just hang out on the beach some more and watch the surfers. I thought maybe I'd check out that tube thing Tara was talking about. We can do Diamond Head another day, can't we?"

Zane had moved closer, and was now perched on the deck railing. He had been doing an admirable job of pretending to ignore us so far, but at the words "tube thing" he rolled his eyes with a groan.

"Sure we can," my father answered, his expression turning thoughtful. "And by the way, I told Keith to let his son know that you'd rather not do Pearl Harbor this afternoon. I told him you'd already seen it."

I smiled back warmly. My parents might not believe that I saw the shadows any more, but my phobia of battlefields was too intense to be denied. After a few thoroughly embarrassing incidents in my elementary years, they seemed to have accepted that, supernatural visions aside, there was something about disaster sites that affected me deeply. Too deeply to fool around with when the unpleasantness—and speculation as to its cause— could so easily be avoided altogether.

"Thanks, Dad," I answered.

He turned to go inside, but looked back over his shoulder with mock sternness. "And it's the world famous *Banzai Pipeline*, not 'that tube thing.' Show a little respect, will you?"

I chuckled. He went inside and closed the door.

"I knew I liked that man," Zane announced from my father's vacated seat. "It's about time you stopped dissing the pipe and learned to worship it like everybody else in Oahu." He leaned closer and smiled at me expectantly. "Let's go surfing."

A flicker of panic made my stomach twist. Maybe it was the mental image of me on a surfboard. Maybe it was the effect his smile had on my insides. More than likely, it was both.

For the thousandth time, I reminded myself that he was dead. "I don't surf," I said flatly.

"Not yet, maybe. But you will. At least come with me and watch? The waves are looking awesome."

He looked so eager, so energetic. He was dressed like one of the pros this morning—wearing a skintight, one-piece, midnight blue surf suit. I wondered vaguely how the whole clothes-changing thing worked for a ghost.

I sighed. Befriending him like he was any other human could not possibly end well for me. Then again, it wasn't like there were any other hot guys asking me to spend the morning on the beach with them, was it? Last night's killer wind had faded to a pleasant breeze. The sky was blue. The air was warm.

Five minutes later, we were strolling down the sand.

"Guess what?" he said cheerfully, when we passed out of earshot of the few other people visible.

"What?"

His green eyes sparkled. "I remembered some things." His face shone with suppressed excitement, causing an effect on me that I can only describe as knee weakening, despite the ripples of translucency—slightly wider than yesterday—that floated periodically across his torso.

I stopped walking and faced him. "Really? Something about your past, you mean?"

He nodded. "Last night, after I left your house, I was thinking about your family, and wondering if I was lucky enough to have one like them. And then some things just came to me, like they were never gone at all."

"Like what?"

He looked away. "Stuff from when I was a little kid. That's all I've got so far. But I know it's real."

We walked for a while in silence, then I prodded him for more.

"So tell me."

He smiled at me again, but this time the smile was hesitant, almost sad. "My family was definitely *not* like yours."

"What difference does that make?" I said quickly. When it came to parental problems, I was a little sensitive to being considered insensitive. My friends from dysfunctional families always seemed to assume that because my parents were happily married, I couldn't understand. Maybe they were right. But I wanted to try.

Zane exhaled with a shrug. "I always lived with my mom. I saw my dad every once in a while, but they were never married. It seemed like they barely knew each other."

I nodded. "Did you have any brothers or sisters?"

He shook his head. "No. It was always just me and my mom." He turned and looked at me, an uneasy smirk on his face. "Would you believe me if I told you that my mother was sort of famous? That she was a television actress?"

The breeze ruffled his dark blond curls, which glinted like gold in the strong sunlight. I resisted the urge to cast another casual glance over his almost perfect form, keeping my gaze on his totally perfect eyes instead. At least he came by it honestly.

"Yeah," I said with a laugh. "I can believe that."

He smiled with relief. "I can remember watching her on TV, and being really proud of her. She was a beautiful person."

I was distracted, suddenly, by the sight of another woman, this one not so beautiful, who was already familiar to me. I was interested in what Zane was saying; and when it came to the shadows, my natural inclination was to ignore first and ask questions never. But something about this particular, very old shadow, faint as a wisp of steam, drew my gaze to her involuntarily.

She was short and relatively stocky, with a squarish head and stringy black hair that hung well below her waist. A dull-colored wrap skirt covered her from just under the breasts to a few inches above the knee, while she clutched a similarly colored shawl around her shoulders. She was pregnant, and heavily so, and appeared young—not much older than me. She stood just as she had the last time I had seen her, watching out to sea, her gaze glued to the horizon, with tears streaming down her cheeks and an occasional wracking sob shaking her small body like a spasm.

It was not her anguish that drew me. I went to great lengths to avoid any shadow that radiated pain, because I had to. Not only did my inevitable empathy hurt me, too; but it was pointless. Whatever I was seeing had already happened; I couldn't change it.

Yet in this woman's case, I knew what was coming, and it was far from painful. I had watched it unfold a couple times yesterday morning, but I was always too far away to catch the highlight. Perhaps today, I would be luckier.

"Kali?" Zane's voice asked me curiously. "Where did you go?" He was waving a hand before my eyes. "Am I boring you?"

"No!" I said emphatically, embarrassed. "I want to hear all about your mother. I'm sorry." I drew my eyes from the shadow with reluctance and set off down the beach again.

"Oh, I get it," Zane said brightly, catching up to me. "You were seeing a shadow, weren't you?" He looked back at the place where I had been staring. "What was it?"

My stomach did a quick flip-flop. My heartbeat quickened.

Covering up my rare moments of shadow watching was something I thought I was good at. My parents never seemed to notice; they just thought I spaced out occasionally. Same thing with my friends. Heck, Kylee spaced out twice as much as I did, and no one ever thought she was seeing dead people.

Zane already knew my secret; but still, talking about it in real time made me uncomfortable. I didn't share this kind of crap with anybody. It didn't feel right. I might as well have been standing there in my underwear.

"Come on, Kali," Zane cajoled, looking somewhat disbelieving. "Don't go all defensive on me, now! You can't seriously believe I'm going to think *you're* weird?"

He shook his head at me and laughed out loud. After a long, thoughtful moment, I laughed with him. "Sorry. It's just that... I don't talk about it. I did once, and everybody thought I was psychotic, or schizophrenic, or something even worse. So now I pretend."

His expression turned serious. "How long ago was that?"

"When I was five."

His eyes widened. "You live with this... seeing these shadows... every day, and you haven't talked to anyone about it since you were five?"

I shrugged. "You get used to it."

He continued to watch me thoughtfully, his gaze drifting back and forth between me and the shadow of the pregnant Polynesian woman, which to him was an empty stretch of beach. "Tell me about it," he said quietly, his voice dropping to the same dreaded, husky whisper he had manipulated me with so successfully yesterday. "Tell me what you see."

My jaw clenched. I knew there was no real risk in being honest with him. He was not going to assume I needed psych meds; and even if he did, he couldn't tell anyone. Still, sharing the shadows seemed so... personal.

"Please, Kali?"

Crap.

Sooner or later, that sexy whisper was going to be the death of me.

"It's a woman, okay?" I said before I could think anymore. "She's very faint. Centuries old, probably. I was watching her yesterday, and I really wanted to see her again..."

I spilled the whole works. Describing the woman in detail, answering every one of Zane's fascinated questions. But as the expected point in the drama neared, I found myself impatient with the inquisition, turning my attention instead to the spot up the beach where the other shadow would soon appear.

"What's up there?" Zane insisted, following my gaze.

The second wispy form appeared, walking slowly across invisible sand drifts that bore no relation to the ones present now. I smiled. "The man she *thinks* is out there," I answered, tossing my head toward the water.

The man's steps quickened, though his legs were obviously weak, and his lips moved as he called out to the woman. I could barely hear him... just the faintest quiver of bass vibration floating above the breeze. He was speaking in another language, so I couldn't have understood him anyway, but his intent was clear. He was shouting to get her attention.

She turned. I moved a few steps closer, not wanting to miss her expression.

"What's happening?" Zane demanded.

"She sees him," I whispered breathlessly. I couldn't begin to describe the look of pure, emphatic joy that transformed her features instantly from the depths of sorrow to the height of ecstasy—the whipping flame of energy that sent her pregnant, unwieldy body into flight. I had never seen any woman *that* pregnant run *that* fast. Barefoot on the sand, her shawl discarded, she sprinted like an extra wide gazelle, breasts and belly bobbing, covering the distance between them in seconds.

I ran along beside her, heedless of how ridiculous I looked, to catch the reunion up close. I was not disappointed.

She threw herself into the man's arms as if compelled there by a suction as powerful as the sea itself, and he held onto her awkward form as if a force just as great threatened to snatch her. They wanted, needed, to touch each other—every inch of skin not in contact seemed unbearable. They did not kiss in the traditional sense, but rubbed their faces together, cheek to cheek, lip to lip, as if trying to absorb one other, to assimilate their two forms into one delirious, satisfied whole.

The man's face was so faint it was difficult to see much detail, but I was certain—whether I could see it or not—that his eyes were tearing. He was no taller than me, with long black hair in a ponytail and no clothes to speak of other than a loin cloth; but for her, he was the perfect fit. I stood there, mesmerized, drinking in the heady joy and warmth that, unaccountably, still radiated from their wispy outlines hundreds of years after the fact—until once again they disappeared together, slowly and gradually, into nothingness.

"You know," Zane prodded good-naturedly, "it's really rude not to narrate for the blind."

I forced my mind back to the present. "Sorry. Just got carried away. I love that scene."

I sighed.

Despite his professed interest, I figured Zane was only

humoring me. But I soon learned that once onto something that intrigued him, the guy was a pit bull. He badgered me mercilessly until I had related every detail of what I had just witnessed, and then some.

"Do you ever research the things you see?" he asked. "Go online, or into a history book, and try to match up the characters and time frame?"

My eyebrows lifted. "Are you kidding? Why would I want to do that? I told you—I try my best to ignore them. It's healthier that way. I only pay attention to the happy ones, because they make me happy. But it doesn't do them any good."

His brow furrowed. "But you could be seeing something important. Something that history has wrong, even."

"What if I am?" I replied defensively. "There's nothing I can do about it. Nobody would believe me. I'd just wind up in a psych ward. Think about it!"

"I suppose," he conceded. "But still... to have that ability..."

My teeth clenched. I knew he wasn't trying to be critical, but I had worked hard, all my life, to stay sane in my own skin—I did not need the one person to whom I had finally confessed my secret telling me I was handling it wrong.

"We're supposed to be talking about you, not me," I said firmly, setting off down the beach again. "Now, tell me more about your mother."

Zane's face lit up again, just as a wide band of transparency settled into the middle of his forehead. "Well, like I said, she was a professional actress," he began, his voice proud. "I can remember watching her in TV commercials. My favorite was one where she had to swing a tennis racket. She wasn't athletic at all, and she used to moan and groan about how many takes it took to make her look like a pro. There was also a dog food one I liked, where she worked with an Airedale in a cowboy outfit. But her main thing was the soaps. She played one particular character a long time—can't remember the name. People would recognize her on the street and call out to us. Sometimes they would look at me funny because her baby on the show was a girl, and they didn't understand that she wasn't her character. But she loved the attention."

His voice trailed off, and he was silent for a moment. His expression had become troubled.

"What is it?" I asked. "You remember something bad?"

He huffed out a breath. "Not yet. No. But I have this feeling that something... happened to her. To both of us. I just can't remember what."

I swallowed. The darkness in his expression troubled me. "Do you think she's still alive?" I asked tentatively.

His eyes narrowed in concentration. "No," he said finally. "I don't think she is."

We walked in silence a while longer, both of us struggling, perhaps, to understand the bizarre dynamic he was operating in. If his mother was alive, where was she? If he could find her again, would she be able to see or hear him like I could? And an even grimmer thought: if she was dead, why wasn't she here, with him, now?

He appeared not to want to discuss it. And I had no idea what to say.

"Look over there," he said at last, changing the subject. "This is 'Ehukai beach. And *that* is the Banzai Pipeline."

I looked. We were not far from where I had laid out my beach mat yesterday, but with Zane's guidance, I took in the vista with more educated eyes. Giant waves rolled in off the ocean regularly here, just as they did a little farther north on Sunset Beach. But the way they rolled in at this particular spot was different. Wave after wave swelled, stood up vertically, then began to peel over at the top— creating a colossal water tunnel that spread sideways along the length of the wave for several seconds before, with the same graceful sweeping motion, it collapsed in on itself in a violent froth of white foam.

I had seen such water tunnels before, when a tall wave spilled over just right; but at this spot it kept happening, over and over again. Not only that, but these waves were so large that the tunnels they created were tall enough for a person to stand up in.

The surfers were doing just that. "Look!" Zane said excitedly, pointing. "See that guy? That's Ezekiel. He *rocks*."

I watched with mingled awe and horror as the surfer, dwarfed in size by the massive swell coming on next, skated fearlessly over its crest to dip down, turn, and slip inside the curl at just the right moment, then zip along the tube's length at a speed that kept him ahead of the massive structure's inevitable collapse. At one point I lost sight of him behind the churning wall of white, but amazingly, he popped up again from its ruins—still upright on his board, still moving, and still in control.

"Wow," was the only comment I could muster.

"Pretty sweet, huh? Not just anyone can do that, by the way. Only the best can handle the pipe on a day like this."

I believed him, as the next surfer I watched screwed up his timing and got caught with the heavy wall of water crashing on top of him, knocking him into the froth and sending his board flying high up into the air. The surfer was fine, however—popping up within seconds to reclaim his board, which had been stalled in its escape by some kind of leash.

"This looks really dangerous," I said stupidly.

"Most deadly surf spot in the world," Zane answered nonchalantly. "The waves may be high but the water underneath is pretty shallow, and you can get banged up bad if you hit the reef or a lava spire. Bust your head without a helmet, and you're a goner." He took a couple steps toward the water.

"So where's your helmet?"

He looked over his shoulder and winked at me. "Being dead does have its perks."

It did not occur to me to wonder, until I watched him run full bore into the water—his lean legs moving through the swells without causing so much as a ripple—exactly how a ghost could surf.

I found out. But I was glad the other surfers didn't, because if they realized that pretty much every time one of them caught a wave, there was a teenage ghost surfer with no regard for personal space totally hijacking their board, they might have been too freaked out for safety.

Watching Zane in action was hysterical. He simply couldn't get enough. He would start out with one surfer, ride through the tube, disappear, and then reappear with another at the crest of the next wave. I had to hand it to him—even with the ability to cheat all the laws of physics, what he was doing couldn't be easy. His position in space seemed to be affected by nothing other than his mind, so staying on the board required—if not physical prowess— no small amount of concentration and sheer athletic instinct. He could sense where the board was going to go, how fast, and which way the surfer would turn. He wasn't perfect by any means—more than once I laughed out loud as the board took a turn he missed, leaving him skating off into oblivion, suspended by nothing, or in one case, absently flying off through the tunnel's back wall. But what sport it was, he clearly enjoyed, sharing as no other human could the charge that each surfer felt during those exhilarating, solitary seconds when they were totally encased within the aqua-white walls of water.

"Did you see that one?" he asked excitedly, appearing next to me quite suddenly after his co-rider had wiped out in spectacular fashion, being kicked a good body's length straight up in the air, upside-down.

"Is he all right?"

"He's fine. Came up laughing, actually. But what a stupid move! I told him he shouldn't take off there—it was never going to work, he was too far inside."

"Let me guess. He didn't take your advice."

Zane's eyes twinkled. "They never do. Idiots."

I noticed that his curls were dripping.

"How do you *do* that?" I asked, curiosity at last overwhelming me. "How do you look wet when the water never touches you? And where do the different outfits come from?"

He smirked. "Mind over no matter. I look however I want to look. Cool, huh? Check that out!" He pointed upwards in the direction of a fluffy white cloud, but I saw nothing noteworthy.

"What?" I asked, looking back at him and answering my own question. He was now dressed, head to toe, in a spotless Air Force pilot's uniform.

"Think Dad would approve?" he asked smugly.

My eyes rolled. "That is *so* unfair. So I suppose you're really short and ugly, too?"

He smirked again. "Can't change the basics. Just the wrapper."

"Glad to hear it."

*Whoops.* Too much?

He smiled, but didn't comment. "So," he said finally, having changed in a blink back into his wet suit. "Are you sold? Are you going to sign up for that surfing lesson with your parents?"

I shuddered. "Hardly."

"Why not?"

"Because I can't swim."

I said it casually enough, as I had trained myself to do. People tended to make less of a big deal out of it then. It was better to throw it out there when it didn't matter than wait until it did.

I had forgotten, for the moment, that it had mattered last night. The sight of Zane's face, frozen in shock, reminded me.

"You... can't swim? Like... at all?"

"Nope," I said lightly, trying hard to think of another subject.

"But you were—" He had turned pale, which for a suntanned ghost was probably a feat. "You were out in the ocean up to—"

"Yeah, I know. Can we not talk about it anymore?"

His voice dropped to a disturbing murmur. "I could have gotten you killed."

I turned to face him. "There's nothing for you to feel guilty about. How could you know? The decision was mine, and I did what I had to do. Everything turned out fine, so let's just forget it, okay?"

He still looked miserable.

"Here I was," he said darkly, "thinking I'd finally found something useful I could do with my... *life*." The word was uncharacteristically bitter. "When all I really did, instead of saving a person, was nearly take out two."

"That's not true," I protested.

"Of course it is!" he argued. "Can you imagine how I felt, seeing that little girl come out of that door, watching her wander off toward the beach, knowing there was nothing that I could do to stop her? Hey, everybody! Look at me! I can walk through walls, I can stay underwater all day without breathing, I can surf the pipe 66 waves in a row... but lift a 25-pound kid out of the ocean before she drowns herself in front of my eyes? *No!*"

He looked away from me, his expression tortured.

"If you hadn't done exactly what you did," I said firmly, catching his eyes again, "that little girl would be dead right now. You *can't* regret what happened."

His expression softened a bit, but his voice was still ragged. "I'm really sorry, Kali."

"*What did I just say?!*" I shouted, forgetting altogether that I was standing on a public beach yelling into empty space.

A long pause followed. Then slowly, ruefully, Zane's mouth twisted into a smile. "Something about how awesome I look catching a wave, and how desperately you want to watch me rip this next set?"

I grinned back at him. "Yeah. Something like that."

# chapter six

I tried to resist. Really, I did. I knew it would only get me into trouble later. But I was so used to sharing everything guy related with Tara and Kylee, it felt like lying not to mention Zane at all. So, I caved.

> Hung out with a hot surfer on the pipe this morning!

That was all it took. It was evening in Wyoming, Kylee's current boyfriend was out of town with his family for break, and Tara's family never went anywhere. They were both probably bored out of their minds.

Tara's response was typical.

> That's the deadliest surf spot on the planet! Is he a pro? Won any contests? Tell me his name; I'll look him up!

Ditto for Kylee.

> SO COOOLLLL!!! Whatd you do? Can u chat online?!

I answered Tara first, because her question intrigued me. If Zane could only remember a little more about himself—she probably could find out the rest. Particularly if his mother was famous. But I would have to be careful. It would be more than a little awkward to tell her I was talking to a guy and then ask her to find out when and where he died.

> No, he's just an amateur. But he's good! We did

> lunch. Later, getting a tour from officer's son. Keep
> you posted!

Answering Kylee was easier. Names and places of origin were not the kind of details she cared about.

> Nope, vacation strictly low tech. Watched him surf,
> did lunch. Later, island tour with officer's son.
> BTW–surfer has curly blond hair! :D

I grinned to myself, even as I made a mental note not to let Zane anywhere near my phone. Kylee not only loved blond guys, she had a serious thing about curls. I could hear her shrieking all the way across the Pacific.

I pocketed the phone, checked myself briefly in the mirror, and headed out of the bedroom. I didn't know when I would see Zane next. After lunch I told him I needed a shower and he had dutifully disappeared, saying something about how he would "rip a few at Log Cabins." After having been with him all morning (and a good part of the night), you might think I would want some alone time. I would have thought so, too. Yet when a quick scan of the condo, deck, and backyard showed no signs of him, I felt oddly disappointed.

"What did you do for lunch?" my mother asked, looking up from her stack of real estate information.

I had to think a moment before answering. In reality I had packed myself a picnic and let Zane lead me to Sunset Point, where I learned more than I had ever wanted to know about shortboards, longboards, beach breaks, reef breaks, northwest swells, tow-ins, and seriously wicked lefts. (To be fair, Zane also learned more than he ever wanted to know about fouettés, battements, rond verses, and arabesques—the last of which, to my supreme amusement, he eventually managed to do on a moving shortboard.) His enthusiasm for everything to do with surfing was contagious, and despite my fear of being anywhere near the actual water myself, I had enjoyed the outing enormously. Never mind that we accomplished next to nothing when it came to addressing his problem; something about picnicking on a beach in perfect weather made both of us forget he had one.

"I made a sandwich," I answered noncommittally. "Did you find us a house yet?"

"No, we're still learning about the different neighborhoods around Honolulu—and the schools. But we found an agent who'll be taking us out tomorrow to look at what's available." She leaned back in her chair and ran a hand absently through her short, dark curls. "Sure would be nice if we could just stay here, wouldn't it?"

I cast a glance out our giant picture windows with a sigh, imagining myself in cyber school. Laptop on the deck in the morning; beach in the afternoon. "Sure would," I agreed.

She glanced at her watch. "Your dad was hoping to get home before Matt got here, but it doesn't look like he's going to make it. You ready to go?"

I nodded. You would think that two people who waited forever to have a baby would be overprotective of their only child; thank God my parents were not. True, they hadn't let me drive at thirteen like some of the other kids in Cheyenne, I was subject to certain dating rules, and if they ever caught me with an illegal substance—not likely—they would ground me for the rest of my natural life. But otherwise, I had always been pretty independent. My dad once cracked that I needed to be self sufficient because they were so old when they had me they didn't know how long they would last.

"Are we supposed to be out over dinner?" I asked,

wishing now that I had asked a few more questions about this setup with the mysterious Matt. I knew from my father's latest conversation with his father that he was seventeen; a junior; had a perfect driving record; was into football, wrestling, and water polo; and wanted to go to the Air Force Academy. Such was the only information my father had deemed necessary.

"All your dad said was that you needed to be home by eight. You should take some money just in case... here." My mother grabbed her wallet off the counter and handed me some bills. Despite my father's old fashioned ideas about chivalry, she had always believed in girls paying their own way.

The sound of a car door slamming out front reached both our ears, and my mother's eyes caught mine. "If you want out of this early, send me a text," she said conspiratorially. "I'll call you with some excuse."

I smiled. "Thanks, Mom."

She went off towards the front door, and I stepped over to look out the back windows again. There was no one in sight. I felt another twinge of disappointment, until I turned around to see Zane's face about three inches from my own. I jumped a foot.

"Sorry about that," he chuckled, stepping back. "You moved a little quicker than I expected."

He had changed clothes again, this time favoring a deep green muscle shirt and cargo shorts. He surveyed my own outfit, a backless Hawaiian beach dress I had picked up in Haleiwa our first day here, with obvious displeasure. "You're not really going out on a blind date, are you?"

I suppressed a grin. "It's not a date. He's just giving me a tour. And he's only doing it because his dad's making him."

Zane's frown deepened. "What do you really know

about this guy, anyway?"

I swallowed, trying hard to hide my amusement. The whole overprotectiveness thing, if that's what this was, was new to me. Girls were supposed to be offended by it for some reason, but I couldn't see why. I thought it was kind of cute.

"Would you be serious?" I said with a smile. "We're not going clubbing in Waikiki. We're going for a drive around the island in broad daylight."

"That's what he'll say while he's deciding whether he's interested," Zane continued, his voice edgy. "Once he *gets* interested, it'll be for dinner. Then, there will be some great local landmark or other that you just *have* to see, and of course, this whatever-it-is will be at its best at sunset..."

"Will you stop?" I interrupted, still smiling. "Where are you getting all this?"

"My mind," he said flatly. "Because if I were going out with you in that dress, that's exactly what I would do."

I stared at him a moment.

I had no response to that.

"Kali?" my mom called out from the hall. Clearly, the guy in question had made his way up the steps to the front door. I could hear a deep voice in the background in addition to her own.

"Thanks for the... compliment," I whispered. "But there's nothing to worry about, really. I happen to be a very good judge of character. If at any point I get the slightest inkling that he's a serial killer, I promise to ditch him and call home. Satisfied?"

"I'll check him out for you."

Footsteps started down the hall.

"You will not!" I hissed. "You promised. No interference!"

He raised one eyebrow, then disappeared.

"Kali, this is Matt," my mother explained, stepping out into the great room and gesturing for her guest to follow. She caught my eye as she said it, her unspoken message clear. *Not bad, eh?*

I turned my gaze on the newcomer. He was a little over six feet tall; not fat, but heavily muscled; with deeply tanned skin and short-cropped, wavy brown hair. His neck was on the thick side, but he had the kind of honest looking, down-home baby face that softened the effect. The instant my eyes met his piercing light blue ones, I could read his thoughts as clearly as I could my own mother's.

Wow, that's a relief. She's not ugly!

I couldn't help but laugh. I was, after all, thinking pretty much the same thing.

"Hi, Matt," I introduced myself casually. "Sorry you got roped into this. But I am looking forward to seeing Oahu—so thanks."

He smiled back, revealing both perfect teeth and undisguised relief at my candor. It got me into trouble with girls sometimes, but guys always seemed to appreciate it. It didn't make them want to date me, of course—they preferred the silly, simpering type for that—but they appreciated it.

After a minimum of polite small talk, my mother excused herself to return to her paperwork, and Matt and I headed for the door.

"Will you get a coat?" Zane's voice demanded irritably. I had no idea where he was, but I could hear him. "You're going to freeze in that dress!"

Matt reached the door and started to open it for me, but after surveying me with another approving look, he stopped. "You might want a jacket or something," he said helpfully. "It can get pretty windy."

"Right," I said tentatively, my head beginning to spin. I appreciated the concern—at some level—but if Zane didn't cut out the disembodied-voice thing, this was going to be a very long afternoon. I grabbed my mother's jacket, since my own fleece hoody was still clammy from last night's adventure, and hurried back toward the door. Zane was still nowhere to be seen, but just in case, I mouthed a silent plea backwards down the hall: "No interference!"

We descended the steps to the driveway and hopped into Matt's car—a modest sedan that probably belonged to his dad. He put his keys in the ignition, then turned to face me. "Anything in particular you want to see? I hear you've already done the base and the North Shore, which is good, because the base is boring and I totally suck at surfing."

I laughed. "Well, I can't even swim, so no problem, there. But I would like to see more of the coast. Or maybe we could drive by some of the high schools around the base? I don't know where I'll be going yet."

He considered a moment. "Okay. We'll drive up to Turtle Bay and down the windward side. You'll like that. Then the high schools. Mine's the best, of course."

"Of course. What do you like about it?"

Our initial awkwardness eased up as I coaxed Matt into talking about what were obviously his favorite topics: football, wrestling, and water polo. He enjoyed talking about them so much I had little opportunity to ask some of the questions that popped into my head as we drove northeast, like why such a huge stretch of beachfront property was devoted to placidly grazing sheep, where the famous Banyan trees from *Lost* were located, and whether it was really safe to buy shrimp out of a van on the side of the road. But I didn't mind. Though a tad self absorbed, Matt was also refreshingly humble, talking more about his screw-ups than his successes. I was soon so at ease with the normalness of it all that I managed to forget about Zane altogether.

"We'll get out here for a minute," Matt announced, turning off the main road into a residential area. "It's called La'ie Point; you'll like it."

I wasn't worried about Matt being a serial killer. Not really. But as he proceeded to drive through a tight maze of small houses and tiny residential alleys that looked like they couldn't possibly lead anywhere, I felt just enough of a flicker of apprehension to let my eyes stray behind me.

Zane lounged casually across the back of the sedan, his hands locked behind his head, his feet stretched out on the seat cushion. Dressed impeccably in a tailored black business suit, crisp white shirt, and polished shoes— complete with opulent watch, mirror-lensed sunglasses, and the unmistakable bulge of a shoulder holster—he was the perfect image of a secret service agent. Or at least the Hollywood version of one.

His expressionless face swiveled my direction. He nodded.

I turned quickly back around.

"Rain's coming," Matt announced, bringing the car to a halt in a parking area by the vast ocean that had appeared out of nowhere. "That's one thing you'll get used to out here—blue sky one minute, pouring rain the next. Makes life interesting, I guess. You want to walk around?"

I opened my door and stepped out.

The weather had indeed changed dramatically. The sun was gone, occluded by one of the many clumps of low-hanging purplish clouds that drifted rapidly across the sky. A wicked wind blew in off the water, which had turned from azure blue to a smoky gray. There were no giant waves here, just a vast, heaving soup of whitecaps that broke and splashed as far out as the eye could see.

I grabbed my jacket as I shut the door, cutting off what was possibly a wind-muffled "I told you so," coming from the back seat. My chivalrous escort—the live one—came quickly around the car to help me get the jacket over my shoulders.

"I've always loved this place," Matt said cheerfully, not the least affected by the ominous feel to the weather. He led me up to the edge of the lot, where gravel and ground changed abruptly to irregular mounds of lava rock. Ahead of us was a spit of land that led far out into the ocean like a pier, and which already hosted a couple pickup trucks and some locals with fishing gear. The view from the end would be fabulous indeed—nearly 360 degrees of ocean, with the mountains of the windward side clearly visible in the distance.

Unfortunately, it was starting to sprinkle.

"Check this out," Matt said, tugging my arm to the left and leading me out onto one of the lava mounds closer to the car. I kept my eyes down as we went; the surface was like walking on mangled iron—full of pits, sharp curves, and jagged edges—and my flip-flops were less than ideal for the task. But before I could sprain an ankle Matt stopped and pointed out toward the ocean. "Isn't that cool?"

He pointed to a long ridge of rock several hundred feet offshore, which rose from the ocean to tower an indeterminate number of stories in the air. Right through its center was a giant, gaping hole. "Tsunami punched that out," Matt explained. "All in one day. *Wham*. Wind and water have got some pretty serious power out here, huh?"

I hugged my jacket tighter around me. The view was beautiful, but I couldn't shake a certain apprehensive feel about the place. Maybe it was the violence of the churning water, or the clearly impending cloudburst. Maybe it was just the shadows. There were an awful lot of them here, which made them harder to ignore. Over Matt's left shoulder, a man in overalls and no shirt perched precariously on the edge of the cliff, reading a letter. Half a dozen fainter people in Polynesian garb milled about all over the rocks, and some hippie types were making out on the land spit, right next to the secret service guy.

I blinked. The latter was Zane, of course, taking in the view. As I watched, he glanced back at me, then gestured dramatically out toward the open sea. I looked in the direction he pointed, and my heart skipped. "Look!" I said excitedly to Matt, pointing myself. I had only seen the movement for a split second, but I had watched enough nature programs to recognize it. The flash of bold black and white that had appeared above the churning gray water was nothing less than a breaching whale.

The animal disappeared again for several seconds, then treated us both to an encore. The fluke of its tail rose high above the surf, then crashed back into the water with a mighty flick.

"A humpback!" Matt said excitedly. "Wow. I've never seen one of those before!"

"Really?" I asked. "Are they rare?"

"Oh, no," he answered honestly. "Other people see them all the time. I've just never gotten lucky. Thanks, Kali. That was pretty cool." He threw an arm around my shoulders and gave me a friendly squeeze.

"You're welcome," another male voice said flatly.

Zane was standing right behind us. "Rain's coming, by the way," he muttered.

The words were hardly out of his mouth before the deluge began. Rain poured down in a sudden torrent as if the sky had opened up like a sieve, and Matt and I couldn't help laughing as we hauled back over the lava rocks as fast as we could—which was not fast at all—to get back to the relative safety of the car. We arrived dripping wet, but fortunately our jackets had taken the brunt of it.

"Don't worry," Matt assured, starting up the car again and turning on the heater. "The sun will be out again before we get to Chinaman's Hat. Promise."

I smiled. Seeing the whale had changed the atmosphere of the place considerably. Perhaps, in sunlight, I would have found La'ie Point perfectly pleasant. It was hard for me to tell, sometimes, which emotions were my own and which I was picking up from something—or someone—else. The fact that I could feel what the shadows were feeling was an aspect of the curse I had always resisted, and at times tried to deny altogether. It was an invasion I found hard to tolerate.

With the car heater running, we dried out and warmed up quickly, and within a few minutes the skies has lightened and we were cruising down the highway with the windows cracked again.

The windward side of the island was gorgeous. Being created by volcanoes, Oahu had no shortage of mountainous terrain; but I could see that its most dramatic peaks were along the eastern coast. Here, sharp points of green and gray stood up acutely, their tops buried in misty purplish clouds, their sides swooping nearly straight down to the water's edge. The road hugged the narrow coastline with spectacular views in either direction, keeping me well entertained while Matt—who admitted he knew virtually nothing about the area—told me more about his high school and why I should go there.

Zane remained in the back seat, but said nothing; and when once or twice I glanced at him he seemed to be absorbed in thought.

Matt stopped the car again near Chinaman's Hat, an interesting cone-shaped island that popped out of the water a couple hundred yards offshore, just begging for a child's game of "king of the mountain." His prediction had been correct. The sun was shining again.

"So," he said, settling next to me on top of a picnic table. "What do you think of The Rock so far?"

"Love The Rock," I said without hesitation. *If only I could move Kylee and Tara here with me.* My phone had been buzzing with texts all afternoon, but I had been waiting for a moment alone to answer them.

"I was thinking," Matt began, looking at me hopefully, "are you hungry yet? One of my favorite restaurants is right around the bay, in Kailua. If we eat an early dinner now, we can skip most of rush hour in Honolulu. We might not make it back to the North Shore by eight, though, if you still want to see the high schools and everything."

I worked hard to suppress a grin. My eyes floated involuntarily toward Zane, who was leaning against a palm tree a few feet away. He removed his sunglasses and threw me a pointed look.

Told you so.

I didn't believe that Matt had any real romantic interest in me—twenty minutes with the football-playing wrestler had shown me that he was a guy who could take his pick where girls were concerned—and to date, I had never been anybody's pick for anything but a gal pal. I was too tall, too bony, and—according to the undisputed queen of flirtation, Kylee—too unwilling to feed a guy's ego with mindless adoration.

Matt, I assessed, was a genuinely friendly enough sort to enjoy spending an afternoon with "the new girl" for a change of pace, if nothing else. But his interest would end there. If I did happen to run into him at school in the fall, I would probably be long since forgotten.

But one never knew.

And I *was* enjoying his company so far.

"Sure," I answered brightly. "I'll just call my parents and give them an update. What kind of restaurant?"

"Oh, they've got everything," Matt answered with a smile. "I like the *kalua* pig—that's barbecued pork, by the way—but you can get burgers, spaghetti, whatever." He sprang up. "I'm making a run to the restroom. Meet you back at the car?"

I nodded, and he headed off.

Zane looked after him, scowling.

"What?" I demanded. "You don't seriously think he's dangerous, do you?"

Zane looked thoughtful for a moment, then came and sat down beside me. "No," he answered. "He's a nice enough guy."

There was a melancholy tone to his voice that disturbed me. A gust of wind blew off the water and whipped my hair around my face; predictably, it didn't stir his curls at all. I frowned. His transparent ripples seemed suddenly more prominent.

"Then what's wrong?" I probed.

He looked at me with surprise. "Nothing's wrong," he said more cheerfully. "I mean, other than being dead, of course. But I'm used to that. Never mind me."

I eyed him suspiciously. "Liar. There is too something wrong. And it doesn't have anything to do with Matt, does it? You've remembered something else. About your mother?"

"Wow," he said brusquely, sliding off the table top. "You're pretty scary. I think I'd better put these back on." He replaced the sunglasses, then gestured toward the car.

"After you. Unless, of course..."

"What?"

"Unless you'd rather I left the two of you alone." I could no longer see his eyes, but his tone had turned serious. "I will, you know," he continued quietly. "If that's what you want."

My mind spun. It was what I *should* want. Wasn't it?

I opened my mouth to answer, but nothing came out. *No-nonsense Kali*, I reminded myself firmly. *Just tell him the truth.*

"Actually," I said matter-of-factly, moving toward the car. "I kind of like having a personal bodyguard."

I was walking a step ahead of him, but threw a quick glance over my shoulder.

He was grinning again.

# chapter seven

I could see why Matt, who had only moved to Hawaii a couple years ago himself, was attracted to the restaurant. A local hangout popular with military types from the nearby Marine base, it offered a comfortable blend of Hawaiian traditional and down-home American ambience. A Polynesian-styled wooden deck, complete with as-yet unlit tiki torches, led into a cozy dining room and bar that could have been plucked from anywhere in generica, except that the giant picture windows on one side offered a pleasantly tropical view of ducks floating on a meandering canal. Matt and I settled into a table by the window where, much to his delight, I joined him in ordering the *kalua* pig. After discovering that a good friend of his was working in the kitchen, he excused himself to go say hello—and to see if he could wheedle us some extra pig meat.

Matt hadn't been gone three seconds when Zane, whom I hadn't seen since we parked the car, appeared in his empty chair. The secret service outfit had been abandoned in favor of a Hawaiian shirt and shorts, but the funky sunglasses remained perched on top of his head, nearly buried by blond curls.

"He likes you, you know," he announced matter-of-factly.

I shrugged. "As a friend, maybe."

Zane's eyebrows lifted. "Not if he can help it."

I shifted my eyes away from him. There was a compliment in there somewhere, but the whole topic made me faintly uncomfortable. As did talking to thin air in a crowded restaurant.

No one seemed to be paying any attention, but just in

case, I pulled out my cell and held it close to my ear. "What did you remember about your mother?" I asked, changing the subject.

He stared at me a moment, clearly aware of my tactics. "I don't want to get into it now. But it wasn't about my mother, it was about my father."

"What about him?" I asked eagerly. "Is he... still alive?"

"No," Zane answered. "He's not. So, how do you feel about this Matt character? What do you really know about him?"

I exhaled. Zane's tone was breezy enough, but I had the feeling that he was covering—that he was, in fact, quite upset about something. Something other than Matt. "What does it matter to your problem?" I challenged. "We were talking about your parents."

He thought a moment. "They're kind of related," he said vaguely. "Let me ask the question another way. How much does Matt know about you? Does he know how many fouettés you can turn?"

I blinked at him, lost. "And that matters... why?"

The green eyes that looked back at me were suddenly awash in sadness—at least for the few seconds I could see them before he replaced the mirrored sunglasses.

"My father was murdered, actually," he said flatly. "Shot at point-blank range by an ex-girlfriend as he walked out of a bar with his current one."

I swallowed. "I'm sorry," I responded weakly, at a loss. "How... how old were you?"

"I was ten when it happened. But I didn't know the truth till a couple years later, when I searched his name online. My mother had told me he died in a bank robbery—that he was a hero."

A long silence followed. I had no idea what to say. The

sounds of the background seemed suddenly magnified: clinking glasses, rattling plates, toddlers babbling, people laughing, the drone of the TV monitors in the bar. There were several shadows around, both inside the restaurant and beside the canal... I hadn't realized they were there before.

Zane sat up suddenly, removed his glasses, and leaned toward me. "Look, Kali, I'm sorry. I shouldn't have said anything while you're in the middle of a date. I wasn't planning to, it just sort of—" he broke off. "Let's forget it for now, okay?"

"I'm the one who's sorry," I said, finding my voice at last. "It must be awful to remember something like that. Does it... I mean, does remembering your childhood seem to have helped... anything?"

He stood up—a feat he could accomplish without bothering to push back his chair. "Not that I can tell," he answered, his tone lighter. "But seriously—don't worry about it. Superjock won't be happy if he comes back to find I've ruined your mood. It will screw up his next move."

"He's not—"

"Yeah, he is," Zane interrupted, managing a grin. "See you."

He dissolved into a blur, leaving me staring into an empty chair. I looked around, but knew I wouldn't find him. When Zane didn't want to be seen, he wasn't. I pulled my phone away from my ear with a sigh, absently checking the screen.

I had four waiting texts. I scrolled down to open Kylee's first.

So... which 1s hotter? surfer or officers son?

Followed ten minutes later by:

> **Answer MEEEEE!!!!!**

Tara was not a whole lot subtler.

> **How is the tour? Are you getting to see the whole island, or just Honolulu?**

Followed a whole half hour later with:

> **You do realize that I have no life, that half of Cheyenne is out of town, and that living vicariously through you is my only source of entertainment? No pressure or anything. TEXT ME!!!**

Before I could answer either, Matt returned to the table and slid into his chair. "Justin's taking care of us," he announced with a smile. Then, with a glance at my phone, "Oh, yeah. This thing's been buzzing all afternoon." He pulled his own phone out of a back pocket and glanced at the screen. "Ten texts! Sheesh." To my surprise, he quickly repocketed it. "They can wait."

He turned his full attention to me, along with a winning smile. I smiled back and put my own phone away. Kylee and Tara would understand. Eventually.

"So," he began with enthusiasm. "What else would you like to see around Honolulu?"

The meal passed pleasantly, with Matt at no loss for words when it came to talking about things within his—admittedly limited—sphere of knowledge of the island. He couldn't tell me a whole lot about tourist destinations or local history, but he was a fount of information when it came to the high school scene. I learned that Hickham had a pretty good social group going, which was nice, because the base kids were spread over a lot of different schools, both public and private. Matt had a lot of opinions on which schools were better than others and why, and I studied him as he talked, musing over what my friends in Cheyenne would make of him. He was no intellectual giant, perhaps, but few of the girls would even notice that, preferring brawn over brains anyway. Tara wouldn't, but she would also be fair enough to admit that, for a jock, he was sweet and uncharacteristically humble. Kylee would swoon, period.

Oahu was treating me well.

We finished dinner by sharing a rather excellent slice of chocolate cake, then headed back to the car for our drive over the mountains to Honolulu. Zane was waiting for us in the parking lot, unaware that he was standing immediately next to a particularly vivid set of shadows—a young airman in uniform running to, and embracing, an elderly man. It was a poignant scene, but with long-practiced will I forced my attention back to the living and got in the car.

Zane slid smoothly into position in the rear seat, but avoided meeting my eye. He had added a pair of earbuds to his accessories, and I wondered vaguely if they were functional or if he was only giving me the illusion he wasn't eavesdropping.

"I thought we'd take the Pali Highway and stop at the lookout," Matt said enthusiastically. "It's an awesome view from the mountains—you'll love it. Sound good?" He reached his hand casually across the car, grasped my own hand, and gave it a friendly squeeze.

"Sounds great," I answered, avoiding the temptation to throw a glance over my shoulder at Zane. The surfer had been right, after all. Matt had crossed over the "I just want to be friends, so don't get any ideas" line pretty fearlessly about halfway through dinner, and was now well into the

"I'm up for whatever, if you are" zone. For the undisputed gal pal of Cheyenne, this was brave new territory, and I had to admit I wasn't hating it.

The drive up into the mountains was beyond beautiful. Since I knew that Hawaii kept pretty much the same temperature all year round, I wasn't expecting March to feel like spring. But everywhere around us the foliage was green, fresh, and bright, with the hint of a rain shower— either just passed or still on its way—around every corner. As we climbed upwards in altitude it appeared as though we were driving into a cloud; the air grew heavy with mist, and increasing winds buffeted against the sedan's now-closed windows. By the time we reached the turnoff to Pali Lookout, the sky had turned uniformly gray. But as we drew near to the site itself, the atmosphere became suddenly, drastically darker... as if some unseen, malevolent hand had surreptitiously drawn down a shade.

My heart beat faster; my shoulders shivered. I told myself it was nothing. Just a trick of the light.

I didn't believe me.

Matt parked his car in the designated lot and pulled out his wallet. "You have to pay to park here," he explained, "which is a kind of a rip-off, since there's no where else you can possibly park, but that's okay. I'll go pay. You can head on up to the point if you want; I'll catch up with you."

It was noisy here. So noisy. Like thunder, but not.

We got out of the car, and as soon as my door was locked Matt headed for the kiosk, where a line had formed behind a befuddled middle-aged woman who was obviously having trouble with the ticket machine.

I moved forward on my own, slowly.

I had to force myself to move at all.

Shadows were everywhere. Half-naked bodies. All

men. Shoulder to shoulder, a writhing mass teeming with sweat-soaked skin, blunt cudgels, and puncturing spears. They surrounded me; I could not take a step without moving straight through them. There were hundreds of them. Thousands.

"Zane?" I heard the voice as though it were someone else's. Weak, far away.

"Yes?" He was beside me in an instant, oblivious to all the shorter, darker skinned men who occupied the exact same space.

My steps halted. My pulse pounded in my ears. "I don't think I can do this."

"Do what?"

His puzzled voice was muffled by the shouting. The groaning. The distant screaming. The incessant roaring, above it all, of a wicked mountain wind.

A sharp chill whipped through me like lightning. A cold sweat broke out on my skin.

"Something happened here," I whispered, in a voice I could barely hear myself. "Something horrible."

I could not explain to him—to anyone—how much more surrounded me than what I was seeing and hearing. I could be blindfolded with earplugs; it wouldn't matter. I could *feel* what was happening, in every fiber of my being, weighing me down like a giant boulder sinking ever deeper into the darkest and coldest of oceans. It was fear. Gut-wrenching fear. So real, so palpable, it was sickening. There was anger, there was rage, there was determination. But above them all, the putrid, sickly fear rose high and biting and merciless... and infinite.

"Stay here a minute," Zane answered firmly. "Don't move."

I could not if I tried. I raised my eyes toward the place where the live humans clustered; a concrete platform, a metal railing... what must undoubtedly be a gorgeous view beyond. The mountains were split by a natural gap here, offering what from this height must be a sweeping eyeful of the windward coast. But I could move no closer. Up ahead... the edge of the cliff... it was worse, there. The bodies were facing away from it but moving toward it, moving backward—against their will. They were fighting the relentless flow, the sea of other bodies, with everything they had. Desperate. Terrified. As one, hundreds of them—before me, behind me, through me—pushed outward, toward the parking lot.

As one, they were pushed back toward the edge.

"Kali?" Zane stood before me now, blocking my view of the platform. "You're right. Something did happen here. There was a battle."

Yes, a battle. Senseless, needless. Brutal, bloody.

"The sign says that in 1795 Oahu was invaded by an army from the big island, and that the defenders were driven here."

They knew what was happening. They could see it. They could hear it. Behind them, their own brothers were vanishing into thin air. In screams and shouts and groans of anguish, they were here one minute, gone the next. Not by bullet, or arrow, or blade... those would be an honorable way to die.

Instead, they were falling.

Tumbling hundreds of feet, propelled through space.

Their bodies smashed to death upon the rocks.

I closed my eyes. It didn't help. My skin was bathed with clammy sweat. My hands trembled violently inside my pockets, and my crossed arms wrapped my jacket so tightly around me I could barely breathe.

"Kali, look at me," Zane urged. "A lot of people died here. They were forced off that cliff to their deaths. That must be what you're seeing. I'm sorry... it must be horrifying."

They knew what was happening. That was the worst of it. They knew they had to press forward, but they couldn't. They were forced back. Farther and farther, closer to the cliff edge. Every step brought more screams from behind, more muffled thumps of shattered body on rock, body on top of body. They couldn't stop it. They couldn't fight it. They couldn't do anything.

They were going to die.

"Do you want to go?"

My nod was mechanical, my movement controlled. I forced myself to look in the direction of the kiosk, where on other side of hundreds of milling shadows Matt had chivalrously stepped forward to help the woman at the front of line with the machine. It seemed impossible that neither group could be aware of the other; impossible that such normalcy and such hideous suffering could coexist at all.

"I can't just leave," I squeaked, bucking myself up with every ounce of strength still in me, which felt like virtually none. "He'll think I'm a nutcase."

*And I am not a nutcase*, I repeated to myself. It was the point that had always helped me keep the shadows at bay. I had conquered them before. I could do it again.

"I have to stay," I proclaimed, swallowing hard and moving determinedly toward the platform. "I can do it."

With every step, the weight on my soul crushed heavier. Their fear pierced through me, consumed me. I could not block it out. The closer I got to the edge of the cliff, the more force their emotions exerted on me. I could *feel* them, all of them, at once. The straining effort, the sting of failure, the disbelief, the stunning knowledge of nothingness behind... and then, in a heartbeat, nothing underfoot. The anguish of pulling at, reaching for friends, fellows, the guilt of knowing that by trying to save themselves, they only moved each other closer to death…

"Kali?" Zane repeated gently. His face was inches from mine; his expression a mask of concern. "You're shaking like a leaf. Go back to the car."

"I can't," I protested, even as the ground beneath me seemed to sway—a seething floor of noise and blood.

Get a hold of yourself!

"Superjock will understand," Zane protested. "Just tell him you're sick. It's not a lie, you're completely green—you look like you're about to throw up or pass out… or both."

The horizon swam.

Shouts. Screams. Spattering.

Fight it!

"I can't act sick," I argued, thanking God for my inborn streak of stubbornness—one trait that had never yet failed me. "He'll think his friend at the restaurant poisoned me. He'll feel awful… he'll take me straight home."

"Then tell him you're afraid of heights," Zane said quickly. "You have all the symptoms. Cold sweat, shaking, vertigo. He'll buy it."

Crush of bone. Wails of agony. Louder now, and louder still…

"You have to go back to the car!" Zane said firmly, shooting out a useless, vaporous arm in a vain attempt to steady me as my top half swayed dangerously to the right. His arm passed through me, and once again I felt the slightest buzz of vibration—just enough to focus my attention and regain my balance. "Kali, trust me," he cajoled. "Matt is the type that likes to take care of delicate females. Just lean on one of those beefy arms of his and tell him you need him—he'll be thrilled. Get your story ready—he's coming now."

No way to stop it. No way out. Nothing to do except fight, push. Frantic, hysterical, flying, falling, striking...

"You didn't get too far!" Matt teased, throwing a careless arm around my shoulders and propelling me closer to death.

Not death! Stop that!

I planted my feet. "Matt?"

He stopped in his tracks and swung round. "What is it?" he asked, one look at my face turning his expression into concern. "What's wrong?"

"I... um..."

"Tell him!" Zane ordered.

"I'm sorry," I spat out. "This is really embarrassing and I should have said something sooner, but you see—"

My sweat had soaked through my dress. The screaming was hideous, gut-wrenching, endless...

"I'm afraid of heights," I blurted, my voice cracking. "I can't do it. I can't go any closer. I'm sorry, but I *just can't.*"

Matt's blue eyes pierced into mine. His concern faded—amazingly—into a smile. With one motion he threw an arm around my middle, hugged me tight, and whirled me around. "Is that all?" he said cheerfully. "Wow, I thought you were really sick or something. Come on— let's get out of here."

With his strong arm guiding me, we made it back to the car in record time, and within seconds we were pulling out of the lot and back onto the road.

The noise faded. The shadows thinned, then gradually disappeared. The biting fear ceased its death grip on my roiling insides... but it refused to leave me altogether. My hands still trembled; my body was still cold.

"Thanks," I said feebly. "I know you must think I'm a

real wimp——"

Matt shot his free hand across the car to grip mine. "Kali, you don't have to say anything. I know what it's like. And by that I mean, *I know what it's like.*"

My eyes widened. "You're... afraid of heights, too?"

He chuckled. "Not heights, no. I'd be a pretty sucky candidate for a pilot with that problem. But mine's almost as bad. I get claustrophobic."

A grin played at the corners of my mouth. The weight of grayness around me began to lift a little. "Really?"

"Like, seriously," he insisted. "My dad's worried about me freaking out in a cockpit or something, but that doesn't bother me. I can get close and personal with walls, as long as there's a window around and some breathing room. But you put me on a stalled elevator with so many people I can't even stretch out my arms——"

He gave an exaggerated shudder. "I swear to God, Kali, I completely lost it in front of half the football team one time. We were going to a banquet in Honolulu on the top floor of this high rise, and there were way too many of us packed in the elevator—the guys were making a joke out of it, you know. And either they broke the stupid thing or our weight tripped some kind of safety sensor—in any event, we were stuck in that god-awful box for twenty minutes before they got the door open, and I was one hundred percent convinced I was going to die."

"I can imagine," I commiserated.

"The funny thing was—I really was about to die," he insisted. "Because if I'd had to stay in that place another five minutes, either I would have had a heart attack or my teammates would have beat the crap out of me for blubbering like an idiot."

He chuckled to himself, and—feeling like I'd been given permission—I laughed with him. "That must have been really awful."

"Yeah, well... the aftermath was no fun either. I *still* get abused about it, and it's been two years!"

"Kids can be cruel," I quipped with a grin. We were moving down out of the mountains now, with views of the city of Honolulu peeking out at us periodically, boasting of much, much more to explore. The horrors of Pali Lookout... the sights, the sounds, the bone-numbing fear... were not yet completely vanquished.

But they were getting there.

Unconsciously, I squeezed Matt's hand.

He smiled at me and squeezed back.

# chapter eight

"And this," Matt announced with a proud flourish, "is Frederick High School."

The sprawling, white plaster building looked more like a motel than a high school, having two stories with outside walkways, both protected by the typical wide-eaved, gently sloping Hawaiian roof. Two taller, boxier buildings which I assumed were a gym and an auditorium rounded out its sides, with an athletic field on one end and a moderately sized parking lot on the other.

"It probably looks small to you," he continued, "compared to public schools on the mainland. But it's the second biggest private school here. Some of them have, like, five kids in a class. And we've got the best facilities by far. Saint Anthony's gym is crap and their field's always flooding."

It was evening already, but clusters of students could still be seen coming and going from the building. There were almost as many dead ones as live ones.

What *was* it about Hawaii and shadows? Cheyenne had its fair share, as did every place else I'd ever lived. But the past few days in Oahu their presence had seemed inescapable—and that was without even considering Zane.

"So," Matt said happily, squeezing my hand again. "What do you think? Do you want to see inside? It looks like something's going on in there—door's probably open."

I tried to concentrate on what Matt was saying as the shadow of a Hawaiian boy, roughly thirteen or fourteen, shirtless and shoeless, shimmied up a nonexistent flagpole twenty yards away.

The kid was upset about something.

"We'd probably better not right now," I said impetuously, anxious to get away from the shadow, who I feared was about to hurt himself. I averted my eyes, irritated greatly by my sudden weakness. I *did* want to see the blasted school. But I couldn't, not now. Something bad was also bound to happen to the two shadow girls in skirts who were smoking by the side entrance... one of them was so afraid I could taste it. And she kept looking over her shoulder...

Ignore them!

With a huge effort, I turned to Matt with a smile. "I wish I could stay longer, but I do want to drive by a couple other schools, too, and we're already running late. Would you mind?"

"No, that's fine," he responded, his disappointment poorly concealed. "When do you have to leave? Maybe we could come back some time."

"I don't know," I answered vaguely, relieved as the car turned and pulled away. I hated seeing the shadows of other kids. Even though I reasoned that just because I saw them in their youth didn't necessarily mean they had *died* young, there was something about it that was unsettling. More unsettling than usual, even.

Come to think of it, a lot of the shadows I'd been seeing lately were more upsetting than usual.

Why *was* that?

My heart began to pound again.

"He thinks you're blowing him off, Kali," a familiar voice said softly from the back seat. "Which—for the record—would be fine by me, but I have a feeling you don't intend to. You're seeing more shadows, aren't you?"

I jerked, pulling my sagging frame up straight again. "I'm sorry, Matt," I said quickly, forcing cheerfulness. "I was thinking about something else. What did you say?"

His face flooded with relief. "I asked how much longer you were staying."

"We planned for a week, originally," I explained. "But we left it flexible. My mother is determined to find a house, and I can get an excuse from school if I need it."

He smiled. "Cool. We'll check out the competition, then. Are you Catholic?"

"Partially," I answered.

He chuckled. "That'll be good enough for Saint Anthony's."

A few minutes later we arrived at the school in question, which I had enough sense not to compliment on its comparatively larger buildings or more spacious grounds. Matt was right about the athletic field, though. It wasn't flooded at the moment, but the ducks that meandered about on its outskirts looked distinctly hopeful.

I drew a breath of relief. There was less traffic here, living or otherwise.

"So, what's the real reason you don't like Saint Anthony's?" I asked teasingly.

He smirked. "Well, mainly because they kick our butts at football," he admitted. "Aside from that, I'm just kidding. It's okay. As good as anywhere. Oahu can be a rough place if you haven't heard—long history of racial tension. Nobody's a majority here. White, Asian, and Hawaiian all have to get along, not to mention the whole local-versus-military thing. But it can be pretty cool, too. I've got friends of all shades here—not like some of the backward, racist holes I got stuck in when I was a kid."

"I hear that," I muttered thoughtfully.

"We can swing by some of the public schools near the base if you want," he suggested. "Does your dad want to stick close to work?"

I looked over his shoulder to notice a guy—a living one, this time—emerging from a side door of what was probably the school's gym. Notable in that he was built remarkably like Matt, including the thick neck, I watched him absently as I answered.

"I doubt it. My dad doesn't mind driving. He's more concerned with finding a house my mother will like. I think they're leaning toward private school for me, though, since I've only got a year left and it's going to be tricky transferring everything before I apply to college. School administrators tend to be more understanding about that sort of thing when you're paying tuition."

"I bet," he agreed with a laugh.

The guy had spotted our car and stopped cold. He was of indeterminate origin, possibly part Hawaiian or part Asian, but also possibly not—his generically dark features could have come from any continent. He would have been quite good looking, had his narrowed eyes not been radiating such intense dislike I could feel a chill sliding up my backbone.

"Matt," I said warningly. "Who is that guy staring at us? Do you know him?"

Matt whirled around. To my surprise, he leaned out the window and threw the still scowling guy a friendly wave.

"Hey, Rod," he called amiably.

Rod's lips broke into a smirking half smile. He offered a begrudging, barely perceptible nod.

"My nemesis," Matt said jokingly, turning to me. "Guy plays every sport I play, and he's awesome at all of them. We crushed them in our last polo match, though. He's probably still ticked."

I tried to relax as I looked again at the figure on the sidewalk. "Ticked" did not begin describe the blatant hostility that flowed from him—nor did a loss at water polo.

Matt turned his attention back to me, seemingly unfazed. "You ready to go?"

"He really looks angry," I commented.

Matt glanced over his shoulder as he pulled the car away from the curb, threw Rod another wave, and drove on. "He's never a barrel of laughs," he said with a shrug, "but he's okay. Where to next, then?"

I started to say something else, but stopped myself. Matt's lack of concern was incomprehensible to me. Could he really not see…

A thought struck. A painful, gut-wrenching thought.

I needed to talk to Zane. But I couldn't say a word. There was no way I could communicate with him with Matt right there. My question would have to wait.

I tried hard to put it out of my mind.

The sun began to set.

The climax of this natural spectacle played out for us just as we reached the North Shore town of Haleiwa, and Matt pulled off the main road to take in the view at the nearest beach park. Zane made himself conspicuously absent as Matt and I walked to Pauena Point, enjoying the symphony of colors that danced over the water's edge, illuminating the clusters of puffy, low-slung clouds that moved lazily across the darkening sky.

"Welcome to Hawaii. Are you sold yet?" Matt asked with a grin, throwing an arm around my shoulders again. I wasn't a fan of handsy guys—not that, if you must know, I'd had much experience with them—but Matt managed to come off more like a giant teddy bear.

I had to admit, it worked for him. I didn't feel in the least bit threatened by his touch; instead, it felt comforting.

By the time we returned to the condo we had

exchanged cell phone numbers and I had committed to checking out the inside of Frederick High. I had also almost forgotten the unpleasant, lingering memories of Pali Lookout and the scowling jock at Saint Anthony's.

Almost.

Matt got out of the car and walked me in, despite my warning that doing so would result in an interrogation by my father about Matt's interest in the Air Force Academy and God only knew what else. I was right, of course. My father lay in ambush in the hallway, pretending to intercept us while taking out a half-full bag of trash. Luckily, Matt didn't seem to mind too much, and since my existence did not, predictably, come up anywhere in their conversation, things never got too awkward. Nevertheless, as an apology, I offered to walk Matt back out to the landing afterward... around the forgotten bag of trash.

"This has been really nice. Thanks," I said genuinely, as we lingered on the wooden platform outside. The continuous crash of the waves behind us floated on the air like music, and a sudden gust of night wind picked up my curls and lashed them across my face.

"You've been great company," Matt said softly, lifting a hand to brush my hair from my eyes. "I'll be your tour guide anytime."

I knew then, by sheer female instinct, that if I didn't say anything or move anywhere, he was going to kiss me. His intentions, like everything else that was going on in his uncomplicated mind, were clearly readable in his eyes.

I just wasn't sure how I felt about them.

I liked him a lot. Who wouldn't? He was sweet and good-looking and honest. He was fun to be around, and he had been remarkably understanding about my meltdown at Pali Lookout.

Still, I wasn't sure, and I had only a split-second to

decide. Because I also knew, by the same instinct, that all I had to do was make the slightest of backward movements, and Matt would abort the plan with no hard feelings. It was, after all, our first date. Not to mention the first time we ever met. He would have other opportunities.

Conflicting feelings swirled mercilessly in my head. Kylee and Tara—neither of whom were probably speaking to me at the moment—would have different takes. Kylee would tell me I was INSANE for not jumping on such a prime dish. Tara would tell me to be careful—he could be a real player back at his school, and how would I know?

How indeed.

A fraction of a second—that was all I had. He looked unquestionably handsome there in the moonlight, so attentive, so hopeful...

Does he know how many fouettés you can turn?

The memory of Zane's random, senseless question popped unbidden into my head, crashing through the rest of my thoughts like a freight train.

And that matters... I had answered... why?

The swirling conflict siphoned suddenly down into a single, unified stream. Matt didn't even know that I was a dancer, did he? Not that I had been keeping it a secret... he had simply never asked. We had never really talked about *me* at all.

I took a tiny step backward.

"I'll take you up on that," I said with a smile. "I do want to see your school again."

He smiled back, his eyes a trifle disappointed, but otherwise unhurt and unfazed. "It's a date, then," he said unequivocally, starting down the steps to his car. "I'll text you."

"See you!" I responded cheerfully, opening the door. Then, with a final wave, I ducked inside.

This time both my parents were waiting for me in the great room, eager to hear all about what parts of the island I had seen and whether or not I had any ideas of my own about schools—among other topics. They showed admirable restraint in not asking me specifically how I felt about Matt, but their endless questions nevertheless left me impatient and fidgety.

I wanted to talk to Zane. I hadn't had so much as a glimpse of him since before sunset, and I wondered if he had left me altogether.

The thought left a pit in my stomach.

After what seemed like an eternity, I escaped the inquisition and stepped out onto the deck. Zane was nowhere in sight, but I took the chance anyway.

"If you can hear me," I whispered, given that some barbecuing neighbors on the next deck were within earshot, "come talk to me in my room. Please?"

There was no response.

I went back inside and excused myself for an early bedtime, which raised no eyebrows, seeing as how we were all, biologically, still half on Mountain Time. As soon as the bedroom door was closed behind me, I looked around hopefully. "Zane?"

"By special invitation," he answered, lounging across the foot of my bed in nothing but board shorts, which along with the rest of him were soaking wet.

Glad as I was to see him, and as well as I knew— rationally—that it was all an illusion, I felt a flare of annoyance at the sight of the gritty sea water dripping onto my spread. I hated clammy sheets. "Do you mind?" I protested mildly.

"What?" he pretended innocently, looking down. "Oh, sorry. Forgot it's bedtime."

He changed in a blink. This time his curls were not

only dry, but perfectly coifed with slick hair gel. He was still bare chested, but now he wore blindingly bright blue oriental-silk sleep bottoms embroidered with neon orange fire and purple dragons—as if he'd stepped straight out of the seduction scene of a really bad movie.

"Zane!"

He dissolved into laughter, changing instantly into a suitably normal-looking tee shirt, shorts, and sandals. "Sorry," he repeated between gasps. "Couldn't resist. What's up?"

I took a few centering breaths, then sat down on the bed beside him. I was pretty sure he hadn't really left me at all this evening, but a part of me was afraid to ask. I knew he was dead and everything, but still, sitting with one gorgeous guy openly discussing one's date with another was beyond weird.

Thankfully, it wasn't "the date" I wanted to discuss.

"Did you see the guy at Saint Anthony's?" I asked. "The one Matt called Rod?"

"The one you were so worried about? Yeah, why?"

I waited for more reaction. "Well, didn't *you* find his attitude disturbing?"

Zane's brow furrowed. "I'm not sure what you mean. They didn't look like best buds, but so what?"

My heart began to race.

It couldn't be.

"Seriously, Kali," Zane began, his voice more concerned. "What is it that's got you so upset? I don't get it."

"I could feel him!" I blurted. My heart beat so hard I could hear my pulse in my ears.

Zane said nothing for a moment. "Okay… so can you please explain *that*? What do you mean, you could 'feel' him?"

"Like the shadows," I continued, trying hard to make more sense, but knowing that there was a limit—seeing as how nothing about the shadows ever made sense. "Some of the shadows... when I'm near to them, I can feel what they're feeling. Like that woman at the beach. I wanted to be near her because I could feel her joy. Not just witness it... I mean, I really *felt* what she was feeling."

Zane sat up straighter on the bed. "You could read her mind?"

"No," I said quickly, "It's not like that. I don't pick up thoughts. There's no language to it, no words. Just emotions."

"You didn't mention that before."

I hesitated. "I didn't always... I mean—" I broke off, unable to put into words what I had refused, for so long, to allow myself to think. "It didn't used to be so obvious. When I was little I didn't really pick up on the emotions. I don't know if it was because I wasn't paying attention, or if something about me changed as I grew up. But now, all of a sudden—"

I faltered again. Zane waited a beat, then prompted. "All of a sudden..."

I pulled myself up and began to pace. "All of a sudden, it's worse than ever. There are shadows *all over* this island! I've never seen so many of them, at least not considering how few people live here—I mean, how many people have *lived* here. And not only that, but I'm feeling them more. Even the older ones. It's like the whole emotion thing has kicked up a notch—and I don't know how to handle it!"

I plopped back down on the bed, exhausted.

"Okay," Zane confirmed. "I get it. But what exactly does that have to do with this guy Rod?"

I closed my eyes. Being able to tell Zane—to tell anyone—a load of seeming nonsense like I had just done without them doubting my sanity was a relief of epic proportions. If I wasn't still so freaked out, I would be overjoyed. But there was more to my story, and the last part was definitely the worst.

I opened my eyes and sat up. I was close enough to Zane that, if he had been alive, we would have been touching. As it was, I felt only the slightest buzz around my knee, where my bent leg grazed his extended one. "You saw Rod looking at Matt," I began carefully, "and you saw nothing except two guys who weren't friends. You didn't see anything... sinister?"

Zane considered. "No. It was a stare. But he smiled later... sort of. Matt knows the guy. He obviously didn't take it as anything threatening."

An involuntary shudder shook my shoulders. "I *saw* the same thing," I explained slowly. "But I *felt* something, too."

Zane's eyes widened. "You mean you felt him, like he was a shadow? You think he *is* a shadow?"

"No!" I protested. "He can't possibly be. Other people see him and interact with him, he's solid... he's definitely alive."

"Then what—"

"I'm *feeling* living people now!" I whisper-shouted, as loudly as I dared without my parents overhearing. I needed to say it out loud; I needed to hear it. "I have to be. There were no shadows anywhere near Rod. It scares me to death to think that this... this *thing* I have is changing, but I can't deny it anymore. It is. It's getting more powerful, more sensitive. Battlefields have always bothered me, but being at Pali Lookout today... it was almost unbearable. I've certainly never encountered anything like you before... a ghost, I mean. I don't know if it's being in Oahu, or if it's something about me, but it *is* happening. It's real. I wish I could make myself believe that I was imagining what I felt with Rod today, but I know that I wasn't!"

My voice cracked, and Zane leaned forward instinctively, as if to reach out a comforting arm. Realizing his mistake, he fell back against the wall instead, his jaw muscles clenched in agitation. He was silent for a moment, then asked quietly, "What did you feel from Rod, then? Something that scared you?"

I nodded. "He hates Matt, Zane. Really and truly hates him. I don't think he did always. The hatred felt, well... fresh. Like something had just happened. Something Matt might not even be aware of."

"Matt was just kidding about the nemesis thing," Zane agreed. "They may be competitive at sports, but I didn't get that he had any hard feelings toward the guy. If there's real hatred, Matt must be in the dark."

"That's what scares me," I said weakly. "I'm scared for Matt, first. That hatred was palpable; I don't know Rod at all, but if I had to guess, I'd say that a feeling that strong was *going* to get acted on, sooner or later. What if he's violent?"

"He may not be," Zane offered. "Most people aren't. Or the anger may resolve itself—maybe there was a misunderstanding of some kind."

"Maybe," I agreed, finding it hard to imagine a guy as friendly and transparent as Matt doing anything to rouse that kind of hatred. "But until I know for sure, it's going to keep scaring me. That... and the whole idea that this *thing* of mine—"

"You mean this gift?"

"This *curse*," I corrected. "The thought that this curse has more power over me than ever... that maybe I *can't* just ignore it anymore—"

"Then you'll use it well," Zane interrupted. His voice was gentle, but firm, and his eyes bore into mine, their green depths sparkling with empathy even as he argued with me. "And I'll do whatever I can to help you. I promise."

Does he know how many fouettés you can turn?

Zane's nearly solid face was inches from mine. For a moment, I had the very odd sensation, not entirely unpleasant, of careening off the cliff of Pali Lookout myself, spinning out into oblivion, weightless, carefree. But over my cliff, there was nothing but azure ocean, and a warm, golden sun was shining.

I drew back, gave my head a shake, and stood up.

It had a been a very, very long day.

Clearly, I needed some sleep.

# chapter nine

*It doesn't get any better than this,* I thought to myself dreamily, stretching out my legs and wiggling my toes in the sand. I couldn't believe that any place as picture perfect as Mokuleia Beach Park could also be so deserted... but it was. Though Mokuleia was part of the North Shore, it lay at the famous surfing strip's westernmost tip, just out of the tourist mainstream. Despite the fact that it was mid-morning on a gorgeous spring day, the wide, straight stretch of sandy beach, crashing turquoise waves, and brisk-but-warm tropical breeze were being enjoyed by only a handful of surfers out on the water, two middle-aged women sitting under a beach umbrella about fifty yards away, Zane (who was currently hanging with the surfers), and me. A few shadows flitted about too, of course, but none with emotions strong enough to disturb me. For once, I could be alone with my own thoughts.

I had quite a few of them.

My parents had been surprised when I declined to join them on today's house tour with the real estate agent, but the opportunity to have the car to myself all day was just too good to pass up. My Wyoming-raised spirit couldn't resist the chance to be behind the wheel again, exploring new territory, enjoying sweet control. My sense of direction left a lot to be desired, true, but I had something better than a GPS. I had Zane.

I smiled as I watched him catching yet another ride with a singularly unskilled surfer in mustard yellow shorts. The surfer wiped out on nearly every wave, allowing Zane to practice his rather eerie "this is where the board *should* be going" move, which involved his skimming over the water suspended in midair. This time he decided to shake things up, wiping out along with the surfer in spectacular fashion, flying head over heels in a back flip. Unlike the flailing mortal, however, Zane threw himself up in a perfect arc, coming down on the board just as it resurfaced, feet perfectly placed for the next ride.

"Showoff!" I yelled over the wind, laughing. Zane grinned back at me, finishing with a stage bow, but my mirth was dampened a bit when I realized that the women under the umbrella were glaring at me.

*Crap.* They no doubt thought I was yelling at the lousy surfer, who was floundering in the rough water, attempting to get back on his (apparently empty) board. I sunk back onto my beach mat, mortified. For all I knew, one of them could be his mother or something.

I pulled my phone quickly out from my pocket, wishing I had had it to my ear just now. I could get away with talking to Zane in public as long as I had my phone around, but yelling on the beach was a little harder to explain.

The phone had gotten a lot of use this morning. Kylee and Tara had begrudgingly forgiven me for ignoring their texts yesterday, but only after I agreed to describe for them every minute detail of my outing with Matt, no matter how many screens it took. I tried, but even leaving out everything to do with Zane and the shadows at Pali Lookout, it took fourteen texts to get them up to speed, and they still weren't satisfied. Kylee kept asking questions about Matt I had no idea how to answer (e.g., Has he ever had a serious girlfriend? Do you think he's the kind that actually *dances* at dances?), while Tara was apparently attempting to track our route geographically on some internet map site (e.g., Did you actually see Kailua Bay or did you just take H3 down to Pali Highway?).

They asked questions about "the surfer guy," too, which I took care to answer a little more vaguely. I really wished, now, that I'd never mentioned Zane in the first place. I wanted so badly to tell *someone* the truth about him—but coming close-but-not-quite was proving more frustrating than satisfying.

Another glider plane sailed overhead, heading for a landing at Dillingham Airfield across the beach road. The gliders were surprisingly loud, but since I'd always lived near air bases the ambience suited me fine. I looked up at the glider just in time to see Zane perched on the top of the tail. He performed a (rather pathetic) arabesque, then dived off and plummeted toward land at lightning speed. He stopped himself just inches from the sand in a dead halt, then relaxed onto its contours with a sigh—as if he had just finished a hard day's work.

My eyes rolled. "Were you this much of a showoff when you were alive?"

His sweat-laden brow (fake of course, but effective) creased in thought. "Couldn't tell you. But probably. I was a ham as a kid, that's for sure. I distinctly remember posing for surf pictures in Malibu when I was nine. The flavor of the month was seriously impressed."

"Flavor of the month?"

"My dad's latest girlfriend," he explained. "I only visited him a couple times a year, but it was never the same woman twice. 'Malibu' I remember, because she was a surfer herself. Got my dad into it—talked him into taking me for a lesson. One of the best days of my life, actually."

His tone turned thoughtful. I relaxed onto my mat and studied him. With a face and body like his, I was not at all surprised to hear that his father had been a chick magnet, but it was interesting that he didn't sound proud of it.

"You got along okay with your dad?" I asked tentatively.

"Oh, sure," he said dismissively. "He always tried hard to make me like him, when he was around. But he wasn't really interested in being a hands-on father. He seemed proud to have a son; he was generous with the child support. But he had no idea how to deal with a kid. That's why he always brought the girlfriends along. Malibu bought me ice cream, took my picture, told me I would be a great surfer someday. My dad spent more time watching her in her bikini."

"You noticed that at nine?" I said skeptically.

He shrugged. "So I was precocious. Dad's genes, you know."

He said it without a smile, seeming lost in thought. I got the distinct impression he wasn't telling me all that he was remembering.

"Zane?" I asked softly.

"Yes?"

"Have you remembered yet who you are... I mean, like your name? If you remember that much about your father, I was thinking maybe you could. Then we could look you up online... find out the rest. Maybe it would help."

I watched, surprised, as a distinct flicker of apprehension shot across his face. He turned his head away from me and gazed out at the ocean. "I didn't say *everything* was clear," he responded vaguely. He started to say something else, but stopped himself. After a moment he turned back to me, smiling again.

"So," he said casually, "What do Kylee and Tara think about our man, Matt? Did you get the girlfriends' seal of approval?"

I blinked at the change of subject. Zane was good at those. "Well, they only know what I tell them, don't they?"

I pointed out.

"You didn't kiss him last night. Why not?"

I blinked again. "Excuse me?"

"You heard me. He would have kissed you, but you stepped back. Why?"

"I thought you were surfing then!"

"No, you didn't."

He was right. I didn't. But pretending to be indignant was more appealing than answering the question. "I'm not going to discuss that with you," I said firmly. "We were talking about your father."

"Details of my life, details of yours. What's the difference?"

I narrowed my eyes at him. "You want to hear about my adventures as a nine year old, fine. You want to know what's going through my head when I'm on a date with a guy, you have to give me something of equal interest."

He smirked. "Such as?"

"Such as... have *you* ever had a serious girlfriend? Do you like to really dance at dances?" *Thanks for the material, Kylee.*

His eyebrows rose. "Good questions," he agreed. "I'd like to know the answers myself. Too bad I don't. You want me to guess? Let's say I had girls hanging all over me all the time, but I never really fell for any of them, because I'm off-the-charts picky. And I'm an awesome dancer, clearly. That good?"

"No!" I protested. "You just made that up!"

"Well, sure," he admitted. "But it's probably true. You can't know it isn't, can you?"

"Fine then," I blurted. "I didn't kiss Matt because he didn't know I was a dancer."

Zane flipped over on his side and looked at me intently. "Really?"

I took a breath. I had meant to make something up—something stupid or funny. Why had I told the truth?

Sheesh, I was pathetic.

"Maybe," I replied, thinking quickly. "But you can't know for sure, can you?"

A broad smile slid slowly across Zane's face, accentuating his too-cute-for-words dimples. "Touché."

He stood up and made a show of brushing nonexistent sand off his limbs. "So, where to next? Your wish is my command."

I looked speculatively down the coast in the direction of Kaena Point, the westernmost tip of the island where mountain slid straight down to water and killer waves of fifty feet or more were rumored to break in winter. It was a sort of wild preserve; no paved road led there. According to Zane, the waves were considered unsurfable because of high winds and poor rescue access. The latter was significant, as the point also boasted rip currents like a river and undertows that could pull your shorts off. For his own purposes, of course, Zane loved the place.

I was feeling adventurous. "Will you take me to Kaena Point?" I asked eagerly.

I had expected sheer, childish delight. Zane always got pumped when I showed interest in his waves. But to my surprise, he frowned.

"No," he replied. "That's not a good idea."

I stood up in protest. "Why not? There's a trail, isn't there? I have a water bottle. I can hike a few miles."

"I know you could; you're in great shape," he affirmed quickly. But then his tone turned melancholy. "Believe me, if I were alive, I'd take you in a minute. But I'm not... and I won't."

I stared at him, confused. "Why not? What difference does it make?"

He looked away from me, seeming uncomfortable. "Just think about it. It's a long hike, the path is full of pits and rocks, it's steep in places, and it can be treacherous. It's the kind of place it would be really stupid to go alone, which is exactly what you'd be doing."

"But I—"

"Don't you get it?" he responded, frustration breaking through his normally mild demeanor. "What would happen if you fell and twisted an ankle or something? It could be hours before anyone else came along—maybe even days. And what could I do? I couldn't help you walk. I couldn't bring you more water. I couldn't even tell anyone where you were!"

"I have my phone," I protested.

"And what if you fell in the ocean?" he continued. "What then? Do I float around next to you and watch you drown? I don't think so, Kali. I nearly got you killed once already. I'm not taking any more chances."

I opened my mouth to argue, but no words came out. I could tell by his expression just how serious he was. He must have been deeply shaken by what had happened with the toddler—and I guess I could understand why. It had made him feel helpless. As much as he had already lost by dying, that feeling in particular must be salt in an open wound. Much worse torture, I was sure, than my hypothetically twisted ankle.

I let out a breath. I was, for the record, perfectly capable of hiking six miles over rough terrain without fatally injuring myself. But I would prefer to make the journey with happy and willing company.

I glanced at my phone. "It'll be lunchtime soon anyway," I conceded, sitting back down on my mat. "Why don't you go out and rip a few more? Then you can take me out to eat in Haleiwa. I think I'll try one of those *kalua* pig tacos."

He smiled with relief. "Sounds great."

"You're buying, right?"

His green eyes twinkled at me. "As always."

His form dematerialized in a flash, rematerializing on
the nose of a board several hundred yards out over the
ocean just as my phone rang. Expecting a check-in call
from my parents, I raised it to my ear without looking at it.
Matt's voice on the other end surprised me.

"Hey, Kali! What's up?"

Just admiring the abs on a dead guy.

"Just chilling on the beach," I answered cheerfully.
"And you? Aren't you in school?"

"Yeah, but it's lunch," he replied. "Listen, there's
something I want to ask you. Are you free tonight?"

My heart skipped. I hadn't been imagining it after all,
had I? As unlikely as it seemed, a really good-looking,
athletic guy was actually interested in me. Not that I had
self-esteem issues or anything. I mean, there was no
reason a great guy *shouldn't* be interested in me. It just had
never happened before.

I pushed the image of Zane forcefully from my mind,
reminding myself, once again, that he didn't count. Aside
from the deadness thing, I was the only girl on the planet
he could talk to... of course he was going to be interested
in me.

Matt, however, had other options. Right?

"Yes, I'm free," I answered, breath held. "What's up?"

"There's this dance at my school tonight—the Spring
Fling. I was wondering if you wanted to go with me. I
would have told you about it yesterday, but I already had a
date. The thing is, she's home sick—she just texted to
cancel. So I thought, I know it's short notice and
everything, but it would be a great way to meet some

people, right?"

My heart thudded against my sternum. It was perfect. A little too perfect?

I fought off suspicion about the conveniently sick date. Hadn't crazier things happened to me in Oahu?

"Sounds great!" I said before I could think too much. "Are you sure it's okay to bring in an outsider?"

"Oh, sure!" he replied, obviously stoked. "Lots of people bring dates from other schools. You'll get to meet people from all over. It starts at eight—can I pick you up around seven? I'd ask you to dinner, too, but I can't get the car early enough to get out there in time—my sister has dibs this afternoon."

He sounded genuinely chagrined. I had no doubt he was telling the truth about the whole situation—broken date, sibling rivalry, and all. "That's fine," I assured, smiling to myself. Then a thought disturbed me.

"Oh, wait!" I asked, my hopes plummeting. "Is this a formal? Because if it is, I don't have a dress. I mean—I just packed for the beach, you know?"

His answering tone was nebulous. "No… it's not a formal. I mean, I don't think it is."

My brow furrowed. "You're not sure?"

There was a pause. "Well, the guys don't wear suits or anything."

I tapped my foot nervously on the sand. "What do the girls wear?"

Another pause. "Oh, you know. Dresses and stuff."

I took in a deep breath, fighting images of myself walking into a gymnasium packed with people I'd never met before, all of whom were wearing stylish formals… and I was in shorts and a cami with my sports bra showing. Or, worse yet, *they* were all wearing beach clothes and I waltzed in wearing a full-length, sequin-studded gown...

I shuddered.

"Matt?" I said tentatively.

"Yeah?"

"No offense or anything, but I really need a girl to tell me what they're wearing."

He exhaled thoughtfully. "Yeah, that would probably be good. Tell you what—I'll ask somebody and text you. Okay?"

I smiled again—tentatively. "Okay."

"Gotta go now. See you later, okay? This is going to be fun. Promise."

We said our goodbyes and hung up.

My heart was still racing. I forced in a few deep breaths. This was good, right? This was just the opportunity I wanted, right?

Crap, I was nervous. Why should I be so nervous? I liked dances. I could dance just fine—no worries about that. So I was used to going with a group of girlfriends rather than a date. What of it? Once you got there, everybody just rocked out in a big circle anyway, right?

Unless they did things differently in Hawaii...

My phone buzzed with a text. I whipped it out and hit the button. It was from Matt.

> **Julia says casual dresses, like sundresses, and nice sandals. That good?**

I sighed with relief.

> **Perfect. Thanx.**

I hit send and dropped the phone back down to my side, the wheels in my head turning rapidly. The nice sandals were no problem. But I had only one dress, casual or otherwise, and I had worn it last night.

I cast a glance out over the water at Zane. He was piggybacking on the shortboard of a hotdogger, who was zigzagging through, up, and over the waves like a skater boy on caffeine.

I wondered how he would feel about some shopping.

# chapter ten

The expression on Zane's face could best be described as a "pained wince."

"Shopping?"

"It'll be fun!" I cajoled, argument at the ready. Truth be told, I wasn't much of a clothes shopper myself, but hanging with Zane was always fun. We'd had a blast of a morning so far, and the thought of having no one to talk to while I got psyched about the dance was too depressing. "We don't have to drive all the way to Honolulu or anything," I assured. "I think I can find what I need at the tourist shops in Haleiwa. You can give me advice!"

The pained expression deepened. "For how long? Like... twenty minutes?"

I hedged. "Well, I will have to try a few dresses on."

He considered a moment. "Dresses? Well, okay. But I'll need to check out the changing rooms for you. Some of them can be pretty dangerous—"

"Zane," I interrupted.

"Yes?" he asked innocently.

"You're not going in the dressing rooms with me."

"Even if I—"

"No."

His lips twisted in chagrin. "Hmm... well, I suppose there could be other girls—"

"Zane!"

He chuckled. "Just kidding, of course. Even as a ghost, I'm always a perfect gentleman."

"Liar."

"Almost always?"

"Can we change the subject, please?"

His appearance morphed, in the blink of an eye, from dripping wet board shorts to a perfectly dry, bright green Hawaiian shirt and cutoffs. "All right, Kali. If you insist. Pig tacos in Haleiwa... and then shopping. But after this, you will officially owe me."

I grinned. "Not a problem."

—✠—

The weather remained obligingly beautiful. Warm but not hot, with blue skies, bright sun, and just the right amount of flower-scented breeze. My high spirits seemed slightly out of place, even to me, in light of the realizations I'd come to last night about the recent "enhancement" of my abilities. Then again, I had a lot of practice at ignoring things I didn't want to think about. And right now, I didn't want to think about anything except finding the perfect dress and having a great time at the dance tonight.

"First stop!" I said cheerfully, pointing ahead to a colorful shop perched mere inches from the cluttered, two-lane road that was Haleiwa's main drag. I had parked the car in a tiny lot at the south end so we could walk the length of the village and back. It was not the most leisurely of strolls, given that Haleiwa's mishmash of storefronts were often set perilously close to a street not nearly wide enough to accommodate the giant tour buses that frequently clogged it. But at least it had character. From high-end original art and hand-carved tikis to tacky shot glasses and hula dolls, you could find all things touristy in Haleiwa. What you wanted might be in a quaint little strip mall decorated with sweet-smelling flowers... but it could just as easily come from an ancient plantation shack with clapboard walls set right next to a dumpster buzzing with flies. Haleiwa's variety was part of its charm.

As was its wildlife. No sooner were the last words out of my mouth than a chicken skittered out from the bushes and ran directly into our path. Zane stepped unconcernedly through its tail feathers, but I nearly broke my neck trying not to trip over it.

I felt a buzz on the arm I thrust behind me as I caught myself—and realized that Zane must have reflexively shot out his hand to help. But when I looked around, his arms were already back at his sides, his expression sober.

"Good save," he commented as I regained my footing.

"Thanks," I responded, watching as the unrepentant hen scuttled off to join the handsome red rooster that lurked under a nearby fender. Both birds stared at me reproachfully.

"So we're buying you a longboard, right?" Zane questioned. "Were you looking to paddle into the big waves, or are we talking tow-in? Because if you're serious about tow-in, you'll need footstraps."

"Nice try," I interrupted. "Like I said, I need a dress. One nice enough for a school dance."

He stopped walking and turned to face me. "A school dance?"

I felt a sharp pricking of guilt. I hadn't meant to keep my plans a secret... the topic just hadn't come up yet. We had spent our taco-eating time chatting about other things, although at the moment I couldn't remember just what. It was easy to get off topic with Zane; he seemed to know something about everything. Everything *except* his own life since puberty, that is.

"Matt just asked me," I explained, feeling distinctly awkward, even as I assured myself that I shouldn't. I had no reason to think Zane would feel jealous. He and I were just friends; he was not technically alive. Looking for any more reasons he should *not* care if I went to a dance with another guy seemed silly.

And yet, as my eyes met his—which currently flickered transparent along with the bridge of his nose—I got the feeling that maybe he did.

A second later, though, the look in question was gone.

"Well, congratulations!" he said with a smile, walking forward again. "How did superjock work that out so fast?"

"His date got sick," I explained. "I'm the sub."

Zane smirked. "Matt have access to arsenic?"

I threw him an appropriate glare. "Stop that. I believe she really got sick. If I didn't, I wouldn't go."

Zane offered a good-natured shrug. "I guess it's fate, then. The timing is perfect—you couldn't ask for a better chance to meet the locals." He stopped dutifully in front of the store I had pointed to, but even as he spoke his gaze drifted longingly across the street, where countless boards of all shapes and sizes stood on the other side of a surf shop window, stacked vertically like a forest of gaudy trees.

"Are you sure you're okay with the shopping thing?" I asked, feeling another, even stronger pang of guilt.

"Absolutely," he responded at once. "No problem. I'm excited."

I frowned. "You don't sound excited."

He stopped looking across the street and considered a moment. "You're right, I don't. That was terrible. I'm normally a much better actor. Wait..." He dropped back a few paces, turned his back, then whirled around and caught up with me again. His face was now flushed with anticipation; his eyes sparkled. For a moment, I thought he had seen something interesting on the ground. "I am SO excited about shopping!" he exclaimed, throwing his whole body into a contortion I could only describe as a skip and a jump. *"Let's go!"*

I laughed so hard three people stopped and stared at me.

"Better?" he demanded, now perfectly calm again.

I groaned, wiping my watering eyes with one hand while pulling my phone self-consciously back to my ear with the other. "Oh, forget it!" I ordered. "Just go stare at the stupid boards, will you?"

"I thought you'd never ask," he said gleefully.

"Will you just... maybe... check in once in a while?" I begged. "I do want your opinion; there's no one else I can ask." It occurred to me, suddenly, that I could easily take a picture of a dress with my phone and send it to Kylee or Tara—or even my mother.

Somehow, that didn't seem like nearly as much fun.

"Will do!" he answered with a salute, barely waiting to get the last word out of his mouth before sprinting across the street through a mountain bike and a minivan and springing into the window of the surf shop like a gazelle.

"Show off," I muttered again.

A sudden cloud seeped over and through me, a wave of sadness so profound it seemed to block out the light, even as I knew from the warmth on my skin and the glare in my eyes that the sun was still shining. The source seemed to be behind me. I whirled around.

The shadow of an old man, haggard and thin, wearing threadbare, damp-looking clothing, leaned wearily against the outside wall of the shop. His rheumy eyes teared. His hands shook.

I dashed forward immediately, down the street and away. I had run a good couple of blocks before I dodged into a shop doorway and paused, chest heaving.

Nothing now. It's all right.

Just forget about it, okay?

The sadness had left me as abruptly as it had come, but it was replaced with a spurt of righteous anger, and I clenched my fists with frustration. This was so unfair! *Why* did whatever had happened to that poor man however many years ago have to make me feel so bad right now? What purpose did it serve?

At least this one wasn't alive, right?

"Can I help you find something?"

The cheerful voice of the shopkeeper—a short, chunky redheaded woman with an accent straight from the Bronx—snapped me back to the regular world. I made an effort to slow my breathing, then scanned the room with eagerness. For a doorway into which I had randomly stumbled, the shop was exactly what I had been looking for: not exactly upscale, but a far cry from plastic flippers and ukulele-strumming Obama dolls. The focus was beach clothing, but there were no "surf's up" tee shirts here— just a few stands of silk and synthetic men's Hawaiian shirts, and rows upon rows of gorgeous, colorful sundresses.

"Yes," I answered heavily. "You can."

—⁓—

Nearly an hour later, I stood in the same shop, my face twisted in an anguish of indecision. I was normally not so fussy about my clothes. Few girls at my school in Cheyenne were uber-concerned with wearing the latest big-city fashion; most of my friends, like me, were happy with whatever looked good with their body type and wasn't too uncomfortable. But this was serious.

Why, oh why, had I agreed to go to this stupid dance in the first place? Could I not see that I was laying my entire social future in Oahu on the line? Like an idiot, I had set myself up to meet a gazillion important strangers in one fell swoop, giving myself only *one* chance to make *one* all-important first impression on everybody, an impression they would then have three whole months to think about and talk about—while I had zero chance to redeem myself!

It was official. I was insane.

My phone buzzed with a text, and I swung the screen quickly into view. It was from my mother, to whom I had texted a picture of both dresses twenty minutes ago.

I think they're both lovely. You can't go wrong!

I groaned. She wasn't blowing me off; I knew that if she said she liked both dresses, she did. My mother was hardly the type to pull punches when it came to expressing opinions on my wardrobe. But it was not the decisive answer I needed.

I stepped to the window and scanned the street again. There had been no sign of Zane since we parted. Where was he? I had expected to see him long before now.

Two more texts buzzed in in quick succession. Thanks to me and my fashion dilemma, Kylee and Tara were currently at war, copying each other on a flurry of transoceanic communications that some phone companies somewhere were loving every minute of.

The first one was from Kylee, who had lined up in favor of the crimson red V-neck right off the bat.

It duz NOT make her look slutty! It makz her look SEXY!!!

Tara, however, had had concerns, preferring instead the yellow print with the purple and blue flowers, whose gathered, form-fitting front was slightly more modest, but still showed off my newly tanned shoulders.

> Her goal is not to get herself mauled in the guy's car! Her goal is to make a good impression on her future friends. The LAST thing she needs is to tick off the girls by stealing all their guys' attention!

I looked fretfully from one dress to the other. Tara had a point. The red with the giant white blossoms *was* really, really striking on a tall frame, even a too-skinny one, like mine. But it was also perilously low cut—lower cut than anything I'd ever worn before. That could definitely cause some anxiety when I was dancing...

My phone buzzed again.

> Guysll drool anyway cuz Kali always looks hot—duh. Let her have FUN!!!

And again.

> She will have more fun if she doesn't get mauled in the guy's car. Or the hallway, or the street... She needs to make the statement, "I'm pretty and confident." Not "I'm easy, do me now."

Seconds later, two more.

> U are SO dramatic! Kali can handle it. GO WITH THE RED, GIRL!!!

> Kali can handle anything. That's why she's going to wear the yellow, look amazing, get the guy, and still make lots of new friends.

I stuffed the phone into my pocket with a groan. Tara was exaggerating about the red, for sure. The girl herself was freakin' gorgeous—long blond hair, big blue eyes, and bone structure like a Greek goddess. But none of the guys in Cheyenne had a clue because her hair was in a ponytail 24/7, she refused to wear contacts, and half her clothes were borrowed from her brothers.

Which made me wonder why I was asking her opinion in the first place.

Kylee had better fashion sense, didn't she? Then again, her tastes differed from mine. I liked a more natural, classy look—she was all about bright colors and bold statements. Of course she would like the red dress.

But was it right for me?

Arrrgghhh!!!

"Kali!"

My spirits leapt instantly; I spun around. "Zane! Where have you been?"

He blinked at me. "Where have *I* been? The question is where have *you* been. I've been looking all over for you!"

I blinked back at him. He looked... not upset, exactly. His voice was calm; his tone was as easygoing as ever. But there was a look in his eyes and a tenseness to his face that was unusual.

"I've been right here the whole time," I explained.

He looked confused. "But I've checked here. At least three times. Along with every other store on the street."

"Maybe I was in the dressing room?" I suggested.

His eyes widened. "Every time? For an hour?"

I chuckled. "You don't go dress shopping often, do you?"

The shop owner's loud voice announced her latest intrusion. "Well, have you made up your mind yet?" she said with a broad smile. "Did the friends vote?"

I quickly pulled my cell phone back out of my pocket, hoping she had not seen me talking into thin air. She probably thought I was nuts already, as indecisive as I was being over one stupid dress.

"They're no help," I admitted. "They can't agree." I stole a look at Zane. "I think I'll try both dresses on just one more time."

The sales lady's smile didn't waver, but her eyes glazed. "If you ask me," she said smoothly, "I think you should wear the red. It's more... sophisticated."

I faked a smile back. The woman meant well, I was sure. But somehow, I couldn't take to heart the fashion advice of a middle-aged, transplanted New Yorker who wore fake eyelashes and had lipstick on her teeth.

"One more time," I insisted. "Then I'll know."

I whisked both garments back into the dressing room, throwing Zane a distinct "stay put" look as I went. I tried each on and came out briefly, whispering for him not to say anything until he'd seen both. The whole time he leaned against the wall without moving, arms crossed over his chest, his expression inscrutable.

"Okay," I said, emerging at last in my own clothes, one dress in each hand. "I know I'm boring you to death, but I really do need help, here. And you're a guy."

His eyebrows lifted. "Oh, so *now* I'm a guy?"

"You know what I mean," I insisted. "Which one looks better?"

He let out a sigh, then considered a moment. "Looks better to who?"

My forehead creased. I started to answer the question, then realized it wasn't so simple. Was I more worried about Matt, or about the girls I was about to meet?

To my surprise, Zane started laughing. "Seriously, Kali," he chuckled. "Do you realize you look more miserable than I do?"

He stood up and faced me squarely. "Look, you want my opinion? Here it is. The guys are going to ogle you either way—deal with it. What the girls like, no mortal being could possibly predict. So how about you just grab the one *you* like, and we get back to the beach already?"

As I looked into his smiling, now familiar face, his warm, sane voice spread through me like a calming drug.

Yes, I thought to myself. Why didn't we?

Within ninety seconds, I had hung the red dress back up on a rack, hastily paid for the yellow (which was *my* favorite, thank you very much), and swept us both back out into the sunshine.

"How was that?" I asked proudly.

"Excellent," he responded, leading me back towards the car. "Glad I could be of service. Sorry I lost track of you earlier, though."

My steps slowed. "You didn't have to worry about me," I insisted, remembering how disturbed he had seemed. "It's not like I was lost."

His expression turned thoughtful. "You weren't, no."

We walked on in silence for a while, taking a detour into the street to get around the long line of Asian tourists waiting patiently for shave ice at Matsumoto's.

An unusually brisk wind kicked up suddenly, whipping some paper trash in cyclones around our ankles. Zane looked up at the sky.

"Surf report was right, I guess," he said gloomily. "The rest of the day's not going to be any good. Too much wind—chops up the waves. I guess I could try sailboarding, though. Or kite surfing, if I can find anyone out. Maybe at Kailua—"

"You're not coming with me to the dance?" I said without thinking.

He turned and looked at me curiously. "Well, I mean… three is a crowd, right? Or do I not count as a guy again?"

An uncomfortable ache rippled through my middle. He was talking half in jest, as he always did, but I could feel the pain behind his words. Alive or not, he was still capable of feeling. He had lost everything he'd ever known, including his physical self, with no consolation except his precious, endless waves and—quite pathetically—me. And all I did was make things harder on him.

"Zane," I said earnestly, halting my steps. "I didn't mean that. I mean... of course you count. Whatever you are in the cosmic scheme of things, you're very real to me."

His expression softened. "Thanks, Kali. But you don't have to invite me along on your dates just because you feel sorry for me. I managed with no one to talk to before I met you, I can manage again. You need your space."

We walked on in silence for several paces as I considered the evening in store. It didn't take me long to realize that every happy scenario I'd been playing out in my head, Zane had been a part of. I had assumed his presence without thinking—without ever questioning that he would want to be with me. Imagining the event without him now seemed hollow.

But what I was expecting of him was totally selfish— and it wasn't fair. Even if we were just friends, how much fun could it be for him to watch me enjoying myself with Matt—doing all the typical teenage things he could never do again?

All of a sudden, I felt totally rotten.

I dragged my feet another half block, then noticed that Zane looked equally melancholy. *How about that honesty thing?*

"Zane," I piped up quickly, hoping not to lose my nerve. "You can do whatever you want, but the truth is, I want you to come along. And not because I feel sorry for you. I *do* feel sorry for you—I'd be a total jerk if I didn't. But I want you to come because I enjoy your company, and if you don't come, I'll miss you. But I realize that's totally selfish of me, and I don't want you to come just because I asked you to." I paused for a breath, my heart racing. "Am I making any sense?"

He stopped and smiled at me. It was the worst one he had—the one that did funny things to my stomach and screwed up my knees. I had thought I was getting immune to it. I was wrong.

"You make perfect sense," he answered. "And as long as we're being honest, I'll tell you this. I want to go. There's no place I'd rather be tonight."

My eyes widened. "Really?"

"Really," he assured, still smiling. "But I don't want to intrude, either. If it won't make you feel too much like you have a stalker, I'd prefer to stay out of your way—where you can't see me. Would that be all right? If you ever *want* to talk to me, though, just call. I'll be there."

My cheeks flushed. He was being entirely too sweet to me, and I couldn't stand it. I didn't think, I just reacted. I wanted to hug him. My arms flew around his shoulders, my weight shifted onto my toes. The shock I felt at my body's meeting not the expected warm, solid chest but instead a total absence of resistance—punctuated with a near audible buzz of vibration—was startling. Equally startling was the realization that, without a swift save, I was about to land facedown on the pavement.

Being a dancer had its benefits. I caught myself in time, throwing out a foot and regaining my balance in a way that looked to passersby—I hoped—like I had simply tripped. But my face was red as a beet.

"Are you okay?" Zane asked with concern.

"I'm such an idiot," I blathered, barely able to look at him. "I just totally forgot. I'm so sorry."

His answer came as a ragged whisper, so soft I could hardly hear it.

"So am I."

# chapter eleven

I was ridiculously, insanely, pathetically nervous. More so than when my date to homecoming in ninth grade called me three hours before the dance to say that he had just "come out" to all his friends and was wondering if I would mind if he took his boyfriend instead. (I didn't, really, once I got over the shock.) I was more nervous than when I got talked into asking a minor crush of mine to the sophomore Sadie Hawkins dance, knowing full well he already had a girlfriend at another school. (He had said no—right there in the middle of the cafeteria. I was mortified.) I was even more nervous than I had been when, three-fourths of the way through last year's semiformal, I had discovered something green and leafy stuck between my front teeth. (Kylee swore that it had not been there the whole night, but I knew darn well people had been looking at me funny since dinner.)

This was worse.

"Come on, Kali," Matt said encouragingly, his blue eyes twinkling. "They're going to love you. I promise."

My eyes roved warily over the front lawn of Frederick High. The troubled boy was headed for the imaginary flagpole again, but I didn't see the smoking girls, and the dozens of living people that buzzed about exuded more than enough positive energy to give the atmosphere an excited, hopeful, almost frenetic air.

I was still nervous.

Matt let out a chuckle and took a few steps back to where I stood, effectively paralyzed, by the side of his car. "If you really hate it, we'll leave," he assured, "but you're not going to hate it. You're going to meet some people you really like—you'll see." He wrapped his muscular arm around the length of mine, took my hand, and propelled me forward.

"You're right," I responded, my voice giving a betraying quiver. I cleared my throat and steadied it. "I'm excited to be here, really... I'm just a lot more nervous than I thought I would be."

"Yeah, I can see that," he answered merrily, swinging my arm as we walked. My traitorous feet tried to dawdle, but Matt's steady pull kept us going.

"Sorry," I offered genuinely. "I'll try not to be too much of a drag on your evening."

Matt looked back at me with a smile. His smile was neither as magnetic nor as mesmerizing as Zane's, but it was friendly and honest. "Oh, I wouldn't worry about that," he said lightly, eyes dancing. "Nothing's going to ruin my evening."

He squeezed my hand, then continued to propel us both forward toward the open double doors of the gymnasium. As we neared them, my heart pounded, and I realized with some amount of shock that I had been unconsciously moving closer to his side.

"Matt!" shouted a short, blonde girl who was stationed at the doors taking tickets. She was slightly overweight, but dressed very attractively in a tie-dyed aquamarine sundress that emphasized her striking blue eyes.

"Hey, Lacey," he answered amicably. I loosened my hold on his hand, giving him the option of dropping it. He responded not only by readjusting his grip, but by throwing in an added thumb caress on the back of my hand. "You look nice," he praised the girl. "Gorgeous dress!"

She smiled widely, showing perfect teeth. "Thanks. You don't look so bad yourself, macho man." She turned to me, her expression pleasant, albeit slightly puzzled. "Hi, I'm Lacey. Have we met?"

"This is Kali," Matt answered for me. "She's from Wyoming, just visiting for a week. But she's moving here this summer—her dad's going to be working with mine on the base."

"Cool!" Lacey answered with enthusiasm. Our eyes met, and a large degree of my nervousness evaporated. "What do you think of Oahu?"

"I love it," I said without hesitation. "Matt's been a great tour guide."

"I'll bet," she said with a chuckle, still looking at me. "Catch up with me later and I'll give you the real story. About something other than water polo."

"Hey!" Matt protested good-naturedly, "I showed her La'ie Point and Chinaman's Hat and everything!"

Lacey's eyes rolled. "While *talking* about water polo?"

I laughed out loud. A few people had come up behind us, and Lacey moved to take their tickets. "I'll find you later," she said conspiratorially, offering a wink.

Matt steered me through the doors and inside, but before he could say anything more we were bombarded by shout-outs from what appeared to be his cheering section. Multiple voices, both male and female, chorused his name as I plastered a smile on my face and hastily scanned the crowd.

First off, my outfit was okay. There were a few girls in shorts, but the vast majority were wearing sun dresses, and no one was in a formal. The guys were a mixed bag, wearing everything from nice tee shirts to polos to button-down shirts, with any manner of shorts and shoes. Hawaiian prints were not considered too touristy, as I had halfway feared; at least half the kids were wearing them. But "party-store luau," the atmosphere was not. The smallish gymnasium was tastefully decorated with nothing but bright-colored table cloths and a few, well-placed clusters of fresh cut flowers.

Perfect.

Second, much to my delight, I could see that these people knew how to dance. In my high school, it would take a good hour before any significant number of people hit the floor. This party was only just starting, and at least half the attendees were already burning it up. Despite my nervousness, my feet began to itch.

"Hey, everybody," Matt announced over my shoulder to whomever was within earshot. "This is Kali. She's just visiting from Wyoming, but she's moving here in June. I'm trying to convince her to come to Frederick, so everybody talk it up, okay?"

A dozen or so friendly faces responded from the dance floor with a smile and a wave, while two couples standing nearby stepped closer to greet us.

"Does that mean we can't tell her about the dog burgers?" laughed a tall, skinny guy with a streak of bright purple in his otherwise dark hair.

"David!" a freckled redheaded girl chastised as she smacked her date on the shoulder. "Shut up about that!" She smiled at me. "I'm Julia. Nice to meet you."

Recognizing the name from Matt's text, I thanked her for the what-to-wear tip. She was wearing a beach dress herself, very similar to mine.

"I'm Madison," said a pretty, dark-skinned girl with long black hair. If I had had to guess, I would say she looked Asian, whereas David looked more traditionally Hawaiian, but I couldn't tell for sure, nor did I really care. "It's good to see you," Madison said with a grin. At lunch we thought Matt was just making you up."

"Yeah, he has a rich fantasy life," quipped the guy

beside her, a hulking football-player type with pale skin and light blond hair. "I'm Ryan," he said with a grin, shaking my hand.

With a stroke of perfect timing, the DJ put on a new song whose first few, obviously familiar chords had the crowd howling with excitement. The group around me headed at once for the dance floor, and I was more than willing to be swept along with them.

I watched as the whole room swelled with motion, myself in the midst of it, moving to the music, letting all cares go—at least for the moment. I laughed inwardly as I noticed that the guys here, though perhaps more *willing* to dance than my classmates in Cheyenne, were no different in their execution. All the guys I knew danced in one of four ways. The stiffest just stood there, swaying a little from side to side, snapping an occasional finger or shifting an occasional foot. Those who were a little more adventurous, but no more coordinated, liked to shake things up by bobbing up and down like corks. Beyond that, you had the guys who *thought* they could dance, but for the most part just managed to look goofy. Matt, like the vast majority of guys in the room, was in the second category. David-with-the-purple-hair was in the third. Only one guy—whom my eyes caught immediately, although he was clear across the room—rated the fourth category: naturals who moved instinctively with the music, effortlessly and without self-consciousness.

As David twirled around in circles, jerking one long leg like he was being electrocuted, my gaze drifted repeatedly from him to the other dancer. Even though that guy was facing away from me, his fluid motion drew my attention to an exceptionally handsome physique, and I found myself wondering why the girls nearer to him weren't watching as raptly as I was. They were, in fact, totally ignoring him—while everyone around David (who was now simultaneously playing air guitar and prancing a hoedown) was egging him on with whoops and hollers.

It made no sense. Couldn't those people see—

I clapped my hand over my mouth as it hit me. I wanted to laugh out loud, but if it looked like I was directing my gaze at anyone but Zane, it would seem very rude indeed. He turned for just a moment, his blond curls bouncing around his face, and caught my eye with a grin. But just as quickly, he turned away again—determined, apparently, to keep the low profile he had promised us both.

I understood completely. Sometimes, when the music calls, you *just gotta dance.*

I turned my attention back to Matt and friends, feeling suddenly much more at ease. These were friendly people, and I liked them—even if Matt did jump up and down so wildly I feared for the safety of my toes. With their smiles and laughter, and the music beating in my ears, I could almost forget everything weird and scary and bizarre that had happened to me since I got to Oahu.

Almost.

I danced with Matt's crowd for nearly an hour before thirst and exhaustion got the better of us and we all decided to take a break. Matt went off to get some drinks while I headed for the restroom.

I was just about to open the stall door when I heard the voices. Maybe I felt something before that—I wasn't sure. I only knew that as little as I wanted to spend any more time than was necessary cooped up in a gym toilet, my hand hung in midair over the bolt, frozen in place.

"I can't believe he's even here," a girl's voice whispered, her tone striking in its simmering hostility. "I mean, it would be bad enough if he showed up by himself, but to bring *somebody else?!"*

A cold prickle of angst swept down my spine. I knew I had no reason to assume the girls were talking about Matt and me. I also knew—beyond any doubt—that they absolutely were.

"I know," another voice answered, this one less hostile, but equally upset. "It's awful what happened. I'm still not convinced, though, that he... does he even know? I mean... why *would* he come, after that? It would be so stupid!"

"Stupid's right," the first girl snapped. "Rod's going to kill him. I know he will."

"Don't say that! Even if Matt did do it, it's not Rod's business."

The hostile speaker let out a snort. "Yeah, try telling him that. Sofia will *always* be his business."

"How bad is..." the second girl paused. "Have you seen her?"

The door to the restroom swung open, admitting several other chatting voices. I waited, breathlessly, until the shuffling footsteps subsided and the restroom door had swung open and shut again. As the new chatter continued (something about an English assignment), I slipped out of the stall, washed my hands, and hastily made my way out the door to see if I could catch sight of the speakers. Two girls, just a few paces ahead of me, were making their way toward the refreshments. I knew instantly that they were the ones. Anger and confused concern, respectively, radiated from them like a bad case of B.O., and whether I was seeing it or feeling it made no difference at the moment.

Rod's going to kill him.

The girls grabbed plastic cups of punch off the drink table and walked out a set of propped-open double doors to the lawn. I was in the process of following, as surreptitiously as possible, when I felt a hand on my elbow.

"Where are you going?" Matt asked jovially. "I've got our drinks over here." He pointed to the table, and with a last, studying look at the girls, I followed him and sat down.

I stared mutely at the drink in front of me, unable to pick it up—my thoughts oscillating between extreme thirst and a fierce, impending nausea.

"You okay?" Matt asked, downing his own, second cup of peach-colored liquid. "You seem a little... preoccupied."

There didn't have to be anything really wrong. The girls could be drama queens. There could be two Matts. Two Rods. I could have been imagining the hatred and rage I had felt pouring out of the guy at Saint Anthony's. The word "kill" could have been used euphemistically. People said it that way all the time.

I noticed that my hands were shaking.

Honesty, Kali.

"Matt," I began, my mouth dry as sandpaper. "I overheard a couple girls talking in the restroom. They were talking about you."

His eyes lit up with nothing more than simple, mischievous pride. "Yeah?" he responded, in a tone that was oddly hopeful.

My own brow furrowed. Either Matt was an incredibly good actor, or he was a guy with amazingly little to be ashamed of.

"What was the name of the girl you were going to bring tonight? The one who got sick?"

His eyebrows rose at the obviously unexpected question. "Sofia. Why?"

I tried to swallow, but my throat was so dry I nearly choked. Matt quickly handed over my drink, and I drained it, gratefully, before answering.

"They seemed to be a little scandalized that you would come," I explained, choosing my words carefully. "Especially that you would bring someone else."

Matt's face crinkled, clearly perplexed. "Who was scandalized? That's the dumbest thing I've ever heard." He drummed his fingers on the table a moment, thinking. "To tell the truth, Kali, I'm not even sure I believe Sofia *was* sick. I think she just wanted out of the date. She's barely talked to me the last couple weeks."

I blinked. "So, you two weren't, like... dating?"

He scoffed. "I barely know the girl. She just transferred to Frederick at Christmas; she used to go to Saint Anthony's. She asked *me* to the dance, weeks ago, but like I said, I've hardly spoken to her since." He gave his head a brisk shake. "Whatever. Girls pull the weirdest crap sometimes. Don't let it bother you, Kali. Everybody here thinks you're great. You ready to dance some more?"

He started to rise, but I stopped him with a hand on his arm. "Were Sofia and Rod ever an item?"

His eyebrows rose; he sank back down into his chair. "Wow, where'd you pick that up? You're like a private investigator or something. Yeah, I heard they used to go out. When she was at Saint Anthony's. But they've been over for a while now. Why?"

I took in a deep breath. It was clear to me, now, why Matt was so unconcerned. Whatever those girls *thought* was going on, he was clueless.

"They seemed to think that Rod was really mad at you."

Matt stared at me, not moving, for several seconds. Then he lifted his hands, palms up, into the air. "What is it with this? You tell me yesterday that he's glaring at me, now people are whispering about it in bathrooms? Why would Rod be mad at me? For *not* dating his ex-girlfriend?"

I gritted my teeth. Put that way, it did sound pretty ridiculous. Furthermore, I had obviously pushed the topic as far as I could push it without seeming like a drama queen myself.

"You're right," I agreed, attempting a smile. "Maybe I misunderstood them or something."

He smiled back, his relief obvious. "Awesome. *Now* are you ready to dance some more?"

I should have been. But I wasn't. Logic was all well and good when it was the only information you had. But when other people's feelings rocked you like a slap, they were harder to ignore. At least two people were harboring a strong degree of malice toward Matt. That wasn't a guess, or a matter of perception; it was a fact I knew to be true.

"Yes," I answered, trying hard to keep my voice cheerful. "Just let me grab another drink first. I'll catch up to you."

Without giving Matt a chance to argue, I slipped away from his side and headed for the punch bowl, which was being guarded by a particularly large Hawaiian man whom I presumed (perhaps wrongly) to be Matt's football coach. Despite his size, he looked less than fearsome as he ladled out another glass of punch, complete with two ice cubes, and handed it to me with a smile.

I thanked him and moved away to my left, where an empty alcove by the vending machines provided some semblance of privacy. "Zane?" I whispered.

Nothing happened.

Frowning, I stepped out of the alcove and scanned the

dance floor. He was still out there, still rocking out, still being completely ignored by the crowds, even as he strategically placed himself in the middle of a large dance circle. It took me a minute to catch his eye, but when I did he was beside me in a second, looking sweaty, exhilarated, and—as always—frustratingly gorgeous.

"Sorry," he said unconvincingly. "Wasn't sure why you were hanging around back here... I love this song. What's up?"

We stepped back into the alcove and I gave him a quick summary, my eyes searching his with no small amount of apprehension. I was afraid he would believe the most obvious explanation—that Matt was lying to me. That he had done Sofia wrong in some way and knew darn well what Rod and bathroom girl #1 were so ticked about. In which case, the whole situation was his own stupid fault, and certainly no business of mine.

I finished talking and took a breath. Zane said nothing for a moment, studying me in turn. "So," he said finally, his words seeming carefully measured, "you really believe Matt has no idea what's going on?"

I exhaled heavily. "I'm sure of it."

Zane's green eyes locked on mine. I braced for the expected lecture about how I had already done all I could do—I had warned Matt, hadn't I? He was a big guy, he could take care of himself. Yada, yada, yada.

"How about this?" Zane suggested. "You point out the girls you overheard, and I'll see if I can overhear some more. I am rather gifted at reconnaissance."

A wave of warm relief swelled up within my chest, and once again my arms lifted, quite unintentionally, to wrap themselves around his strong, sun-bronzed neck. This time, however, I caught myself in time and replaced them at my sides.

"Thanks," I offered, my voice choked with a sudden, acute sense of loss. I could not hug him, would never be able to. But what did it matter, really? I had plenty of guy friends with whom I was not on hugging terms.

The painful, hollow feeling would go away.

"I'll point out the girls," I murmured, pulling my gaze away from his and leading him toward the exit to the lawn. When I turned back to face him again, my melancholy dissolved.

The figure that followed me was wearing a double-breasted tweed overcoat, pinstripe trousers, and a deerstalker hat. "Just point out the suspects, Madam," he said with a British accent, taking a drag on a curvy pipe that exuded a wisp of very real looking smoke. "And I'll attend to the necessary inquiries."

Suppressing a giggle, I cast a glance out the doors and over the green space outside the gym. The girls in question were not hard to find; they had joined a group of several others hanging out under a tree about twenty yards away. I described them to Zane as succinctly as possible, being careful not to point—or move my lips too much. He nodded in understanding. My eyes caught his again, and I tried hard to make them convey the gratitude a hug could not. "Thank you, Zane," I whispered.

His returning gaze held a sparkle of pure pleasure, which would have warmed me had it not been for the unexpected flash of anguish I thought I glimpsed, ever so briefly, behind it.

He winked at me and disappeared.

# chapter twelve

Matt's friend Lacey was true to her word. She "found" me midway through the evening, appearing quite conveniently just as the DJ decided it was time to slow things down.

As the gal pal of Cheyenne, I was used to timing my rest breaks over slow dances, so heading off to "get some air" with Lacey seemed a natural enough move. Still, I couldn't help feeling a little guilty when I saw disappointment written so largely on Matt's previously cheerful baby face. "We'll catch the next one then," he said charitably, turning to join some guy friends who were talking in a cluster in the far corner.

"Matt's a sweetheart, isn't he?" Lacey gushed, leading us to a door on the opposite side of the gym from where I had sent Zane. "I hope he's been introducing you around—not keeping you all to himself."

"He's been great," I answered, following her up a flight of stairs. She opened the door onto a balcony that attached to the classroom building, and we were hit with a welcome breath of brisk, misty Oahu wind. About six feet to my left, a couple of shadow teenagers lounged against the corner of the railing, making out.

"He seems to be a pretty popular guy around here," I said quickly, turning my back on the shadows before they did something embarrassing.

Lacey laughed. "Oh, everybody loves Matt," she confirmed.

I nodded, though it felt like a lie. In the last 24 hours I had met at least two people from whom Matt was definitely *not* feeling the love.

"He's a hopeless flirt, of course," she added matter-of-factly, "but you've known him at least—what—a day? So I suppose I don't have to tell you that!" She let out another of her merry laughs, but on catching my concerned expression, sobered instantly. "Oh, don't get me wrong," she hastened to explain. "Matt's no operator. In fact, he's quite the gentleman, compared to most of the guys around here. It's just that he's not one to get attached, if you know what I mean. He's dated practically every girl in school at one point or another, but it never turns into anything. At least, it never has before." She studied me, her eyes sparkling. "I keep telling him, though, one day he's going to fall for somebody. And then he's going to make a total fool out of himself."

I looked back at Lacey with a guarded smile. I liked her already, had liked her instinctively, but there was no way I was responding to that. "Have the two of you ever dated?" I asked, oddly certain that I already knew the answer.

"Oh, no," she said dismissively, confirming my impression of a longstanding friendship. "I have a boyfriend. Had the same once since eighth grade. Ty and Matt are buds, too, or at least they used to be, before Ty started working all the time. Like tonight, for instance," she finished bitterly, blowing a stray bang out of her eyes with a puff of air. "If Ty misses prom this year, I swear to God, I'll kill him."

Rod's going to kill him.

I pushed the ominous echo away from my brain. It was a common enough expression. Lacey obviously didn't mean it. Who would?

"Do you know Sofia?" I blurted.

Lacey's fetching blue eyes widened slightly. "Sofia Liang? A little bit. Why?"

I shrugged, attempting to conceal my interest. "I just

thought it was a little weird, her breaking the date with Matt for tonight. Do you think she was really sick?"

Lacey didn't answer for a moment. Instead, she brought a hand to her mouth and began to nibble absently on a professionally polished nail. "To tell you the truth, Kali, I don't know what the heck is up with that girl. She seems nice and all, but she hasn't made a lot of friends here. I get the idea she hangs with an older crowd—as in dropouts, mainly. When she asked Matt to the dance, it was, like, totally out of the blue. He was happy and all—I mean, she's *really* good looking—but then she just kind of disappeared again. I have a couple classes with her, and she's not there half the time. She's not involved in anything after school, either. It's weird."

I was possessed suddenly by an odd wave of warmth, an all-consuming feeling of happiness, elation, and— particularly strange, given the conversation—a fierce, raw sort of hunger...

Oh, crap.

With a sudden flash of understanding, I cast a furtive look back at the shadow couple. They were now prone on the concrete; the girl had the guy's shirt off.

"Let's take a walk!" I suggested quickly, passing Lacey on the balcony and moving off... wherever. "Does this wrap all the way around to front of the building?"

She shot me a quizzical look, but kept up. "No, but there's a staircase on the end. We can go down and around."

"Sounds good," I said lightly, trying to squelch the image of Zane in his favorite board shorts that had crept, unbidden, into my mind. "I love how all the buildings here have walkways outside, rather than hallways. The fresh air is so invigorating," I prattled on, trying desperately to shake the couple's lingering, ever-so-beguiling feelings from my relatively innocent psyche. I could not help wondering, if I had stayed where I was, what else I might have seen…

"I used to live in Detroit," Lacey said, presumably responding to something I had already forgotten saying. "So I know what you mean. You get so used to the ocean breezes here, you forget how the rest of the world lives."

I reached the staircase and started down. The hijacked feelings—thank God—were finally fading. Then I gasped out loud. Zane was standing right in front of me on the stairs, not subconsciously in board shorts, but quite visibly (minus a few transparent streaks) in his dance outfit. In the next instant, he was gone again.

My heart thumped like a jackhammer.

"What?" Lacey asked, coming up beside me, "Did you see something?"

"Um… no," I said, thinking fast. "I just… realized I forgot something. But it's no big deal." I turned at the bottom of the steps and faced her, attempting a carefree smile. "So, Matt keeps telling me how great Frederick is. Do you like it here?"

Lacey happily launched into an entertaining description of the pros and cons of Frederick High, and I tried my best to pay attention as we meandered across the grounds and back to the gymnasium, passing shadows right and left along the way. My head spun as they seemed to come out of nowhere… tons of them, their emotions all over the place… like a badly organized Halloween parade. It hadn't been this bad when Matt and I arrived. Why now?

"So, you should definitely tell your parents you want to go here," Lacey finished, pausing at the corner by the smoking girls, who were, regrettably, back in place and as fearful as ever.

I moved as far away from them as I politely could.

"Sounds like a plan," I agreed.

"Besides," she added, a mischievous glint in her eye, "I'm thinking that Matt might really like you."

I threw her a skeptical look. "Oh, please. We only just met!"

"Yeah," she said thoughtfully. "Seems unlikely, I know, given his track record. But I was watching you earlier, when you were dancing. The way he was looking at you... You're an awesome dancer, by the way."

"Oh. Thanks." My cheeks flushed at more than the compliment.

"There's a certain spring to his step tonight that I can't say I've seen before," she continued. "I noticed it as soon as the two of you walked up. Plus..." she reached into a pocket, hidden in the folds of her sundress, and pulled out a cell phone. "Unless I'm mistaken, he's texted me, like, six times in the past twenty minutes—bugging me to bring you back inside."

She flipped open her phone and punched a few buttons, her grin broadening all the while. "Okay," she corrected, "only four times. But the last two had frowny faces."

She sighed. "All right. I'd better follow orders, or he'll tell Ty about that ultimate Frisbee tournament in Waimanalo tomorrow. The guy has one day off in three weeks—he darn well better spend it with me!"

She turned the corner and began walking toward the side doors of the gym, and I held my breath as we walked past the cluster of girls, still sitting under the tree, to which I had directed Zane. He was there now, standing in the midst of them, his face an unreadable mask of concentration.

I felt a sudden sense of unease; one of the bathroom girls had spotted me and was staring. I turned quickly back to Lacey. "Those girls," I whispered, "are they friends of Sofia's?"

She cast a glance over my shoulder. "Maybe," she said vaguely, as if not completely sure herself. "One of them is a cousin of hers. Why?" But with another glance, she answered her own question. "Oh. They're looking at you, aren't they? Hmm."

We moved out of earshot and slipped back into the gym. "No idea what that was all about!" she mused out loud. "They can't possibly resent Matt's asking another date. Sofia's been a total jerk to him. Well, Krystal was with them. She's cool. I'll ask her later. Now, let's get you—"

"Kali!" Matt's arm appeared from nowhere and wrapped around me like a tentacle. "We thought you'd never come back! Ready to dance some more?"

Lacey threw me a knowing smirk and melted away.

"Whatever Lacey told you about me," he said teasingly, "It's a lie. The girl's been out to get me ever since ninth grade gym."

Despite the swirl of confused thoughts already in my head, I had to ask. "What happened in ninth grade gym?"

He sighed. "I gave her a concussion."

My eyes widened. "Seriously?"

He nodded gravely. "We were playing badminton. I kind of backed up over her."

"You didn't!" I protested, stifling a laugh. "In *badminton*? Really?"

"It wasn't funny at the time," he insisted, though he began to grin himself as he led me back onto the dance floor. "I thought I'd killed her. Never left my position again, I can tell you that. I hate playing sports with girls— makes me nervous. Took a C in gym that semester trying to get out of it. Shall we dance?"

I felt a sudden desire to withdraw my toes out of his range.

I took a deep breath instead. "Sure. Let's do it."

—m—

We had been dancing for quite a while when I realized that, at some point, Zane had come back inside. He had been keeping tabs on me all evening, presumably, but now he stayed visible, hanging out by the refreshment area. I got the idea he was waiting to talk to me, but he did not pop over beside me to say so, or even try to get my attention.

He didn't really have to. Even as David showed off some of the most bizarre hip action I'd ever seen, and Julia and Madison graciously took the time to teach me some funky local dance called the *limu*, my eyes continued to stray in Zane's direction. He had changed, inexplicably, into worn looking jeans, sneakers, and a plain gray tee shirt, and he appeared wholly preoccupied—though with what, I wasn't sure. Other than one brief glance at the start of the next slow dance, he did not even look my way.

There was no escaping Matt's embrace this time, nor was I entirely sure I wanted to. I was a little apprehensive at first, given the way David and Ryan both crunched their dates against them like ragdolls; but, just as Lacey had led me to believe, Matt was neither pushy nor clingy, and I found myself surprisingly comfortable in his arms. I just wasn't comfortable otherwise.

I knew that Zane had something to tell me—something he had overheard. But it must not be emergency worthy, or he would have told me already. So why was he lurking just out of reach?

I could not help feeling awkward dancing with Matt in

front of him, illogical as I knew that to be. Whether Zane
cared or not, I couldn't tell. He was too far away for me to
read his face, and I never had been able to sense his
feelings like the other shadows.

Shortly after the slow dance ended, however, I did
sense hostility coming from somewhere. It took me a
moment to locate her, but I knew who I was looking for:
she was short and bronze-skinned with close-cropped
black hair, Chinese, or perhaps Hawaiian—very likely a
little of both. She watched my date from a distance, eyes
narrowed, mouth drawn into a singularly unattractive
scowl. As I stepped in between her and Matt, the heat of
her glare hit my bare shoulders like a sunburn.

"I need a drink," I announced brusquely, taking Matt's
hand and leading him away from her and back toward his
friends in the corner. "You hang here a minute; I'll be
right back."

I gave him no chance to argue, but slipped away
toward the refreshments without looking back. Zane had
seen; he was there, waiting for me.

"I have a lot to tell you," he said simply.

"I know," I responded, breathing heavily. "And we
can't wait any longer. That girl is out for blood."

"He's coming after you."

"What?" I spun around to see that Matt had not, after
all, been so easy to shake.

"I'll get us some drinks," he insisted with a smile,
wrapping an arm around my waist again. "What would you
like?"

I tried hard not to show my frustration. "Punch is
fine," I offered. "I'll just run to the restroom first."

There was no place else to go. I could not get back to
the alcove without Matt seeing me. My phone was in my
purse on the table; the very place he would take our

drinks. If I stepped outside alone, he would undoubtedly follow.

"We'll have to talk in the bathroom," I muttered to Zane as I weaved through the crowd.

"I'm allowed in the women's room? Wow."

"Good point," I quipped. "Maybe we should go in the men's instead."

"I'll avert my eyes," he suggested dryly.

As luck would have it, the women's room was empty.

"All right," I said, steeling myself. "Tell me everything. What's going on?"

Zane settled himself on the hard countertop, balanced over the sink holes, looking perfectly comfortable in a pose no live person could possibly be comfortable in. His countenance, however, was grave.

"I'm afraid it's pretty bad, Kali."

My breathing quickened. "Just tell me!"

"This girl, Sofia. She didn't cancel the date because she got sick. She cancelled the date because she was in the hospital getting ready for surgery, after spending most of last night in the ER."

I shook my head in confusion. "But why would she—"

"She didn't want Matt to know what had happened to her. She didn't want anyone to know. But the girl in the black dress—the one you overheard in the bathroom—that's her cousin. She heard her mother talking about it to her aunt, trying to figure out who was responsible."

A sick feeling stirred in my stomach.

"Sofia was beat up, Kali," Zane continued, his voice sober. "And badly. Somebody punched her in the face so hard they broke the bone above her eye. That's what the surgery was for. To wire it back into place."

A wave of nausea rolled through my middle, so intense I felt like clutching my stomach. But as the bigger reality of the situation hit me, the nausea was replaced with a white heat of indignation. "But they can't possibly think--"

"That Matt did it?" Zane finished for me, quietly. "Of course they do. Sofia's family, anyway. None of them know him, and he's apparently the only guy she's mentioned lately."

"But that's insane!" I protested, unable to picture Matt striking another guy in the face, much less a girl. He was big, but he was a total teddy bear—surely anyone who knew him even a little bit could see that.

Zane hopped off the counter and stood beside me. "I agree with you. I don't think Matt had anything to do with it. In fact, I don't think he has a clue what's going on."

"But he needs to know!" I insisted. "He could be in trouble!"

Zane hesitated a moment. "He *is* in trouble, Kali. You were right about Rod. Apparently he and Sofia have this on-again, off-again undying love/possession thing that's been going on since they were in middle school. Whether they're dating now or not, Rod thinks of her as his personal property."

My eyes widened. "Then maybe *he*—"

"I don't think so. Sofia's family does know Rod very well, and he's above suspicion. But they must have told him what happened—asked his opinion about who might have assaulted her. Because he definitely knows about it."

Anger. Hatred. Rage…

"But Rod should know better than to suspect Matt!" I argued helplessly. "They know each other!"

Zane let out an exhale. "Rod's a guy, Kali," he said patiently. "He's bound to be furious over what happened, his own pride is hurt because he didn't stop it, couldn't protect her—he's probably just desperate to find a scapegoat."

I closed my eyes with frustration.

"Not everyone believes it," Zane continued. "Sofia's cousin—her name is Morgan—she's been whispering about it to her girlfriends, trying to convince them, but none of the Frederick girls who know Matt believe he had anything to do with it. Even Sofia's family isn't sure enough to bring in the police, not when she's refusing to cooperate."

"What is Sofia saying?" I asked.

"She's not saying anything. She told the ER staff she fell down some stairs, but they knew she was lying." He caught my eyes. "Here's the thing, Kali. What I've been thinking about ever since I heard all this. You saw Rod glaring at Matt yesterday, while it was still light out. But there's no way he could have known about Sofia's injuries then, because it didn't happen until late last night. That means Rod was already suspicious of Matt, even before this assault."

My stomach did a flip-flop. Lacey had said that Sofia hung out with older kids... *drop outs, mainly.* The wheels in my brain turned, and I took a steadying breath. "This probably wasn't the first time, then," I thought out loud. "I'll bet Sofia has a bad-news boyfriend who's been beating her up for a while now. A boyfriend she's been keeping a secret—particularly from Rod."

Zane's response was interrupted by a cluster of chattering girls banging into the bathroom. I pretended to fix my hair in the mirror, then walked back out into the gym.

"What are you going to do, Kali?" Zane asked, a warning note in his voice.

"Talk sense into Matt, of course," I murmured, weaving through the crowd toward where the football player sat, currently alone. Yet even as I walked, I could see Morgan, flanked by several of the girls she had been talking to earlier, move deliberately toward him, her face steeled for confrontation...

"Kali," Zane whispered urgently, "do you see—"

"I'm on it."

My pace doubled. I cut the girls off in their tracks and swooped in on the table like a diving bird, grabbing up both cups of punch and gesturing Matt toward the doors. "Let's take a walk," I suggested.

He blinked at me, then rose with a smile. "Sure, whatever."

We set off toward the exit, and my peripheral vision caught Morgan and her inquisitorial squad huddled in discussion. I threw Zane a look. He nodded, and his form blurred. In the next instant, he had joined them.

I led Matt outside into the breeze.

"Are you having a good time?" he asked, seeming concerned. We polished off our punches with a few gulps each, threw our cups away, and began a slow saunter around the courtyard. I really didn't want to walk too far from the crowd, figuring that Morgan would be more tempted to confront him—or us—if we were alone. And Morgan's confronting him was an event to be avoided.

"I was having a great time," I said honestly, choosing not to delay. "But I overheard something else, Matt. And it's got me really worried."

I did overhear it, I rationalized to my lie-sensitive conscience. I overheard it when Zane told me about it.

"Oh, Kali," Matt said dismissively. "Will you stop worrying about this thing with Sofia? It's just a bunch of drama."

"No, it's not," I insisted. "She's in the hospital. Last night somebody beat her up so bad they broke a bone in her face."

Matt's feet stopped walking. He turned toward me, the color drained from his face. "What?"

"It's true," I continued. "Her cousin has been telling people. Sofia insists she had a fall, but the family knows better. They just don't know *who* did it, because Sofia's been keeping the guy—assuming it is a guy, which is pretty likely—a secret."

Matt stared back at me for several seconds, evidently unable to take it in. "Is she going to be okay?" he asked finally.

I wanted to stomp my foot in frustration. It was nice of him to ask after her health, yes. But seriously. Could he *still* not see the connection?

"I don't know," I stammered. "But right now, I'm more worried about you. Rod is protective of her, her cousin and her whole family are protective of her, and right now they consider you suspect number one!"

Matt blinked at me for another moment. Then, unaccountably, he broke into a chuckle. "Are you kidding me? That's ridiculous. I told you, I barely know—"

He stopped suddenly, looking at me with undisguised alarm. "Kali, you can't possibly believe—"

This time I did stomp my foot. "Of course I don't!" I declared. "No one who knows you would! But Sofia's family *doesn't* know you. And you're the guy she asked to the dance! Don't you get it?"

Matt's brow creased into a frown. He put his hands squarely on my shoulders. "So I'll set them straight," he said in a low voice. "But it's nothing for you to worry about."

I stared back into his uncomplicated blue eyes. He understood the basics; he just wasn't particularly worried about the situation. And it seemed to annoy him that I was.

"Matt—"

"Drop it, Kali," Zane's voice broke suddenly into my thoughts, confusing me into silence. He seemed to be standing right behind me. "You've said all you can say. Any more is going to backfire."

"What?" Matt said shortly, dropping his hands from my shoulders.

"It's just that—"

"Will you stop?" Zane insisted, his voice harsher. "He's *a guy*, Kali. You think he wants to be saved by you? You keep it up and he'll get reckless on purpose."

My jaws clenched. I could see it with my own eyes— Zane was right. The more I played up the danger of the situation to Matt, the more he would downplay it.

The male ego was *so* freakin' irritating!

"Nothing," I finished, attempting to regroup. "So long as you know, I guess you can handle it."

"Thanks," he replied, with an uncharacteristic hint of sarcasm.

We resumed walking, this time in an awkward silence, across the green space and back toward the parking lot. The shadows were so thick we walked through a few, but if they were casting off any emotion, my own angst was drowning it out.

Matt stopped suddenly. "Kali," he said softly, taking my hand again. "I do appreciate your looking out for me. Really."

I looked up into his honest baby blues, and melted a little. "No problem," I whispered.

We were too far inland to hear the waves, but an ocean breeze still managed to reach us. It would have been a wonderful night for a walk... *if only*. I felt a drop of water on my arm and looked up into a starless, inky sky.

"So," Matt said finally, his voice back to its usual, jovial tone. "You're telling your parents you want to go to Frederick, right?"

The feeling hit me like a blast from a paint gun. The entire left side of my body stung with its venom, and for a moment, I thought my knees would buckle.

Pure, unadulterated *rage*.

"Zane!" I squeaked, unable to think, unable to move.

"What?" Matt asked, puzzled.

"What?" Zane asked, surprised.

I let out a string of curses... but this time was smart enough to keep them in my head. My legs trembled. I broke out in a sweat. The brisk wind hit my newly clammy skin—and I shivered.

"Kali," Matt said with concern, "are you all right?"

Rod was here. I knew it with as much certainty as I had ever known anything. He was here somewhere, just out of sight. He was watching us. He was waiting for Matt.

I opened my mouth again, but snapped it shut. I could not tell Zane what I felt—not with Matt here. And I could *not* let Matt confront the source of that feeling... that raw, burning, *murderous* feeling...

Think, Kali! Think!

I whirled around, but could not tell where Rod might be. The sensation seemed to be everywhere now, pressing in on us like a pack of circling wolves.

Inspiration struck. I forced the words into my throat. "I'm sorry," I apologized, looking around with what I hoped appeared like mild, curious interest. "You know how sometimes you get the feeling that someone is watching you?" As I twirled, my gaze met Zane, and I stared at him hard.

"Yeah," Matt said, "you feel that now?"

"I do," I confirmed.

"You think Rod is here?" Zane asked pointedly.

If I could, I would have kissed him.

I directed the slightest of nods at Zane, then turned back to Matt. I even managed to smile. "But then, I'm always getting random feelings like that. I really do like this school, even if it is a little creepy at night. So, it's official— I'm telling my parents I want to go here."

Matt grinned back at me, blissfully unaware of my charade. He took both my hands in his. "That's great, Kali. Best news I've had all night." His eyes twinkled as he spoke, and for one nail-biting moment, I thought for sure he would kiss me. But perhaps I had acted too weird tonight, after all. Instead of leaning in, he contented himself by throwing his arm around my shoulders. "I guess it can seem a little creepy around here," he said lightly, hugging me to his side. "Particularly when it's about to rain. Not to mention the fact that Oahu is known for its ghosts. You want to go back in now? The nearest door's this way."

I nodded gratefully, and he turned and steered me back in the direction of the building.

We had not moved three steps before Zane appeared directly in front of us. "*Stop!*" he ordered, his hands upraised.

Matt continued forward, walking halfway through him. I stalled in my steps, colliding with Zane's outstretched arm, noting its familiar, rippling buzz in my flesh even as my sudden halt caused Matt to stumble and nearly trip us both.

"Rod's hiding right around that corner," Zane said urgently, his green eyes blazing into mine. "And, Kali…"

I felt my heart drop into my shoes.

"He has a knife."

# chapter thirteen

"Sorry," I squeaked, having trouble finding my voice again. "I don't know what I tripped over."

Matt's clueless blue eyes sparkled again. "Better watch those ankles," he said smoothly, supporting me with a firm hand around the waist. "If you couldn't dance anymore, it would be a crime. Which reminds me... are you a dancer, like, for real?"

"Let's go back in the other doors," I said nonsensically, hoping against hope that he would dismiss the bizarre request the same way he was dismissing every other bizarre thing I had said and done all evening.

He did. As I pulled him away from the corner where Rod lay in wait and back toward the same doors we had exited, he made no complaint, asked for no explanation... even though the promised rain was already starting to fall.

"Yes, I'm a dancer," I babbled, irritated, despite myself, that we had finally gotten to this particular discussion only to have it play out under duress. "I've been taking lessons since I was six."

"I knew it," he said smugly. "What kind of dance?"

The rain fell harder. But with every step we took, the poisonous vibe emanating from Matt's pursuer seemed to lessen.

"Ballet, jazz, hip hop, modern, tap," I listed mechanically, trying to calm my mind, even as my heart still pounded with adrenaline. "But I suck at tap. And hip hop's not really my thing, either. Jazz is my favorite."

"You look like a ballerina," Matt commented.

My eyebrows rose. That was what my teachers always said—that my body type was better suited to ballet. Why he would think that was beyond me, but as the image of dull steel glinting in Rod's unsteady hand continued to flash in my mind, I put reaching the gym doors ahead of conversation and maintained our hurried pace.

We stepped out of the rain and into the safety of the building none too soon. Never mind that my sundress was already so soggy the skirt was clinging to my thighs. Sofia's cousin hovered just inside the door like a vulture, making me wonder if she had planned to pursue Matt outside, whether he was with me or not. But upon our reappearance my popular date—who did not even notice Morgan standing there glaring at him—was immediately surrounded by friends again.

"Hey, quit disappearing on us!" Ryan chided. "The party's not over yet!"

"Yeah," David added, "We're going to make Mr. Hagiwara kick our butts out again."

"Which he will, in twenty minutes," Madison announced, looking at her phone.

"Stay with the group," Zane ordered from behind me. "Rod's alone—he won't try anything with these guys around."

"So let's get back out there!" David whooped, taking his date by the hand.

"Just... go dance some more," Zane suggested, his tone unusually clipped. "The other girls talked Morgan out of confronting Matt, at least tonight. You'll be all right."

"Let's do it!" Julia hooted.

"Come on, Kali!" Matt said with enthusiasm, all drama forgotten. He darted behind me, swooping me up with an arm around the waist and propelling me forward in a move that, had Zane been alive, would have given both guys concussions. I winced at the imagined collision, but when my eyes reopened, Zane was nowhere to be seen.

He stayed out of sight through the next three numbers, and the slow dance that followed them. I tried to put thoughts of Rod out of my head, at least temporarily, in order to finish what would otherwise have been an enjoyable dance on a positive note. But though Matt appeared completely unencumbered by any concerns about his own wellbeing, I was not the only one worrying on his behalf. No sooner had the last chords of the slow dance been struck than a female hand appeared on his upper arm, interrupting what appeared to be another session of deliberation, on his part, about whether or not to kiss me.

"What do you want, Lacey?" He said with annoyance, releasing his hold on me. "Whatever it is, your timing seriously sucks."

"Yeah, well, so does your sense of self preservation," Lacey snapped. "Can we talk a minute?"

Matt looked from her to me, then rolled his eyes. "Not if you're going to tell me the same lame story about how Rod's out to get me because he thinks I beat up his girl, no."

Lacey cast a questioning glance at me, then planted her hands on her generous hips. "Look, Matt. Krystal said—"

"Lace!" he interrupted. His tone was gruff, but as he laid his large hands heavily on both her shoulders, it was obvious he did so with an affectionate familiarity. "I've heard this already. I'll talk to Rod about it over the weekend, all right? I appreciate the concern, but as you can clearly see, I'm on a date."

"You wish," she quipped. "All the more reason to watch your back."

Still gripping her shoulders, Matt leaned in, planted a loud smack of a kiss on her cheek, then turned her around and released her with a push. "Thank you! Now go away.

Doesn't Ty get off at eleven?"

"Midnight," she said sulkily, "and I'm not waiting up this time, either." She offered me a smile. "It was nice meeting you, Kali. I'll see you again sometime, I hope."

"Absolutely." I smiled back, suddenly warmed by the realization that—even as I struggled with how to handle my unnaturally acquired information—Matt's friends were watching out for him the old fashioned way. Various girls who liked and trusted him had been talking Morgan down all night, and Lacey had been sent to warn him specifically about Rod. The guys might still be clueless, but they would be there for him if needed, I was sure of that.

I took an easy, deep breath—quite possibly my first of the night. Everything would be okay. We would walk to the parking lot as a group, and Matt and I would safely drive away. Rod would give up, go home, and—with luck—cool down and come to his senses before meeting Matt again.

"Now," Matt continued smoothly, sliding his arms around my waist once more. "Where were we?"

Another slow song had already begun. I wrapped my arms around Matt's neck and allowed myself to relax—a little—and enjoy the music. I knew that people were watching us, as they had all night, but I chose to believe it was intrigue over the new girl, rather than Morgan's gossip, that was behind most of the sly smiles and awkwardly averted glances. Perhaps, as Lacey had hinted, Matt was showing more interest in me than his crowd was used to seeing.

And if he was?

I wasn't sure how I felt about that.

The last slow dance of the night, as it turned out, offered no chance for dying-chords canoodling but segued immediately—and loudly—into a raucous number that brought down the house. Julia and Madison offered me a fine tribute by perfecting a particular Cheyenne-born move I had taught them earlier in the evening, and David's attempts at break dancing had us all laughing until we cried. We swept out of the school and into the parking lot in the midst of a wave of chattering people, and as we reached Matt's car and said our goodbyes I felt a dramatic sense of relief—even as I scanned the area for any signs of a lurking Rod.

I could see no sign of him, nor of Zane. I did not believe that Rod had left the school; the negative vibe created by his wrath still lingered, even though I sensed that we were out of his immediate range. Zane's own absence was mildly disturbing, but I calmed myself by rationalizing that if Rod *was* making a move toward us, Zane would certainly appear to warn me.

And he did.

Matt and I were several miles outside of Honolulu, traveling north on the road that led back to the North Shore, before our perfectly enjoyable, albeit mundane conversation about car engines was interrupted by Zane's sudden appearance in the back seat. I did not need to look at him twice to know that he was worried.

Zane could appear to wear whatever he wanted when he was thinking about it, but at the moment, he didn't appear to be thinking about it at all. The result was the sort of outfit a living person would reach for on a rainy, cold morning when they felt like crap and had no intention of going out anyway.

He appeared in grungy jeans and a solid, dark-colored tee shirt, his hands sunk deep into the pockets of a medium gray hoody that looped partway over his head, hiding all but a few, rather mussed looking curls. He did not speak immediately, but studied Matt and me for a moment, seeming to take the measure of the conversation. He also seemed to be deliberating within himself.

After another five or so minutes, during which time the conversation had turned to motorcycles, I could stand it no longer. I turned my head over my right shoulder, out of Matt's view, and threw Zane an emphatic "What is it?" look he couldn't possibly misinterpret.

He had the gall to look away.

My stomach flip-flopped. I tried again, this time conveying a threat along with my silent plea.

"I'm sorry, Kali," he said finally, in a voice so low I had to work to hear it over Matt's monologue—a monologue I was no longer following in the slightest. "I'm only stalling in telling you this because I can't decide the best thing to do about it. And you're going to need a cool head."

Matt had paused. He was looking at me. I made a suitably generic response, and he resumed talking.

Zane's face bore a pained expression. "Rod isn't giving up, Kali. He's following you in his car."

My heart skipped a beat. Surely not. That was insane.

"I don't know exactly where his head's at—I can't read people like you can," Zane continued. "But he's upset, there's no question about that. Sweating bullets, hands clenched on the wheel. I just don't know what he would do if he met Matt face to face right now."

My pulse hammered in my ears as I looked out the rear window, but there was nothing much to see. Several pairs of headlights were visible behind us on the road, but even the closest remained at a safe distance. I couldn't really make out any specifics on the car, much less see the driver's face.

"The thing is," Zane said calmly, "if you tell Matt about this, I'm almost certain he would pull the car over right now and go out to confront the guy, which would be a really bad idea."

"Right," I dared to answer, hoping that the word made sense with whatever Matt was still on about. Apparently it did, because as long as I kept my head turned primarily in Matt's direction, he seemed content to keep on talking.

He seemed to be on the topic of popcorn, now.

"Perhaps if we could steer Matt to someplace Rod wouldn't dare pull anything, like a police station—"

Zane's comment was interrupted by a sharp cry from Matt. I jumped in my seat so much my head nearly hit the ceiling; Zane sat up so fast and so violently that part of his head actually *did* go through the ceiling.

But Matt merely laughed, and took my hand in his. "Sorry, Kali. Didn't mean to scare you. Sheesh! It's just that I forgot I'm low on gas. We'll have to stop before I get you home. Sorry about that."

"That's... fine," I said hesitantly, thinking the exact opposite as I turned to catch Zane's eye again. *What now?* I mouthed.

"Try to steer him someplace well lighted and busy," Zane responded. "The busier the better. Rod's going to want to get him alone."

The image those words burned into my brain did not make for a very comfortable drive. I did my best to engage myself more fully in Matt's conversation, but it was tough to appear interested in the contrast between Hawaiian and Kansas City barbecue when all I could think about was an over-emotional Rod lashing out with a knife to skewer Matt's own rib cage.

It seemed like years before Matt slowed the car and pulled off at a gas station. I scanned the place critically, prepared—if it proved dark and deserted—to pitch an uncharacteristic hissy fit about the state of the bathrooms and demand we move on. But what I saw was reassuring.

The brightly lit station had a convenience store attached, and several other cars were also stopped. Furthermore, there was a bar next door at whose outdoor tables a dozen or so surfer types loitered in the night air.

Matt would be fine.

The second my date was out of the car and out of earshot, I pulled my phone out of my purse, put it to my ear, and swiveled to look backward. "I think he'll be okay, don't you?"

Zane moved instantaneously into the empty driver's seat. "I'll check." He disappeared for several seconds, then reappeared in a blur of muted light. "Rod pulled off, too. He's parked just around the side of the store, where Matt can't see him. I don't think he'll try anything here."

The tone of Zane's last word disturbed me. "What do you mean *here*? Where are we supposed to go, then? How can we lose him?"

Zane considered a moment, then leaned forward. "I don't think you can. Rod seems determined to have it out with Matt tonight." His steady gaze met mine. "You have two options, Kali. The best one would be for you to let Matt take you home. Then, once you're safe, you tell Matt everything that's happened and suggest he call the police, tell them he's being followed, and let them confront Rod."

"And what if he won't?" I argued. "What if his response is to storm right out of my house and confront Rod in my driveway?"

Zane looked at me sharply. "Then *you* call the police. And stay the heck out of it."

I crossed my arms over my chest and looked away. Clearly, my priorities and Zane's were not identical. "And the second option?"

He exhaled. "You tell Matt right now and let him confront Rod here, with an audience. You could call the police yourself, tell them everything."

"And how long would it take them to come?" I protested. "If Rod goes wild in the meantime, how likely are these drunks at the bar to intervene?"

Zane's eyes narrowed. "The important thing is to keep *yourself* safe. Matt's a big guy, Kali. Give him some credit. He brought this mess on himself, he can get out of it by himself—without you being collateral damage!"

I started to retort, but stopped myself. Arguing this particular point was hopeless. Zane was an intelligent guy, but he was still a guy, and dead or alive he *thought* like a guy. Protect the helpless little woman, that was priority numero uno; she couldn't possibly protect herself in a knife fight. An entirely true fact, but hardly the only consideration. What was it about high testosterone levels that prevented guys from seeing the obvious?

There didn't need to be a knife fight. There didn't need to be a fight at all. The whole situation was just plain stupid, and as far as I was concerned, one helpless little female was *exactly* what was needed to fix it.

I tossed my phone on the seat, opened the door, and got out of the car. "I'm running to the restroom," I announced to Matt, heading for the building.

Matt merely nodded. Zane was by my side in an instant, shouting into my ear.

"Kali! What do you think you're doing?"

"Stop worrying about me," I muttered, striding with rapid paces toward the store. I could just see the hood of a rather dilapidated sports car parked around its far side. "I'll be perfectly fine."

As I neared the door through which the rest rooms were located, I cast a glance over my shoulder. Matt wasn't watching. I made a sharp left turn and darted toward the corner of the building.

"Kali, NO!" Zane tried to block my path, but I walked right through him. The sensation was unsettling, rather like a mild electric shock, but I forged on. In a few seconds I was around the bend and safely out of Matt's line of sight.

Six feet in front of me was a car. And in the car was Rod. His windshield was tinted so dark I could barely see him, but his emotional aura was as heated, as violent, and as vile as any I'd ever felt.

I strode up to his window and rapped on it.

# chapter fourteen

After a second that lasted an hour, the window in front of me buzzed and began to lower. I stood at a comfortable distance; close enough to talk, yet far enough away to make an easy retreat.

"Kali," Zane pleaded, "This isn't going to help anything. Just go back inside—"

"Hi, Rod," I said calmly, doing my best to tune out Zane's insistent voice. "My name is Kali. I'm just visiting from Wyoming. It's nice to meet you."

The dark pair of eyes that met mine were red rimmed. The lids were swollen. His brow was creased into a scowl.

"What do you want?"

His voice, which was higher pitched than I expected, coming from such a large guy, quavered a little. But its tone was less than friendly.

"I want to clear up a misunderstanding," I explained, my voice dropping to a soothing tone. "And I want to do something to help Sofia."

The dark eyes fixed on mine like laser beams. I felt the heat of his anger spike sharply, then recede.

"Why would you?" he growled.

"Because," I continued smoothly, "I agree that Sofia needs to be protected from whoever hurt her. But you've got the wrong guy, Rod. I know you do."

His eyes left mine. His fingers clutched the steering wheel in a death grip; his upper body tensed. "You don't know anything," he said menacingly. "You're just trying to get your lover boy off the hook."

Zane was saying something else now. Screaming it, actually. But I blocked him out. I knew exactly what I was doing. Despite Rod's outward bravado, he was clearly unsettled ... and uncertain. I could feel it.

"I met Matt for the first time yesterday," I stated matter of factly, "at about four o'clock in the afternoon. His dad and my dad set it up so he could give me a tour of the island. I was with him until late—at our condo on the North Shore. He wasn't anywhere near Honolulu."

I took in a breath. Matt hadn't left my house all that late, and I had no idea where or at what hour Sofia had been assaulted. But it was worth a shot.

Rod showed no visible reaction.

"I know Sofia asked Matt to the dance, but I think she only did that as a cover," I rolled on. "There's nothing going on between them and there never has been. If there were, Matt's friends would have known about it, and they're all completely clueless. I asked them."

A little more fudging, perhaps. But I was getting to Rod. He was no less angry... in fact, he seemed to be getting even angrier. But his focus was shifting, his emotions were roiling in general.

"You got a lot of nerve throwing yourself into the middle of this!" he snarled, training his eyes on mine again. "And what's in it for you, huh? You just met this asshole yesterday and now you're desperately in love with him?"

My shoulders slumped. Guys were *so* freakin' predictable. Feeling sheepish? Strike out harder. Doesn't matter who—just make a show; pick a fight.

Not this chick. Not taking the bait.

"Somebody hurt Sofia," I retorted calmly. "It wasn't Matt, so there must be somebody else. Somebody who's still out there."

I said the last words slowly, gauging his response at every syllable. He tore his eyes away; stared straight ahead. Breaths came heavy and ragged in his chest. Then he released one set of whitened knuckles from the steering wheel and ran a hand through his inky black hair.

"I just want to beat the crap out of somebody," he muttered. His expression was dark; his tone, laced with venom. But inside, I could tell that his anger was slowly, painfully defusing. It was taking a mortal hit, overcome by guilt... and shame. "Doesn't really matter who."

"Well, it *should!*" I blurted. "What good is it doing Sofia for you to chase some random guy around the North Shore?"

"Maybe none," he snapped. "But it will make me feel better."

He didn't mean it. I knew he didn't. There was something else here, something eating him.

"Well," I said softly, "It's not about you, is it? It's about Sofia."

Rod's features hardened, but the emotions I felt from him didn't match. The dominant one right now was hurt.

"Sofia doesn't give a damn about me," he mumbled.

I allowed myself a smile. The emotions in this very passionate—and potentially dangerous—soul might be complex, multilayered, and churning around in his gut like froth at the Pipeline, but at bottom, he was not evil. He really loved that girl.

"Rod," I said gently, "I think you're wrong about that. Do you have any other idea who could have done this to her? Some older guy maybe?"

His swollen eyes slid toward mine. "She's been hanging with some people she's got no business with. I've tried to tell her that, but she won't listen to me. Her whole family's tried to tell her."

"Dangerous people? Like what... criminals?"

He snorted. "Whatever. Gang stuff. But I didn't know there was a guy." He paused a moment, lost in thought.

"There's got to be a guy."

"I think you're right," I agreed.

"She's had these bruises," he went on, more to himself than to me. "I saw them, and I kept asking her about it, but she just kept blowing it off. A couple weeks ago her whole cheek was purple, and when I asked her about that, she got mad—told me it was none of my business. Then she started in hassling me about how cute she thought Matt was, and how she was going to ask him to that stupid dance." He snorted again. "She knew that would get to me. Him in particular."

His rage had all but subsided. Regret, irritation, sorrow... then suddenly, a flare of ire again.

"And the day before he's supposed to take *her* to the dance, he's out screwing around with *you!*" Rod flung at me, his lips curled into a snarl. I was taken aback, but only for a second, until I remembered the scene at Saint Anthony's. Rod might not have known about the assault then, but he was already suspicious that Sofia was being mistreated. Seeing the guy she claimed to like out with another girl, publicly dissing Sofia without a care, had been too much for him.

The boy had it bad.

He was also not the brightest bulb in the factory. And I was getting a little irritated myself. "Sofia doesn't give a damn about Matt!" I fired at him. "She never did! Can't you see that?"

"No!" He said sulkily.

I resisted rolling my eyes, but just barely.

"Whoever beat Sofia up is clearly dangerous, that's why she's been keeping her relationship with *him* a secret— from you, from her family, from everybody. At first, she was probably just afraid her family wouldn't approve, but then when things got violent, she got scared. Maybe he's threatened her family if she tells. Did you think of that?"

Rod considered a moment, then shook his head. "She would tell me."

"She would not!" I argued. "She wouldn't want you anywhere near the guy!"

He scoffed. "So why is she running around with Matt, then?"

I resisted a strong urge to smack him.

"Because she wants to throw you off track, you moron! She's *not* running around with Matt; they barely know each other—she only asked him to the dance to keep you and everybody else from figuring out what was really going on!"

The wheels in his brain seemed to turn at last... slowly.

"So," he said flatly, meeting my gaze. "She never did like Matt."

I exhaled with a huff. "If she did, do you really think she'd lead you to believe that he was the one slapping her around? Knowing perfectly well that you'd go beat the crap out of him?"

His      tightened     lips      suddenly     twisted     into— unbelievably—a grin.

I felt a stab of disloyalty in purporting that Rod would, in fact, get the best of Matt in a fair fight. But Matt would have to forgive me. Rod's anger was all but quenched—I needed only to pump him up a little, get his focus on helping Sofia and off the macho vendetta.

"Whoever this guy is, he's seriously dangerous, Rod. And Sofia's going to need professional help to get out of it. You've got to get her to call a hotline—for domestic violence. They know how to deal with this stuff."

Rod scowled again. "If she'd only tell me who—"

"Well, she's not going to," I interrupted. "And I don't blame her. Because your hot head would only make things worse. She's got to want to help herself, Rod. She's got to make the decision to get away from this guy. You can help her by—"

"She obviously doesn't want my help!" he snapped. "Don't you get that? She doesn't care about me at all!"

Now I really, *really* wanted to smack him.

"Will you please stop and think about it!" I practically yelled. "She's kept her mouth shut, she went to all the effort to lay a false trail with Matt, all to keep you from finding out who this guy is! Why would she do that? Because, you idiot, she's scared to death that if you went after him, this maniac would beat the crap out of *you*!"

My voice seemed to bounce off the concrete block wall behind me, echoing in an otherwise surprisingly quiet moment. I threw a worried glance over my shoulder, wondering if Matt could hear. Zane, whose presence I had forgotten, caught my eye and promptly disappeared. He returned two seconds later, shaking his head. "Matt didn't hear," he said quietly. "He's inside."

I turned my attention back to Rod. He sat hunched over the wheel now, shoulders slumped. He looked exhausted. His emotional storm of rage had broken at last, replaced with a gurgling mixture of relief, regret, and— much to my delight—a brewing warmth I could only attribute to love.

He said nothing further.

I took a step away. "Get online and search on domestic violence," I suggested. "Get a hotline number and give it to her. Call it yourself and see what they say. It's the best thing you can do for her. Really."

He did not look at me again. My words were met with a barely perceptible, grudging nod.

He rolled up the window. I watched him drive away.

Unfortunately, so did Matt.

"Kali!" he called out, nearly colliding with me as I turned the corner of the building. "Where were you? Was that Rod's Mustang?"

I took Matt's hand in mine and led him back towards his own car. "Yes, it was," I said simply. "We had a nice conversation. Everything's fine." Feeling a sudden, almost giddy surge of relief, I swung our hands merrily in the air. "Do you need to get home," I asked with a smile, "or do you want to take a walk on the beach?"

—⟡—

I told Matt everything. Well, everything except the parts that would totally freak him out—like my ability to sense Rod's emotions, and of course, anything about Zane. It wasn't all that difficult to let him believe, without my specifically saying so, that I had spied Rod lurking at the school myself, or that I was just particularly good at reading people. The last part was true anyway, or at least I always thought it was. Now I had to wonder how much of my perceptiveness was based on cues anyone could see or hear, and how much was really... something else.

We checked in with my parents, who were still awake and cuddled up on the couch watching a rerun of *Hawaii 5-0*, then left our shoes on the deck and headed out toward the sand.

It was a relatively windless night. The stars had returned to the sky, and the waves were as low as I had seen them. Zane would be disappointed. I wondered where the surfer had gotten to; I hadn't seen him since we reached the condo. He hadn't said a word since the gas station.

Matt took my hand. "Kali, girl," he said cheerfully, "I don't even know what to say to you. You fly onto this rock and within two days you've got everybody at Frederick High half in love with you. You showed all my friends how to Dance with a capital D, you helped some girl you've never even met get some real help—hopefully—and you kept me from busting up my knuckles on Rod's ugly face. Not a bad showing at all."

I smiled back. Matt didn't know about Rod's knife. I couldn't explain how I knew about it, but mainly I'd left it out because Matt was ticked enough already that I had confronted Rod alone in the parking lot. He got over it quickly, but I wasn't inclined to take chances on an even longer lecture—or add fuel to the fire of the guys' ongoing rivalry. Matt was under the impression that if he and Rod had clashed tonight, Rod would have gotten the worst of it.

I was content to let him think that.

"Well, what can I say?" I said lightly. "Frederick High knows how to show a girl an exciting time."

Matt's blue eyes twinkled at me. Feeling a twinge of unease, I looked away. "I can't believe how tame the waves are tonight," I commented. "I guess it's like this most of the summer, though."

Matt shrugged. "The North Shore goes pretty flat, yeah. I've seen it a lot flatter than this."

I saw Zane, then. He was far away, body surfing on the open ocean, his khaki board shorts barely visible in the moonlight. By his standards, the waves were offering no more than a gentle float. But he would rather be there than here.

Matt put his arms around me. He turned me toward him, raising my chin to look up at his face. "I've never met anybody like you, Kali," he said softly. "I can't wait till you move here for good."

I felt myself seized with a sudden, uncharacteristic

panic. I didn't want him to kiss me, and I didn't know why. Had I had not just asked him for a night walk on the beach, knowing perfectly well what that implied?

"I'm looking forward to it myself, now," I answered quickly, keeping my own tone light. "I just wish my friends in Cheyenne could come with me, you know?"

"Are they military?" he asked. It occurred to me that he knew nothing of Tara and Kylee yet. Though I had told them plenty about him.

"No," I answered. "Kylee's stepdad has a civilian job on the base. Tara's parents are cops."

"Hmm," he sympathized. "No convenient transfers, then."

"Afraid not."

I was stalling now, and he seemed to know it. He sighed a little—a gesture that might not have registered on anyone but me—and we began walking down the beach again.

"Did your parents decide how much longer you can stay?" he asked.

I drew a breath. My eyes scanned the ocean for another glimpse of Zane. I could barely see him; he had drifted even farther away. "Not yet," I answered, unable to keep a tinge of sadness out of my voice. "My mom said they have a few more houses to look at tomorrow. I'm almost hoping they can't make up their minds."

Matt smiled. "Well, as long as you're around for the weekend, maybe we could get together again? My mom was talking about having your parents over to dinner. But even if they don't work that out, we could still squeeze in another hit of *kalua* pig somewhere—if you want."

I smiled back. I did like Matt, a lot. As did most everyone who knew him. The attention he was paying me—particularly given Lacey's claim that he didn't fall for girls easily—would have any female over the moon. I liked being with him; I liked holding his hand and dancing in his arms. It seemed natural, comfortable. The whole idea of having a boyfriend was wonderfully exciting.

We had stopped walking again. He raised a hand and pushed a shock of curls from my eyes. Then he leaned down and kissed me.

# chapter fifteen

It was a very nice kiss. Gentle at first, then growing gradually more intent—but never too demanding. The foam of a breaking wave lapped at our bare ankles. A light breeze whistled around our ears.

He broke away himself, first. With a smile, he took my hand again and led me back up the beach. We didn't talk—the sounds of the beach seemed too perfect to intrude upon. The subdued rush of the waves, the calmest of winds. Only occasional engine noise from the nearby Kamehameha Highway.

I scanned the ocean's horizon for a glimpse of Zane. He wasn't there.

"We'll set something up for tomorrow," Matt said finally, as we reached my deck again. "I'll text you. I hope my mother does invite your parents over—it would be fun to show you around the neighborhood. Julia lives three doors down, believe it or not, and Ryan's only a couple blocks the opposite direction."

"Sounds cozy," I said with a grin. Cheyenne wasn't a particularly big city, but my friends' houses were pretty spread out. Just one more thing to like about Oahu.

Matt collected his shoes, kissed me once more, said goodnight, and drove off.

I remained, sitting, on the deck. I stared at the sliver of beach that I could see. I wondered what the heck was wrong with me.

The evening—aside from the whole knife-wielding maniac thing—had been picture perfect. I'd never had more fun at a school dance, and that was saying something. I'd never had as romantic an experience, period.

So why was I so freakin' *sad?*

"Zane!" I called suddenly, standing up and looking around into the shadows. There was an edge of anger to my voice, and I didn't understand that either. So he had taken off on me. Was that so terrible? It wasn't like I even needed a bodyguard anymore.

I wasn't supposed to need *him* at all.

I was the one doing the favor, right?

Some job I'd been doing of that. Several times, earlier in the day, I had tried to ask him about what he was remembering, but every time he had changed the subject. Since the dance, I hadn't asked him at all. The entire evening had been about me.

"Zane?" I called again, my voice apologetic.

There was no response.

I let out a breath, slowly. The inside of the house was dark, except for one light in the hallway. My parents had already gone to bed. I might as well do the same.

I turned and put my hand on the knob.

"Yes?"

I whirled to see Zane lounging against the deck railing, looking mellow in jeans and a soft Hawaiian shirt covered with green palm fronds. His expression was inscrutable.

My spirits rose instantly. I reined in what would otherwise have been a goofy smile.

"You're back," I said stupidly. "I'm glad."

He studied me a moment. "I never went very far."

I took a step toward him. "I didn't want to leave things between us with what happened at the gas station," I explained. "I know you were only trying to keep me safe. I really do appreciate that."

His eyebrows rose. "I'm not sure you need me or anybody else for that. You do pretty well on your own."

I frowned. His voice wasn't sulky or bitter, but it was unmistakably melancholy. "Everybody needs somebody watching their back," I protested. "Tonight would have been a disaster without you."

He smiled a little. But only a very little. He shifted his position against the railing. I could see the neighbor's grill through the left side of his face.

"You don't need me, Kali," he said softly. "You were brilliant tonight. Really. I'm in awe of the way you read people; your ability to stay cool in a crisis. You knew just what Rod needed to hear, and you weren't afraid to confront him with it. You're amazing."

His eyes caught mine—or at least, the solid one did—and my heart began to race. As much as his praise meant to me, I got the feeling he was leading up to something. Something I didn't want to hear.

"Thanks for that," I said quickly. "But don't tell me you didn't help. Matt and I would have walked right into Rod back at the school if you hadn't warned me."

Zane shrugged. "You probably would have sensed where he was when you got closer. Even if you didn't, I doubt he would have confronted Matt with you there."

"Then he would have confronted him after he dropped me off at home," I insisted. "We would have had no idea Rod was following us, and Matt would have walked into an ambush in my driveway. How well would that have gone, do you think?"

Zane stared back at me, and the pain in his expression hit my gut like a fist. After a long moment, he turned his gaze back out toward the sea. Then he said the words I was dreading. "I think it's wrong for me to stay with you, Kali. You have a normal life—you need to lead it. Whatever's going on with me, whatever I need to do, I'll figure it out eventually. But it doesn't have to be your problem."

My heart pounded harder. The fear that spread through my veins was irrational, nonsensical. Worse than any threat I'd felt from Rod and his knife.

"But I *want* it to be my problem!" I practically screeched. "I want to help you figure it out. Selfish or not, it's true!"

Zane refused to look at me. He raised a hand and ran it absently through his curls. "And maybe if I weren't so selfish," he said quietly, "I'd be okay with that. But I can't do this anymore, Kali. I'm sorry."

"Can't do what anymore?" I demanded, rapidly losing what was left of my composure. "What do you mean?"

He faced me, his voice calm, but firm. His emerald eyes bore into mine. "I can't stand by and watch you fall in love with Matt. I just can't do it. It hurts too much."

My insides trembled. My outsides, too. My legs felt like rubber.

"I know that sounds insane," he continued. "You don't need to remind me that I'm dead—that I'm of no use to you as a human being, and never will be. I remind myself of that every second. It doesn't help."

He looked away from me again. He made a poor effort at a smile. "Sorry to freak you out, but I thought I owed you the truth. I didn't want you to think I'd left you because I didn't care."

"You *can't* leave me!" I protested again, my voice close to breaking. So much for the calm-in-a-crisis thing. My entire body was dissolving into gelatin. "You just can't. Not yet."

He swung his head back toward me, his expression puzzled. "Why not? Does it really matter? There are plenty of other people you can talk to, hang out with. Live people you can talk to without getting stared at."

I made no response. None of the myriad thoughts racing across my brain made any sense at all.

"I've been dependent on you because of your gift," he continued. "But you don't owe me anything. Especially not when all I'd be doing for you is infecting your happy little romance with a bunch of weird, negative vibes."

"I—"

He tilted his head to hear more, but I had nothing else. The word had escaped of its own accord.

"I'm sorry you're upset, Kali," he said quietly. "I really didn't think you would be."

"And I didn't think—" The words came out on their own again, but this time I knew where I was going with them. "I didn't think seeing me with another guy would bother you," I finished in a rush. "I thought that... even thinking you might care would be just... well, stupid. And conceited. If I had known I would never have—" Words failed me again. "I'm really sorry."

"You don't have to be sorry," he answered. "You didn't do anything wrong."

"Yes, I did," I argued, my voice strengthening. "It was dumb and insensitive and I'm not letting you leave me because of it. I'm just not. So you can forget about that plan right now!"

His eyebrows rose again. The corners of his mouth lifted a little. "Oh?"

I was in desperation mode. A million thoughts, some uncomfortable, some anything but, were swirling in my head like a cyclone. Later on, I would figure it out. But right now, I had one goal and one goal only. To keep Zane around.

"Tomorrow morning, we're going to work on your problem," I announced. "We're going to go through everything you remember, we're going to figure out who you were, and we're going to get you wherever you're supposed to be. Just you and me. On Sunset Beach. No talk of Matt or anyone else. Especially no talk of your deserting me when I least expect it. Because that would make me really, *really* upset. Got it?"

His mouth drew into a real smile this time. The full-blown, dimple-showing model that made my knees weak even when they weren't already wobbly. This one nearly undid me. I lurched and grabbed onto the railing.

But his smile was short-lived, muted all too quickly by the look of sadness that crept back into his eyes. "Are you absolutely sure you want to do that?"

"Do I look sure?" I demanded.

He flashed another smile. I tightened my grip on the railing.

"You're a difficult person to say no to," he whispered.

"Then don't."

We faced off, for a long moment, in silence. At last, he turned his gaze toward the beach again. "I'm taking advantage of you, Kali."

I stepped around into his line of sight. If I could have, I would have touched my fingers to his chin, turned his face back toward mine. "You're not," I said emphatically. "If you don't believe anything else I've said, please believe that. I'm not helping you because I feel sorry for you, or because I feel obligated. I *want* to help you because…"

The words wouldn't come. I couldn't fill in my own blanks. Even as I stood there, my brain grappling for something coherent to say, the rest of me pulsed its desire in no uncertain terms. I wanted to wrap my arms around him. I wanted to bury my face in the curve of his shoulder, feel the warmth of his chest against my cheek. I wanted to hold him. I wanted him to hold me back.

But none of that was going to happen.

Ever.

Hot liquid swelled behind my eyes. I took a sharp breath and swallowed. "I want to help you because I care about you, too," I said mechanically, stepping quickly away from him and back toward the door. "So deal with it. I'm going to bed now, and when I come out for breakfast I want to see you here, ready to roll. All right?"

I dared one last glance over my shoulder. He hadn't moved, but remained leaning against the railing, watching me with a smile I could afford myself only the briefest glimpse of, lest I crumble to the deck right then and there—a quivering heap of raw, hopelessly confused emotion.

"Whatever you say, Beautiful."

Beautiful.

I wrenched open the door and stepped hurriedly inside. I did not look over my shoulder again.

"Goodnight, Zane."

# chapter sixteen

"Pathetic," Zane said with a sigh, looking out over a fantastically beautiful seascape of azure water, moderately sized churning waves (moderate for Hawaii, meaning as big as any I'd ever seen on the East Coast), and golden sunshine. A steady, moist wind blew strongly in our faces, but the air was still comfortably warm.

"Worthless."

My eyebrows rose. Sunset Beach looked idyllic this morning. The red flags that ordinarily signaled "Do not swim here or you will die a horrible death" were conspicuously absent. A sprinkling of kids played in the sand. A few people waded. The now familiar shadows that haunted this particular stretch of beach near my condo were all in their usual places. But not a surfer was in sight.

"What's wrong with it?" I asked.

"Onshore wind," he said simply.

As if that explained anything.

Ordinarily, I would ask for more. This morning, I had other things on my mind. "Sit down with me," I urged, unrolling my beach mat in a prime location under a cluster of palms. "I want to talk."

He sat.

Things were a little awkward between us this morning, but it wasn't too bad. What had been harder was convincing my parents that I would rather hang out on the beach again—presumably alone—than join them in a second day of house hunting. My mother in particular had been disappointed, even a little hurt. But I knew I could make it up to her later. How much time I had left with Zane, I couldn't bear to think about.

I had been tossing and turning all night.

"So, how much do you remember now?" I asked quietly. "Do you know your name? Where you came from?"

He sighed and ran a hand absently through his curls. His body was tense, his expression cheerless. It was a long time before he answered. "For a while, I was trying to remember," he said finally, his voice low. "But then I quit."

There was a profound sadness in his voice. I couldn't feel it like I could feel the emotions of the shadows—or Rod's particularly passionate anger—but it affected me, nevertheless. "Why?" I asked.

"Because," he began tentatively, idly plucking at a strand of sea grass which his fingers coursed right through. "I have this feeling... that my past is not somewhere I really want to be."

A wave of something, part sympathetic sorrow, part fear of hurting him further, wafted through me like a dark cloud. I wanted to tell him to forget it, that we should bag the drama and go do something fun. I wanted to see him smile again. I wanted to *have* some fun. But a larger part of me knew that avoiding the elephant that was Zane's predicament would be selfishness. If we had been brought together for some cosmic reason, it certainly was not for my entertainment. We needed to do this thing. I needed to help him. *Really* help him.

"You have to remember, Zane," I insisted. "One piece at a time. You remembered when your father died. You remembered a couple years later, when you found out how. Have you remembered anything else since? Middle school? High school?"

He offered no response.

I coaxed him with a smile. "You remembered you were

an awesome dancer."

He turned his head slowly toward mine. He smiled back. But only a little. "Like riding a bike, I guess. I do remember a few school dances. But they couldn't have been in high school, because I remember I was shorter than the girls."

I laughed. "I'm sure the preteens found you adorable, despite the height challenge."

Slowly, his smile began to broaden, as if he was remembering something he didn't mind at all. Then he downright smirked.

"Maybe," he replied.

I cracked up. "*Shocked*, I am!" I teased. "Holy crap, Zane, whenever you do remember high school, you're going to be impossible. Once the growth spurt hit the girls must have been all over you."

His green eyes looked into mine. "If they were," he said with sudden seriousness, "none of them were anything like you."

My heart skipped a beat. "What do you mean?"

He held my gaze. "I'm not sure. I just feel like, if I'd had you around then—maybe I wouldn't be here, now."

I drew in a breath and held it. "I don't understand."

His head turned. He exhaled roughly and trained his eyes out on the water. "It's why I don't want to remember, Kali. Because I know, somehow, that where I came from—I mean, whatever was happening with me more recently, before I died—it wasn't good. It was horrible. I wanted away from there. And I don't want to go back now, either in my mind or... any other way."

I released my pent-up breath. This was hard. He didn't want to remember, didn't want to face his demons. And I didn't want to make him. But he could not go on like he was. Not forever. There had to be something better for him. Something more... satisfying.

"I'm not sure, Kali," he continued, his voice barely above a whisper. "But I'm afraid I might have—" he broke off, not wanting to voice the thought. "I'm afraid I might have killed myself."

No!

The word reverberated in my brain like the clang of a gong. I didn't want to accept it. I would not accept it. It was all wrong.

"Maybe that's why I—" he began miserably.

"No!" I said again, this time out loud. "You did not. There's no way."

He looked at me curiously. "How can you be so sure?"

"I don't know," I said stubbornly, "but I am." I looked at him. At the healthy glow of his sun-kissed skin, the red blush of his cheeks, the normally laughing eyes. Not this soul. No way. "Zane, I've never met anyone who loved life quite the way you do. You exude optimism. You reek with humor. Everything about you is passionate, hopeful, resourceful. No matter how bad things got, you would *not* give up on yourself. You would find a way to turn it around. I know you would."

His eyes flashed; I saw a glimmer of relief. "You really think so?"

I smiled. "I know so. So if you've been blaming yourself for the state you're in, please cut it out. Sheesh— if every person who committed suicide ended up like you, I'd be talking to ghosts 24/7. Whatever happened to you, I promise you, it was *not* your choice."

He smiled back at me, but he was clearly still troubled. "I wish I could be as sure of that as you are."

With a flash of inspiration, I sat up on my mat. "Do you have any scars?" I asked. "Like, from when you were a kid?"

His eyebrows rose. "Sure, on my forehead. Do you see it?" His face was conveniently solid at the moment, and when he raised a sheaf of curls with his hand I could just see a moon-shaped scar high on his left temple. I nodded.

"I got that flying over the handle bars of my bike when I was eight," he continued. "Not my fault, for the record... stupid ramp collapsed. I got six stitches."

"So, your scars do stay with you," I deduced. "Stretch out your arms."

He complied warily. "Is there a point to this?"

My gaze traced the length of his upper and forearms, which were mostly solid, though the edge of his right hand was missing. The limbs were lean, muscular, and smooth skinned.

Not a mark on them.

"Look at yourself," I prompted. "Do these look like the arms of a cutter to you? Almost everyone who thinks about suicide screws around with less dangerous stuff first. Your arms are perfect. All of you is perfect. You're the picture of health, Zane. You obviously took care of yourself."

His answering smile was genuinely grateful, but the glint in his eyes was wicked. "Really? You think *all* of me is perfect? Do tell."

Heedless of annoying vibrations, I smacked playfully at his still outstretched hands. "Shut up! What I mean is, there's no reason to think you suffered from depression before you died. No cuts, no needle tracks, no picked scabs—"

I paused. Somewhere between "depression" and "scabs" he had withdrawn his arms abruptly. His face was like a stone. "Zane? What is it?"

He didn't answer. His mind seemed far away. For a long moment, all of him seemed far away. A wide band of transparency floated through his chest. His tanned torso blended disturbingly well with the sand beyond, making him, for a moment, look almost invisible.

"Zane!" I repeated.

He stood up. "Sorry," he said vaguely. "What were we talking about?"

I stood up with him. "We were talking about you, and you obviously just remembered something important. What was it?"

He hesitated.

"Please tell me," I begged. "Don't worry about what I'll think—this is all about getting you to a better place, remember?"

His eyes flashed with pain. A deep, bitter pain I would give anything not to see.

"A better place," he echoed dully. Then he turned and took a step toward the water. "I'm thinking this is a pretty great place right here. How about a walk? Or a drive? Your parents left the car, didn't they?"

I could not let him off the hook that easily. I stepped back to his side. "Don't do this, Zane. Don't avoid it. Whatever it is, I'll help you deal with it. I promise. Just try me."

He was a silent a moment longer. His gaze remained on the horizon. The muscles in his jaw clenched. "I hate this," he whispered huskily.

Everything in me wanted to touch him, to comfort him. But he wouldn't even look at me. All I could use was my voice.

"I know."

We stood a long time, the wind blowing my hair into a mass of tangles, his own curls still as death.

"I remembered a lot just now," he said finally. "It happens like that sometimes—in a rush. But I don't want to talk about it. It's not you... I just need some time. Do you mind?"

I took a breath. Despite the gravity of his words, his tone sounded steadier. Perhaps whatever he had remembered, bad as it was, was an improvement over the wondering.

"No," I said, deciding. "I don't mind. For now. If you promise—"

"I promise," he interrupted. "Let's talk about you instead."

I groaned. "We talk about me constantly!"

"Oh, I don't want to talk about superjock, believe me," he retorted. His voice had turned playful again, and its familiar, cheerful tone enfolded me like a warm blanket. "I want to talk about the pre-Oahu you."

I grinned back at him. I had to admit that I was flattered by the interest he showed in my life—even the little, boring stuff. A short break in the seriousness would be okay, wouldn't it? We had all day, after all.

I turned to sit back down on my beach mat, but jumped to notice the sudden appearance of a particularly grungy looking biker dude, a little too solid for comfort, standing over the spot of beach I had just vacated. He was drinking a brand of beer I didn't recognize, smoking a cigarette butt so short he could barely hold it, and staring aimlessly down at the sand. As I watched, wondering why I'd never seen this particular spectacle before, he let out a belch and flopped down, sprawling one incredibly disgusting looking foot—in dire need of a good wash, not to mention a toenail trim—right over the spot of mat where my head should be.

"Ugh!" I groaned out loud. I grabbed a corner of my mat and tugged on it, but as I did, a curious sensation washed over me.

His heart is breaking.

"Kali?" Zane asked, "Is it a shadow?"

I stared at the apparition, one of so many unpleasant ones that, over the years, I had ignored without a second thought. It was easier when I didn't feel them.

"Yes," I answered absently, still studying. The biker was just about the ugliest man I ever saw—early thirties maybe, but already with a pot belly and thinning hair. His face was acne scarred; his nose far too big for his face, and crooked besides. He had a pouch rigged up to hang from a belt loop that poorly concealed some type of knife. And, although odor wasn't usually part of the equation with the shadows, I could swear I caught a whiff of B.O.

"What's it doing?"

I dragged my beach mat a few yards away and laid it back down, still unable to take my eyes off the shadow. "He's mourning a lost love," I answered. *And very soon, he's going to slit his wrists.*

I shook my head to clear the image. I didn't know that for sure. I couldn't possibly. But his despair went deep; his sense of worthlessness was profound.

And, as always with the shadows, there wasn't a single thing I could do about it.

"Is it bothering you?" Zane asked. "We can move somewhere else."

Without answering, I dragged my mat several more yards out of the shade of the palms and into full sun. What the heck? I wanted a tan.

I plopped back down on my beach mat, determined to put the shadow out of my mind. So what if I could feel them all more now? I had learned to ignore the sight of them; I could learn to ignore their feelings, too.

I had to.

"What were we talking about?" I asked, as cheerfully as

I could manage.

Surprisingly, Zane did not pursue the question of the shadow, but sat back down beside me with a smile. "We were talking about you," he explained. "Like why you never learned to swim."

My eyes rolled. "We were? Funny, I don't remember that."

"How is it possible?" he continued doggedly. "You're a natural athlete."

I grimaced. "It's embarrassing."

"Tell me."

"You'll laugh."

"I won't!" he insisted. "I promise."

I let out an exaggerated sigh. It was hardly my favorite topic, but it beat thinking about the biker dude. I couldn't help him. I *could* help Zane. At least, I hoped I could.

"When I was three years old," I began with resignation, "my day care went on a field trip to a Japanese garden."

Zane's eyebrows rose. "And?"

"And I fell into a koi pond."

The corners of his mouth twitched. His cheeks reddened. His whole face began to contort.

"Oh... FINE!" I shouted at him. "Go ahead and laugh already!"

He did. The laughter exploded from him like a volcano, and as he rolled on the sand I could not help but laugh along with him. "You're terrible!" I accused.

"I'm sorry," he said finally, wiping away faux tears with a finger. "Really, I am. It's just... not exactly what I was expecting to hear. I mean... you're so graceful, and coordinated, not to mention brave—"

"Oh, spare me," I snapped. "I know it's stupid; you think I don't? My parents made me take swimming lessons every summer for years. I was twelve before they gave up.

It was *so* humiliating."

"But what was the problem?" he asked intently, now all ears. "Wouldn't you even try?"

I sighed. "I was too scared."

"How deep a fish pond was it?"

"A foot and a half," I said sharply. "Whether or not my life was ever in danger is not the point. The point is, for a couple seconds, I thought I was drowning, and I've never gotten over that feeling. I can't put my face in the water. It terrifies me."

He studied me seriously for a moment. "Very interesting," he concluded. "Particularly for a girl who isn't afraid to talk down a crazed football player with a knife. But I think I understand. I could help you, you know."

I looked at him skeptically. "Many have tried. All have failed."

He smirked. "Well, they're not me. I could teach you to swim." His face lit up. "I could teach you to *surf.*"

I laughed. "Can you teach me how to fly, too? Be serious. It's hopeless."

His expression sobered. "Under the circumstances, probably so. It's not like I could save you if you got into trouble."

I had a fleeting image of what it would feel like to be pulled out of the water by Zane's strong, solid arms, to be held against his dripping wet chest—

I squelched it.

"Still," he continued, his voice more hopeful again. "There are things we could do that would be safe." He considered. "Have you ever been out on a glass-bottom boat?"

"Yes!" I said brightly. "I loved it. Seeing underwater was the coolest thing... I've always wished I could snorkel."

His eyes gleamed. "You do realize you're vacationing in the midst of some of the greatest snorkeling on the planet?"

"That hardly does me any good if I can't swim!" I protested. "Not to mention the whole face-in-the-water thing. I told you, I'm hopeless. It ain't happening."

Eyes still gleaming, he stood up and offered me his hand.

I looked at it quizzically.

"Oh, just fake it," he quipped.

I reached my own hand into empty air, felt a faint buzz, and pretended to let him help me up.

"Get your car keys," he ordered. "We're taking another field trip."

# chapter seventeen

"Come on," Zane cajoled. "That's not a bad price. And it will make a perfect souvenir."

"It's a kid's toy!" I protested, looking at the picture on the box of a grinning preschooler.

I glanced around self-consciously, but what was undoubtedly the least sophisticated retail establishment in Haleiwa was so crowded with tourists I had little fear of drawing anyone's attention. I took another look at the picture. The item Zane had so enthusiastically led me to was an inflatable raft—more like a boogie board in size— with a clear plastic window. Supposedly you filled the window with water, and then could float on the raft and see clearly into the ocean below. Smiling child or not, the mere thought of floating out on the open sea made my blood run cold.

"So what?" Zane argued. "It's perfect for our purposes. This isn't about ego is it? About being afraid of looking silly?"

"No!" I protested. "It's about being afraid of drowning. Or being eaten by a shark, or—"

"Kali," Zane interrupted, holding my gaze firmly with his own. "You know I wouldn't suggest anything that wasn't perfectly safe for you. Where we're going is a protected cove. The waves are cut off by walls of rock and the water is only a few feet deep—it's like a glorified kiddy pool. But at the same time, it's real ocean—with coral and fish and plants. You'll love it."

I wavered. "Really?"

In truth, he had already won. I *did* love the glass-bottom boat ride, and when it came to my safety, bodiless ghost or not, I trusted him completely.

My phone buzzed in my pocket. Kylee and Tara were driving me crazy. I hadn't said a word about having kissed Matt last night—much less everything that was going on with Zane, but I could swear they knew anyway. It was like some kind of weird best-friend telepathy.

"Go ahead and answer," Zane said patiently. "I know you want to. I can tell it's been ringing all morning."

My brow furrowed. "How? I've had it on vibrate."

He shrugged, but his perceptive eyes twinkled at me. "You get a certain look on your face."

Wondering how transparent I really was, I reached into my bag. "I told you that Matt would not be on my agenda this morning, and he's not," I insisted. "But I'll see what everyone else wants."

I flipped through the texts with haste. There *was* one from Matt, but I didn't open it. The others were from Kylee and Tara.

> U R holding out, girl! Talk to me!!!

Tara was usually more subtle. But not today.

> Secrecy doesn't suit you, and it's irritating me. We know you totally kissed this guy. And you'd better start talking. Or else Miss Scarlett spends the rest of break in your room. WITHOUT a litter box.

I winced. I loved animals as much as anybody, but I could hardly stand ten minutes at Tara's house with my allergies... having her cat in my bedroom could kill me. Luckily, she was only kidding.

At least I hoped she was only kidding. I *had* given her my house key so she could feed the gerbils...

U have 2hr, then im calling u. Deal w it!

On this point, Kylee was dead serious. And she would not be happy when I didn't answer.

I composed a quick message to both, explaining that I was with someone and would fill them in later. I clicked send and dropped the phone back in my bag.

"You did answer him, didn't you?" Zane asked.

I looked at him in surprise. "No. I had a text from Matt, but I didn't open it. Let's go."

I put the box with the raft in it under my arm and started toward the register, but stopped when I realized Zane wasn't following.

"You should answer him," he said from a few feet away.

I stepped back over. "It's fine," I assured.

"No, it's not," he responded flatly. "You can't kiss a guy and then ignore his texts. It'll mess with his head. That's not you."

"No," I agreed quietly. "It's not. But I promised—"

"Forget     that,"     he     interrupted,     his     tone uncharacteristically gruff. "You're not screwing up this thing with Matt because of me. Now text him, dammit. I'll be waiting outside."

In a blur of light, he was gone.

I stood still a moment, watching the spot where he had stood. Not a thing remained to mark his presence. Not a brush of air as he passed by, not a whiff of sea breeze and manly deodorant, not a scuff mark on the dusty store floor.

Nothing.

I pulled the phone back out of my bag and texted Matt.

—⟶⟵—

"Now, did I lie? Is this place perfect, or what?"

I looked up into Zane's eager, optimistic, drop-dead gorgeous face, and couldn't bring myself to tell him the truth. It had been an awkward ride up from Haleiwa, despite his concerted effort to prove that he was perfectly okay, and I would do just about anything at this particular moment to lift his spirits. But shallow or not, scenic or not, the body of wild, unbridled ocean that loomed mere feet from my person terrified the crap out of me.

"You said there wouldn't be any waves," I squeaked, the now-inflated child's raft clutched tightly to my side. I felt like a moron anyway, wading into the water in a leotard and bike shorts, but I hadn't packed a swimsuit because I didn't own one. I used to have a one-piece I wore whenever Kylee put up the giant water slide on the hill behind her house, but the butt had gotten fuzzy and I had trashed it.

"Waves?" Zane said with disbelief, looking down at the crystal clear ocean water that lapped lazily against the sandy beach.

I supposed an unbiased observer could see his point. The snorkeling cove at Turtle Bay was bordered by the resort itself on one side and a solid pier of lava rock on the other. Its connection with the ocean, several hundred yards from the shore, was buffered by multiple layers of rocky reefs that systematically reduced the incoming waves down to languid sloshes.

The place still scared the crap out of me.

Unaccountably, Zane laughed out loud.

I fixed him with a glare.

"Kali," he continued, chuckling between words, "You are *so* lucky I'm a ghost."

My eyebrows rose. At least my misery was having a

good effect on his spirits. "How do you figure?"

"Because if I could, I swear I would pick you up, carry you out in the middle of this gorgeous, God-given paradise, and throw you in."

"You would not."

His grin was devilish. "Yeah, I would. But I'd be right there to catch you again."

His dimples were back, in full force. His green eyes sparkled.

My knees forgot their function.

I steadied myself with a start and turned my gaze away from him. "I can't do it, Zane."

Any of it. It's too hard.

"One step at a time," he said confidently, coming to stand close beside me. "For now, let's just sit on the beach, and you can get used to the feel of the water."

He dropped down on the sand where the water lapped just high enough to cover his legs. Or at least it would, if he had legs.

I glanced around. There truly wasn't any danger. No more than a bathtub, anyway. The cove was crowded with tourists—the open water was dotted liberally with snorkeling swimmers, and more than one toddler with inflatable arm bands splashed around happily several yards out from shore. The sea bottom was clearly visible and I could walk out a good twenty feet before the water even reached my waist.

"Kali…" Zane cajoled.

"Oh, fine!" I snapped, plopping down beside him with a splash. "Are you happy now?"

He grinned back. "Ecstatic."

"As long as we're here," I began, desperate to distract myself from the slightly sick feeling I got as the coolish water soaked through my clothes, "we can do something constructive. You promised me you'd talk about yourself later—and it's later. Now, what have you remembered?"

Zane let out a sigh. But thankfully, he didn't resist. "I don't really know where to start."

"Let's start with your mother," I suggested. The water seeping around my butt was uncomfortably cold, but a stream of warmer water had encircled my feet, and I wiggled my toes nervously inside my aqua shoes.

"Her name was Alisha," he said stiffly. "Alisha Bayne. At least that was her stage name. She had naturally blond hair—curly, like mine, except that she usually straightened it. Her eyes were blue. She was beautiful and she was talented, and she lived a kind of a charmed life... and so did I. For a while."

"Go on," I said mercilessly. The warm stream had vanished. The sun was behind a cloud. I was cold again, and I shivered.

Zane made an involuntarily move to circle his arm around my shoulders—but with a frown, quickly aborted it. "My childhood was happy enough," he continued. "But everything changed when my mother turned forty. Her friends had a big party for her; she claimed she never felt better. But three days later, the soap dropped her contract."

I sucked in a breath. "That's pretty brutal."

"Acting is a brutal business," he agreed. "She knew that; the modeling work she used to do on the side had dried up long before. But I think she always secretly hoped to beat the odds."

He was quiet for a moment, and I decided to press. "You had money problems?" I prompted.

He shook his head. "Not then. Not right away. The child support from my father's estate was generous; we could have lived off that and done fine. It was more about the blow to her self confidence. She tried to find other work and couldn't. Money for the extras dried up. Former "friends" stopped calling. She had a breast cancer scare the same week there was an electrical fire in our apartment. For a while, it seemed like everything was going wrong, and she didn't know how to handle it. She started feeling desperate."

He leaned back on his elbows. I watched as the water coursed through him, and realized that I could see sand, even parts of shells, quite clearly on the other side of his torso. In fact, the only solid part of him at the moment was his face.

"Zane!" I said sharply, alarmed.

"What?" he answered, springing up. He looked out at the ocean first, perhaps expecting to see a rogue wave— then focused his eyes back on me. "What is it?"

His form was solid again. His arms were still iffy and one leg was gone, but for the most part, he was back to normal.

"You—" I faltered. "You went all transparent on me. Cut that out!"

He looked down at himself quizzically. "Really? I didn't notice." His eyes caught mine. "I don't think I can control that. Sorry if I scared you."

"You didn't—" I cut myself off again. Who was I kidding? Seeing him faded away like that *had* scared me. It had scared me a lot.

"Sorry if I yelled at you," I apologized. "I was just startled, I guess."

The intensity of his gaze was unnerving.

I grabbed the raft and stepped a few feet out into the water. "Are we going to do this thing, or not?" I blurted, my heart beating fast. "I believe I was promised fish?"

His eyes stayed on me as he came to my side. "And

fish you shall see. Stay right here a minute. Don't go any deeper."

Like *that* was a possibility!

He disappeared in another blur, and from time to time I could see him underwater, poking around the convoluted ridges of coral and lava rock that protruded from the sea floor, making wandering around the cove all but impossible for anyone without water shoes.

The sun remained in hiding, and I dropped down to a squat to put more of myself in the water, which at the moment felt considerably warmer than the air. When standing, the ocean came to just above my knees, so I wasn't *too* nervous.

When Zane reappeared at my side again, he was smiling. "You're going to love this. Follow me."

I picked my way over the uneven surface, wary of the shifting currents and bizarre difference in temperature between indistinguishable streams. I had never been in the ocean before—not even to knee high—before a couple nights ago. Surprisingly, I wasn't as afraid now as I thought I would be.

"What you do," Zane instructed, stopping near a stand of twisted lava spires that just breached the surface, "is put the board on the surface of the water, right around here." He pointed. "Then lower yourself enough to look through the window."

The lapping water pitched suddenly against the breaching spire of lava, sending up a blip of water that splashed onto my waist. I hesitated.

"Kali," Zane prompted gently, "Trust me. It'll be worth it."

His voice radiated with something so warm and beguiling that a flush of heat sprang from my toes and flooded clear to the roots of my hair. My eyes were drawn

involuntarily to his—but I could look at him for only a
second. It was all I could stand without launching myself
through empty space in a hopeless quest to touch him.

The sun reappeared at last, and as the air began to
warm I gathered my nerve and dropped down onto the
water—my feet and knees drifting on the ocean floor
while my upper body rested on the raft. I stared into the
plastic window.

My breath caught.

There really *were* fish here. And not just one or two dull
gray ones, either. Dozens of brightly colored, curiously
shaped ocean fish milled around the twists and turns of
lava, nibbling at the equally colorful spreads of plant life
that clung to the rock's chaotic contours. Things that
looked like anemones shot out their eerie looking tentacles
to sway in the currents, while more hesitant fish poked
their noses out of a honeycomb of tiny lava caves, ready to
retreat at the first sign of danger. It was not an aquarium.
It was not a movie. All these awesome creatures were real,
they were living, and their watery home went on and on…
stretching far beyond me and this cove… clear to the ends
of the earth.

It was totally, freakin', *amazing*.

I found myself slowly moving, turning and reorienting
the board toward other interesting things I saw in the
distance. It was as if an entirely new world was unfolding
before me—a world I had previously been blind to. When
at last I heard Zane's voice, it took me by surprise. I had
no idea how long I had scooted and stepped and splashed
around, eager to get closer to the main stands of lava rock
on the west side of the cove, which housed even more
fish. It was tough going without scratching myself on the
coral, but I was managing so far.

"Careful, Kali," he warned. "You're not paying

attention to the depth."

I stood up sharply, and realized that I was standing in water to mid-thigh. A couple more steps in the direction I was headed, and I would be up to my waist.

"Crap!" I exclaimed, splashing back into safer territory. "Why didn't you warn me?"

"I did!" he protested, chuckling. "I'm glad you're getting comfortable."

I looked back toward the beach, which was considerably farther away than I would have guessed. But I was okay. The water was just above my knees, and though there were deeper pits here and there, I could see exactly where I was stepping.

"Oh, wow," Zane said suddenly, looking off toward the resort. "You're going to love this."

He led me a few steps away into water that was no deeper, but considerably harder to maneuver through because of thicker lava formations. "You don't need the board," he instructed. "Just look."

My gaze followed the direction he was pointing to see a familiar smooth, dark shape gliding serenely just beneath the surface.

"A sea turtle!" I exclaimed. "A giant sea turtle!"

The creature, which gleamed greenish yellow in the sun, was hardly a giant of its species, sporting a shell about a foot and a half long. But to me, seeing it swim around in the wild waters of the ocean while I was standing right there next to it was too cool for words.

"Have you ever seen one before?" Zane asked.

I shook my head. "Only in zoo aquariums. I can't believe there's one right here in this cove—with all these people around!"

"I've seen turtles here before," he remarked matter-of-factly. "But not usually this time of day. There are even more in Kawela Bay."

We stood a long time, watching the turtle tool around in the gentle current, unconcernedly exploring the curls and caverns of lava rock. Zane, of course, could get as close to it as he wanted, but although the turtle didn't seem to mind my presence in the general area, whenever I got within a few feet, it would flipper slowly away.

"That's far enough," Zane warned again as, transfixed by the turtle's hypnotic, gliding movement, I found myself unthinkingly following it. "The water gets deeper that way."

I stopped in my tracks. I had been paying no attention whatsoever, which was so unlike me, it was absurd. Yet here I was—doing something I had never before in my life had the nerve to try. I threw Zane a sheepish look. Maybe he was right. Maybe, given enough time, he really could teach me to swim.

If we had time.

I turned back to the turtle.

It had disappeared.

The sun moved behind a cloud again, and I gazed upward to note its position. It was afternoon already. Where had the day gone?

My parents were due back by five o'clock, after which we were all going to Matt's house for dinner. He was excited about it; that was why he had texted me. I thought it would be fun, too. But I had hoped to accomplish something first. Something a lot more important than my seeing a giant sea turtle.

"Let's go in," I said to Zane, feigning a cheerfulness I didn't feel. "You've accomplished your goal—I no longer fear the ocean. At least, not all of it. But it's getting kind of cold."

Standing up in the water with wet skin and no sun, I

had no trouble producing another shiver. But I wasn't really cold this time.

Just worried.

—⚏—

A half hour later I was back in dry clothes, being led by Zane on a scenic tour of the rest of the resort grounds. We walked around the shore of Turtle Bay proper and then out onto a narrow land spit that hosted a curious concrete block structure.

"It's a bunker, from World War II," Zane explained, answering my unspoken question as I examined the tiny square building, which was laid half-in, half-out of the sand. It had a solid roof and open doorway in the back, while inside two open windows were strategically placed to offer views of the ocean North and West. The inside was dank and cool, but the concrete roof was doing a nice job of catching the fickle sunshine, and I climbed up on it and sat down.

Zane stood a few feet away, watching me curiously.

"What?" I asked.

His brow furrowed. "Don't you see anything here? I mean, like shadows?"

I glanced around. I hadn't felt anything. As for what I saw, I had successfully blocked it out as it happened—a feat that was easy when I was preoccupied. "There's a man and a little boy, playing," I answered. "The usual amount of fainter Polynesian shadows... they're always around. A woman is taking a picture a couple of feet away from you—camera's huge, probably something from the seventies. That's about it, right here. Why?"

He blinked at me. "You see all that?"

I nodded.

"But you don't see anything... military?"

I was puzzled for a moment, but then understood. "Oh. You mean because of the bunker. You thought I would see history reenacted?"

He let out a breath. "I guess so, yes. That's... kind of why I wanted to walk this way."

"Disappointed?" I teased. "I told you, the ability is worthless. I don't see things I want to see, or the kind of things historians think are important. It's more about the shadows themselves—their emotions. Every time I think I have it figured out, I see a shadow that doesn't fit. But for the most part, I think that what I'm seeing are moments that were turning points for people—what they would remember most about their lives."

Zane came and sat next to me on the bunker roof. "It *is* a gift, Kali," he insisted, "even if you can't always see the value in it. I wish you would realize that."

My lips twisted. "Look, you got me out in the ocean today, didn't you? That's a pretty big accomplishment in the Kali improvement program. Don't even try to make me happy I see dead people. You're good, but lightning isn't going to strike twice. Give it up."

He grinned. "I'll never give up."

I swallowed. For the hundredth time, I found myself biting back something I wanted to say. Something about how much I looked forward to his teaching me to swim—or, what the heck?—to surf. Something about how incredibly fun and exhilarating this day, and every other day I had spent with him, had been. About how often my subconscious mind turned to thoughts of doing other fun things with him—biking, hiking, taking a flight across the Pacific, exploring Cheyenne, meeting my friends, taking up ballroom dancing and performing a ridiculously sexy salsa routine at prom. I wanted to take walks, sip cool drinks, cuddle up on a couch and watch a movie, play cards, write stories, go out to dinner, pack a picnic lunch, have a fight and make up, take a road trip...

We would never do any of it.

"Zane," I said heavily. "I don't know how much time I have left here. For all I know, my parents are deciding on a house right now. I want to help you out of this... this limbo that you're in. But you have to cooperate. No more distractions. And absolutely no more putting me and my stupid issues first—no matter how much I like it and how pathetically easy it is to get me off point. Okay?"

Zane laid back flat on the bunker, both his face and voice expressionless. "Okay. Thanks. What do you want me to do?"

Hold me.

"I want you to finish telling me everything you've remembered about yourself." I answered. "Starting where you left off before. When your mother lost her job. What happened next? How old were you?"

It took a moment for him to answer. "I was midway through high school," he said in a monotone, the solidness of his chest wavering again, "when I realized my mother was a drug addict."

# chapter eighteen

"Your mother started taking drugs?" I asked, my voice thin. "What kind of drugs?"

He shrugged. "I'm not sure what she started with. But she ended up on heroin. And there were pills, too. At the end, she wasn't particularly picky."

I swallowed. I had no idea what to say. Maybe I didn't need to say anything. For once, he seemed willing to share without prompting.

"My mother was a really wonderful person," he said quietly. "And I loved her. But even as a kid, I could tell she wasn't strong. She was talented and successful and charming, but she never had any real confidence in herself."

Zane looked away from me, seemingly embarrassed. "My mother was the kind of woman who *had* to have a man around. Always. She could manage her own finances, cook her own meals, raise a child... she was perfectly capable of doing everything any other single person had to do. But she couldn't stand being alone. She needed the constant attention, the adoration, the ego boosting. She needed to feel like she was part of a couple, be seen as part of a couple. Having a man around was as crucial to her as having heat and electricity."

He squelched a sigh, then continued.

"When she was successful, she dated successful men, and they more or less treated her well, until they got tired of her. And they all got tired of her. They got tired because they were prescreened to be operators who feared commitment and craved variety. The kind of man who was *looking* for a long-term relationship was never the kind of man she was attracted to. Don't ask me why, because I don't know. I never could figure it out. When I got old enough to see what was happening I used to do a little matchmaking. You know... my widowed biology teacher, the engineer two floors down. Honest, solid guys who I thought would respect her.

"She was never interested. She wanted Antonio from the club, Richard the indicted broker, Ryan the anchorman. And, at the end, Devon, the unemployed playwright-cum-pusher. When her self-esteem suffered from being out of work, her standards in men sunk even lower. She used to be reasonably careful about who she brought home, how long they stayed, and whether or not I was comfortable with them being there. But once she started using, she didn't care about anything anymore except making herself feel good."

My heart beat fast. Zane's form was as transparent as I had ever seen it. Even his voice wavered from clear to faint as he talked.

"Things got really bad, then. I didn't realize she was using at first. But I saw the kind of men she was bringing home, and it made me angry. My room smelled like cigarettes; there was trash everywhere. She never cooked anymore; half the time, I had no idea where she was. I got a part-time job and fed myself. I stayed away as much as I could."

He paused, and his voice caught. "That was selfish of me, I know. If only I'd paid a little more attention to what was happening with her—"

"Stop it!" I commanded, my cheeks flushed with heat. "Don't even bother blaming yourself—I won't listen to it. It's completely ridiculous. Now, go on."

His eyes turned misty. They avoided mine. His body remained disturbingly faint.

"Eventually, I caught her using," he continued, his voice steadied. "But she shrugged it off. Told me she was stressed out and needed something to help her relax. I didn't buy it, of course, but I didn't know what to do about it, either. She wasn't the kind of parent to lean on her kid; despite the fact that I was old enough to drive and work, she treated me like I needed protection—she would never tell me her problems, or admit how bad things really were. Whenever I tried to talk to her she would tell me that everything would be fine—that she'd just had a fabulous job interview and that she was sure *this* would be the one. I had no idea how much trouble we were in until I started noticing the bills.

"Everything was overdue. Her credit cards were maxed. The money from my father's estate had been disappearing as quickly as it came in. We were behind in the rent; the only food in the house was what I bought. I gave up delivering pizzas and took a job in a warehouse that paid better—but between school and work, I was hardly ever home, and mom got worse. I begged her to drop the guys. I begged her to go into rehab. She wouldn't listen to me. She *just wouldn't.*"

The pain in his voice was so deep, I could feel it in my own gut. Hot liquid swelled behind my eyes. "You did everything you could," I said inadequately. "She put you in an impossible situation. You know that."

He made no response. "I tried to get someone else to talk to her. Someone whose opinion she would respect more than mine. And a few of her longtime girlfriends did try. But they'd been telling her the same things for months already; my mother wouldn't listen to anybody. We didn't have any family to turn to. My father was dead, my grandparents had been dead a long time, and I never had any aunts or uncles or cousins. The more desperate I got, I kept coming back to the same conclusion—that she wasn't going to get help on her own. And that if she didn't get help, she was going to end up killing herself."

His voice turned deadpan.

"I started thinking about talking to the guidance counselors at my school. I'd put it off because I knew that talking to anyone in authority could get her into legal trouble, but I figured at least she would get court-ordered rehab—which was the only thing likely to save her."

"That was a good idea," I affirmed.

"Was it?" he asked dryly. "I was still only seventeen. I had no other family. What do you think happens to kids in that situation when their legal guardian is declared unfit?"

I drew in a breath, disbelieving. "Not... foster care?"

He smiled at me, weakly. "Yes, foster care. I wasn't stupid; I knew it would happen. But I was less than a year away from my eighteenth birthday. I figured all I had to do was stick it out. The bulk of my father's estate money was tied up in trust till I turned twenty one; but I knew that once I turned eighteen, I'd at least have access to enough to support myself. I wasn't worried about being a prisoner in the system forever, and I knew I could manage just fine when I got out. It seemed a reasonable price to pay for getting my mother healthy again."

"You did a very selfless thing, then," I assured. His words seemed to be leading to a happy conclusion, but his expression told otherwise, and my stomach twisted with anxiety. "What happened?"

He was quiet a long while. Very little of his body was solid now; and the mere sight of him, pale and nebulous, frightened me. It was all I could do not to shout at him, as I had before, to release him from his reverie. I wasn't sure what the transparency meant, but clearly, its timing was no coincidence. Whenever his thoughts took him to his past, they carried a chunk of his substance with them.

"My memory isn't perfect yet," he said ruefully. "I have no idea how much time has passed between the last thing I remember and now, so I'm not sure what I'm missing. I know that I did end up in foster care. My mother was horrified at having 'lost' me to the department; it shook her up enough that she agreed to go to rehab right away."

I let out a pent-up breath. "That's good."

"It was a voluntary commitment," Zane continued. "She walked out three days later. Two days after that, she overdosed and died."

My hand clapped over my mouth. It was unfair. So horribly, brutally unfair. "Oh, Zane," I cried, having no idea what to say.

He sprang up and walked to edge of the bunker. His form took on a more solid shape as he moved. "You don't have to say anything," he responded, not facing me. "There's nothing to say. Except that I guess now you can understand why I didn't want to get into it."

He looked out over the open ocean, which was hosting an impressive display of pent-up power at the moment—a series of ridges that rose seemingly simultaneously out in the open water, swelling higher and higher, rolling in toward the break zone in almost military formation. The sun seemed to be shining again, though I couldn't feel its warmth.

I wanted, more than anything, to jump up behind him, wrap my arms around his waist and hold him, comforting without words. But my limbs seemed too cold and heavy to move, and my mind knew better than to try.

"Awesome set!" he said more brightly, a welcome splash of color returning to his semitranslucent skin. "I think I'll go for a dip."

He dove off the bunker into thin air, but instead of

landing on the sand below, his form blurred and disappeared. He rematerialized just off shore, and I watched as he swam freestyle out toward the approaching giants, heedless of their pulverizing strength.

The waves broke right through him, easily as mist.

—ᴍᴍ—

I sat on the bunker, alone, for a long time.

Zane worked out his grief on the water. I used the time to process my own.

In my heart, I knew it was a good thing. Zane was regaining his memory, and his ghostly form was... well... fading. It was what we had both wanted. His leaving Oahu—and me—could only mean that he was moving closer to the light, whatever and wherever that might be. It would be a good place, because he was a good person. He would be reunited with both his parents, perhaps other family as well.

It was the best thing I could hope for him. Wishing anything else was pure selfishness.

I felt a buzz at my side. My phone was ringing. I pulled it out of my bag and saw that it was my mother, who would have texted if it wasn't urgent. I hit the button and put the phone to my ear.

"Hi, mom," I said distractedly. "What's up?"

"What's up is dinner," she responded, her voice agitated. "We're supposed to leave in half an hour. Where are you?"

*Crap. The time.* I hadn't checked in ages. First, we were having too much fun. And then...

"Sorry, mom," I apologized. "We're up at Turtle Bay. I'll be right home."

"We who?"

Double crap.

I thought fast. "Just some guy I met." Should I say he was teaching me to snorkel? No way... it was too unbelievable. And why hadn't I said it was a girl?

Triple crap!

"I decided to check out the resort, and there are a bunch of kids my age here," I improvised. There had to be some here somewhere, didn't there? "They're just tourists, though. I'm heading home now, okay?"

My mother was silent a moment. "Kali, when we get home tonight, you and I are going to talk."

I groaned inwardly. Though I was proud to have her genes, there were times when I could really use a mother who wasn't so irritatingly intuitive. "No problem, Mom," I answered with pretend lightheartedness. "What do you think we'll have for dinner?" Food distraction... it was always worth a try.

"Nothing if you don't get here in the next fifteen minutes."

*Swing and a miss.* "I will. Promise. Bye."

We hung up.

I rose and waved my arms in Zane's direction. "I have to go!" I shouted, my voice hardly carrying to my own ears over the roiling sounds of the ocean.

He saw me, though, and appeared instantly at my side. "What's up?" he asked. Both his body and his hair were dripping wet again, as appropriate. But my breath caught nevertheless. The solidness of form that had always separated him from the shadows was gone. He was visible, and he was whole. But whereas before he had been solid with occasional see-through ripples, his body was now mostly semitransparent, with only patches of solid.

"What's wrong?" he asked, alarmed.

I stammered, trying to get a hold of myself. I could not

let him see my distress. This was supposed to be a good thing.

I forced a smile. "I think it's working, Zane. You remembering your past. Your form is fading. Look. Can you tell?"

He looked down; held out an arm and then a leg, examining them. His expression was wooden. "Well, what do you know?" he said with the same forced cheerfulness I had just used myself. "I do feel a little different. Like I'm not... well... totally here."

His eyes turned toward mine. "Does that make any sense?"

I blinked. His eyes were no longer solid either; I couldn't read them as I once had. My insides lurched uncomfortably. "It makes perfect sense," I answered. "You're doing what you're supposed to do. You're moving toward the light."

His gaze left mine; his expression turned thoughtful. "I don't see any light. But I definitely feel different." He was silent a moment. "Kali?"

My heart pounded. I was frightened, and growing more so. I knew I shouldn't be. But I couldn't seem to help it.

"Thank you," he continued softly. "You're a genius."

I looked back into his face, and for a few, beautiful seconds, one eye turned solid enough that I could make out the familiar twinkle.

"I just want you to be happy," I replied.

He smiled at me. But he made no response.

I held his gaze another moment, then shook myself roughly. "I have to get home fast," I explained, grabbing my bag and jumping off the bunker. "I'm late, and the whole family's been invited over to Matt's parents' house for dinner."

Zane had no response to that, either. He merely
appeared at my side a few yards down the beach and kept
pace with me, silently, as we made our way to my car.

We were off the resort grounds and back out on the
Kamehameha Highway before we spoke again. I didn't
know what he was thinking, but in my own mind, I was
hearing his story over and over again.

"Zane," I said tentatively, breaking into the
awkwardness with a seemingly random thought. "You said
your mother's name was Bayne. You can't seriously be
Zane Bayne?"

To my delight, he chuckled. It was a sound we both
needed to hear. "No," he answered. "I told you Zane was a
nickname. My mother used her name as my middle
name—Zachary Bayne, ergo Zane. I went by my father's
last name."

"And what was that?" I asked quickly. "Do you
remember?"

He looked uncomfortable. "Yes, I do. I'm afraid I owe
you an apology about that. I've remembered my name for
a while, but I didn't want to tell you."

My brow creased. "Why not?"

"Because you would have looked me up online," he
answered simply. "And I wanted to remember for myself.
I didn't want you or anyone else knowing things about me
that I didn't know myself. Does that make sense?"

I nodded, feeling sheepish. He was right—I would
have looked him up. I wouldn't have been able to resist.
"You don't have to tell me if you don't want to," I agreed.

He shook his head. "It doesn't matter now. It's
Svenson. Zachary Bayne Svenson. My mother and I lived
in Hackensack."

An unexpected smile escaped my lips. "New Jersey?
You grew up in *New Jersey?*"

He offered a mock glare. "You have something against the East Coast?"

"No," I said, laughing. "It's just... I assumed your mother worked in LA and you grew up in California... you know... surfing."

"Hey," he defended, "Manasquan's got some decent waves in the fall. A kid has to start somewhere, you know."

I continued to chuckle. "Your mom worked in New York City, then?"

He smiled with me. "Yeah. She thought Hackensack was a better place to raise a kid, though, so she commuted. We had a nice apartment, with a big playground complex to run around in, and there were plenty of other kids."

He grew quiet, and I braved a glance in his direction. Once again, his form was eerily faint.

"We had to move out of it at the end, though," he said absently. "To someplace cheaper. The next neighborhood wasn't so good."

I was at a loss. "I'm really sorry, Zane," I said softly.

He shrugged.

I drove on, conscious that my parents were waiting anxiously for me at the condo, but also aware that my concentration for driving was less than optimal. Driving was harder for me than most people. The shadows drifted across the road just like anywhere else, which meant I was constantly making snap judgments. I couldn't brake at every shadow—if I did, I'd cause a multi-car pileup every time I hit the highway. But I couldn't take chances when I wasn't sure, either, which resulted in a fair amount of "Sorry, I thought I saw something in the road" explanations to confused passengers. My father called me "brake happy." My mother just shook her head and held on.

Zane said nothing further, and after a few moments I glanced his way again. It was a compulsion, and I knew it. A part of me was half afraid that the next time I looked at him, he might not be there.

He was still there, all right. But the sight of him made me gasp out loud.

He was slumped in his seat, looking idly out the window. His form was largely transparent, with a few solid patches. His legs, from mid-thigh down, were bare, and his skin was pale. He was wearing a blue cotton hospital gown.

"Zane!" I shouted, and the car swerved suddenly toward the shoulder. I righted the wheel and forced myself to breathe slowly.

"What?" he asked, sitting up straight, his eyes searching the road ahead. The gown was gone. He was wearing a tee shirt and cargo shorts. He was fine. "Did you see something?"

I shook my head without thinking. It would have made the perfect explanation, since I was always seeing things in the road. I didn't want to tell him the truth. I couldn't.

"Zane," I said with a squeak, unable to restrain myself, "do you remember what happened... I mean... how you died?"

He did not appear thrilled at the question. I couldn't blame him. He had remembered enough rotten stuff already. His own death must surely be the worst.

"Don't answer that," I said quickly. "It doesn't matter. I'm sorry."

"You don't have to apologize," he answered. "But for the record, no, I don't. I can't remember anything past when my mother died."

"Maybe you shouldn't, for now," I announced, filling my voice with a positive energy I was nowhere close to feeling. We had reached the turnoff to my condo, and I pulled in with relief. Freakin' shadows were everywhere this afternoon, especially near the beach lots. "I think you should just relax for a while," I suggested.

"Yeah," he answered brightly, rubbing his hands together. His voice was cheerful, vintage Zane, but I didn't believe he felt any better than I did. I just figured he was a better actor. "If you don't mind, I think I'll hang around the condo tonight while you guys are gone. Catch some basketball on TV, make myself a sandwich. That okay?"

I offered a smile. I wasn't surprised that he didn't want to go with me to Matt's house. It was better for everyone that he didn't. How much I would miss him wasn't an issue.

I would miss him for the rest of my life.

I pulled into our drive and shifted the car into park, fighting hard to contain the moisture building up, once again, behind my eyes.

"That's cool," I agreed. "Just do me a favor, surfer boy."

He smiled at me, dimples and all. "Anything."

"Be here when I get back."

# chapter nineteen

I knew my mother would be annoyed with me. But when my dad, who was usually the epitome of easygoing, offered little more than a glare as I hustled down the stairs of the condo two at a time to join them in the idling car, I knew I was in trouble.

"I don't like to keep a colleague waiting, Kali," he said shortly, steering out of the drive before I could get my seat belt fastened. I'd had no time for a shower and felt totally grubby—my hair was still clammy with sea water from the cove.

"I know, Dad," I apologized. "I'm sorry. I just lost track of time. I'll tell them it was my fault."

We rode in uncomfortable silence a few more minutes; but lucky for me, my father never stayed mad long. Besides which, it was obvious there was something he was dying to say.

"Looks like we've found a house!" he announced finally, his voice back to its usual buoyant tone. "Your mother and I both really like it, and we think you will, too."

"That's great!" I said sincerely. "What's it like?"

My mother showed me some pictures she had taken on her cell phone, while my father described every aspect of the house and neighborhood in glowing detail. It was smaller than our house in Cheyenne, as we all knew it would be, given local housing prices. But clearly, it had character. Funky multiple levels, wide, gently sloping eaves, and over-large windows made it look wonderfully Hawaiian.

"The rooms are small, and it needs a lot of updating,"

my mother admitted. "But the house is definitely livable. And I know you'll like your room, Kali. It has its own door leading to a lanai that looks out over the backyard."

I smiled broadly. Having my own personal deck would be too cool for words. I could see myself now, nibbling on fresh mango, sipping some tropical concoction while filling out college applications on my laptop. The sun would be shining; there would be a nice breeze, scented with flowers. Zane would pop over and perch on the railing, telling me how great the surfing was—

My smile faded. I had to stop.

"It looks fabulous," I answered, handing the phone back to my mom. "I don't mind if it's smaller. I'll be off to college in a year anyway."

"We can drive by it tonight," my dad explained, "but we can't get inside. We've scheduled with the agent for all three of us to take another walk-through tomorrow afternoon."

It was clear from his tone that the outing was not optional.

My parents finished the rest of the drive talking mainly to each other, which was a relief. I knew that my mother suspected I was keeping something from her, and that she expected—at the very least—a more detailed accounting of how I had been spending my "alone" time. I could hardly blame her. But mercifully, she did not raise the subject in the car. Most likely because she figured she'd have better luck interrogating me on her own.

I used the down time, instead, to placate Tara and Kylee.

Thanx for waiting. Walk on beach after dance was nice. You are psychic—yes, he kissed me. On way with parents to dinner at his house. Not sure how I feel, but like him a lot. I am SO not used to

> hanging out with a jock!

I must have rewritten the text twenty times before I sent it. It was all true, but the tone was a lie. I sounded happy and excited, which is how I figured I should feel. I couldn't describe in a thousand texts the hopelessly confused, murky muddle of excitement, hope, sadness, and raw terror that was actually coursing through me.

Their responses were immediate.

> KNEW IT!! Kali's 1st real kiss! Don't worry jocks can b sweet!

> That's exciting! Meeting the parents already? Wow! This guy must be super serious!

I frowned, realizing I hadn't explained the parent connection very well. I hadn't explained anything very well, but that couldn't be helped. I could satisfy their curiosity only after I had a very long return flight over the Pacific during which to think up some version of events that actually made sense.

I tried, for a moment, to focus only on Matt and my feelings for him—or what I *might* be feeling if I weren't otherwise so distracted.

> My dad knows his dad. I've never met a guy like Matt before. He seems really into me, and his friends say he's never been serious about anybody. But he's sweet and honest and really good looking. Whole thing seems surreal.

I hit send without trying to overthink. The phone buzzed again within seconds.

> U are SO set, girl! Hang onto this 1!

Kylee's rampant enthusiasm always made me smile. But Tara's response was unexpected.

I know I usually advise caution in such situations... but what the heck? Jock is a stereotype. You have good instincts. Follow them. Luv U, Tar

I replaced the phone in my bag, feeling oddly adrift. I would have been much more comfortable if Tara had started spouting off statistics on athletes and domestic violence. Having the all-wise, no-nonsense Tara trust my judgment in a matter of the heart would have pleased me... if I trusted my own judgment. But how could I?

I had kissed Matt less than twenty-four hours ago. Right now all I could think about was Zane.

"This is it!" my father declared in his military voice, making me jump in my seat. The time to Honolulu had flown by—I had not even realized we were close.

We piled out of the car and headed for the front door of a modest one-story house with a small front yard, but what appeared to be a monstrous deck looking over a lush hillside out back. Smoke curled around the side of the house as the delicious scent of smoldering charcoal met our noses.

"Good eating tonight!" My father mused, ringing the bell. "Keith said he liked to barbecue."

The door was opened almost immediately by a big, handsome guy with bright blue eyes and a broad smile. It took me an unforgivably long moment to realize it was Matt.

"So, how's it going, Kali?" he asked a few moments later, when the introductions (and apologies) were over and he had managed to steer me aside. We were standing on his deck, ostensibly checking the grill. The aroma was

mouthwatering; the view exotic and lovely. By Cheyenne
standards, all the houses in Honolulu were small and
packed way too close together, but when one had what
was practically a rain forest ascending up a steep green
slope into the clouds mere feet from one's door, such
disadvantages could be overlooked. "You look kind of
freaked out," he continued good-naturedly. "My dad
doesn't scare you, does he? I mean, he scares a lot of
people, but I figured you'd already be used to that."

To my surprise, I chuckled. "No, your dad doesn't
scare me. If you can put up with mine, we're cool." Having
a father who tends to intimidate your friends was part of
being a military brat. It was nice that Matt understood.

I met his eyes, which looked friendly and open as
usual, and wished I could tell him the truth about my day.
But there wasn't a soul alive I could share that with.

"I got in the ocean a little bit this afternoon, and it did
freak me out, seeing as how I can't swim," I explained,
attempting a shred of honesty. "But I was only knee-deep
in a cove. What have you been up to?"

He shrugged. "Same old, same old. Working out.
Getting texts from Lacey yelling at me because Ty took off
to that ultimate Frisbee tournament."

I grinned. Lacey's texts on the topic would be colorful,
I was sure. "You told him about that?"

"Hell, no!" Matt protested. "Dude doesn't need me for
that. I think he was already planning to go. He just didn't
want to tell Lace about it. Last thing I need is to get in the
middle of their business."

"Do they get along okay?" I probed, realizing it wasn't
any of my business either, but curious nevertheless. I was
hoping Lacey and I could get to be buds when I got back.

"Ty and Lace?" Matt responded. "Yeah, I guess so.
They've been together forever." He paused a moment,

looking thoughtful. "Actually, if you want the truth, I think it's pretty lousy between them. Ty's a good guy and all, but he takes her for granted."

I leaned in attentively, hoping for more. Nothing gave a better window into what a guy thought about relationships than listening to him talk about his friends. But apparently, all Matt had to say on the subject, he had already said.

Our conversation turned, as it so often did, to sports, and within a few minutes we had been summoned back inside for some obligatory socializing. I liked Matt's parents, whose casual attitude toward dinner and life in general was much like my own parents', and I was amused by the self-absorption of his older sister, who barely said three words to anyone as she rummaged about the house looking for sunglasses and car keys and some other, unidentified item that was apparently ultracrucial to the hot date she was already late for. It was enough to keep my mind sufficiently occupied that I could—at least for a little while—stop worrying so much about what was happening to Zane.

There was still, however, the matter of the Buddha shadow.

He wasn't a real Buddha, of course, just a really fat, middle-aged Asian looking man who happened to be sitting cross-legged on the floor, barefoot and shirtless. I might have been able to tune him out if the dining room were bigger, or if he were smaller, but the fact that his corpulent form sat staring at me about eighteen inches from my assigned chair was maddening. The man did absolutely nothing during the entire meal but glower—and occasionally belch—in an endless, revolting loop of wasted ectoplasm. The only emotion I could sense from him was a vague disgust, which was doubly annoying given that his eyes were trained solidly in my direction.

*Gift, indeed,* I thought irritably as the Buddha burped so loudly it drowned out the punchline of Matt's mother's joke about grocery shopping on the island. What possible emotional turning point could *this* be for the man? For anyone?

I would never understand the shadows.

The belching Buddha was so distracting that I could barely engage in the conversation like an intelligent person, and after the third time I had to ask Matt's mother to repeat something, I started worrying that his parents would think I was either partially deaf or—worse—some kind of flake. Luckily Matt, who was seated across from me, had no such trouble. He seemed perfectly at ease fraternizing with my parents—seeming, in fact, to enjoy it—and judging from the look on my father's face I had no doubt the man had us mentally married already... pending Matt's graduation from The Academy, of course. Only when the conversation broke into two, with the women talking schools and the men talking real estate, did Matt turn his undivided attention back to me.

He didn't say anything, two simultaneous conversations being enough for the small table, even without the noxious burps only I could hear. But I could guess what he was thinking. It was in his body language, and the smile behind his eyes. He wanted to be closer to me. He wanted an excuse to deliver another of his friendly hugs, or to slide an arm around my waist. He couldn't seem to come up with one, given the company. But, as if to prove my powers of observation correct, he slid a foot over beneath the table and bumped it up against mine. "Doing okay?" he mouthed.

I smiled and nodded. His foot stayed where it was, and so did mine.

The doorbell rang, and Matt's father excused himself to go get it. Playing footsie under the table made me feel like a small child misbehaving, but the sensation was too pleasant to give up. There was something to be said for the power of a friendly touch.

"Matt?" the Colonel announced, returning and taking his seat. "Rod Lee's out front for you."

A dry lump rose in my throat. I swallowed.

Rod? Here now?

"Okay," Matt said matter-of-factly, swinging his legs out from under the table and rising. He offered a perfunctory wink in my direction, then headed off toward the front door.

"Excuse me," I mumbled weakly, wiping my mouth with a napkin. I would have made more explanation, but I had none to give. I only knew I was going to see what was up, no matter what anyone thought. Luckily for me, the adults' conversation continued without concern.

Why on earth would Rod confront Matt here? I had been so sure I had gotten through to him...

Heart pounding, I swept through the folds of shadow fat engulfing the only route out of my chair, and followed Matt as he went out the open door and stepped onto his front lawn.

Rod was waiting on the sidewalk, hands in his pockets, one foot idly kicking a small stone off the concrete and onto the grass. He was dressed in nice jeans and a school jersey; his hair was neatly combed.

"Hey, man," he said casually.

"Hey," Matt returned, his own tone slightly stiffer.

My eyes darted nervously from one to the other. I was still standing in the doorway; if Rod noticed me there, he gave no indication of it. And if Matt's dad hadn't announced the name, I might not recognize him, either.

The burning anger I had felt from him so acutely last night was gone, and its absence had changed his entire aura. Although I was sure he was still awash with emotion, there was nothing left that I could feel. I could read him no better, or worse, than I could anyone else.

"Hey, uh..." Rod continued uncomfortably. "You might hear some stuff about last night. I was pretty messed up. You know—about Sofia."

My body tensed. I didn't know what Rod was up to, but I didn't like the fact that his hands were hidden in his pockets. Still, he seemed... well, calm.

He took an exaggerated breath. "I know you didn't have nothing to do with it," he said seriously, looking Matt straight in the face. Then his lips twisted into a smirk. "Should have known that all along. Wuss like you couldn't beat up a fourth grader."

"Wouldn't be fair," Matt quipped, his tone even. "Not since second grade, anyway."

Rod's smirk deepened. "I just wanted to make sure we were cool, you know?"

I couldn't see Matt's expression. But I was proud of his words.

"Sure, man. We're cool."

Rod's face broke, unaccountably, into the faintest of genuine smiles. The effect was transforming; he looked like another person entirely from the knife-wielding maniac of last night. This Rod was rational. This Rod also was, now that I had the inclination to notice, quite devilishly cute.

"Awright," he returned, taking a step closer to Matt and extending his arm in the air. The guys didn't shake, though—what followed was some weird, football player thing that started with fists and ended with a shoulder bump, one-half the force of which would have sent me sprawling into the grass.

My eyes rolled. *Guys.*

"Hey, Kalia," Rod said offhandedly, noticing me for the first time—or maybe not—in the doorway. I stepped out onto the lawn beside Matt, intrigued by his use of my whole name. Being a local, he must have heard it before and assumed it from my nickname. I liked the sound of it.

"Didn't expect to see you here," he continued, glancing sideways at Matt. "But whatever. Look, what you said... about that number?"

The domestic abuse hotline? I nodded.

"I looked it up and gave it to Sofia's mom. She's going to try to get her to call."

I felt a flush of warmth. "That's fabulous," I said sincerely. "I hope it helps."

Rod's dark eyes met mine, and in their depths I could see a flicker of gratitude—a gratitude that would go unspoken. That was fine by me.

An awkward silence followed. Rod took a step back. "Well, that's all, man," he said, his attention back on Matt. "Later."

"Later," Matt returned.

We watched as Rod walked away down the street. There was no Mustang in sight. "Does he live near here?" I asked.

"About a half mile that way," Matt said, tossing his head to the west. Then he looked down at me and smiled. The subject of Rod, I knew, was already off his mind.

He pulled me into a quick bear hug—an undemanding, comforting gesture that felt so good my eyes watered. It lasted for only a second or two, but I didn't want it to end. Maybe just because I had had such an emotional day, and any strong arms would do. Maybe because I was so frustrated at not being able to comfort Zane the same way.

Or maybe, because I cared about Matt for his own sake.

I honestly had no idea.

Matt released me, but kept one arm loosely around my shoulders. We were still standing in front of his house with the door wide open, and he made no attempt to kiss me. Given my present state of mind, I was grateful.

"Been wanting to do that all evening," he said lightly. "So... you're coming back into Honolulu tomorrow to see a house?"

I nodded. My eyes were still watery, and I didn't entirely trust my voice. But Matt didn't seem to notice.

"I tell you what," he continued. "I've got dibs on the car tomorrow. How about if I come up to the North Shore and pick you up... say, around noon? We can do lunch, and I can show you a few more things around Honolulu. Then I'll take you to meet your parents at the house. I'd do dinner instead, but I have practice tomorrow night. What do you say?"

His arm around my shoulders was warm and solid, his blue eyes optimistic and sincere. A couple more hours of Honolulu sightseeing did sound like fun, and I had no good reason not to go. No reason except a creeping, uneasy feeling that lay somewhere between guilt and fear of impending doom.

Neither made any sense to me. Both my mind and my heart were all over the place, and I stood there, not answering, like a total flake. Only this time I couldn't blame the belching Buddha.

Matt looked at me for a moment, waiting patiently for an answer. Then he hugged me to his side and dropped a kiss on the top of my hair. "You can think about it for a while if you want to," he said easily. "No pressure." He dropped his arm and turned as if to walk back into the house.

I stopped him with a hand on his wrist, my stupid eyes getting watery again. "I don't need to think about it," I answered. "Tomorrow sounds great."

# chapter twenty

I knew my mother planned to corner me. It was only a matter of when and where. The when turned out to be as soon as we reached the condo and my father headed into the bathroom for a shower. The where turned out to be the deck, on which I was pacing anxiously, searching for Zane.

"All right, Kali," she began, closing the doors behind her and seating herself at the table. "Let's have it. I don't know why you've been so secretive lately, but it's not like you, and that worries me. You've met somebody here on the beach, haven't you? Somebody you'd rather your father and I didn't know about?"

I drew in a deep breath. My mind turned cartwheels. I had been thinking all day about what I could say to her, and I hadn't come up with a thing. But her theory—which, for the record, was amazingly accurate—provided a helpful idea. "I told you I met some other kids who were tourists," I began carefully. "Up at Turtle Bay. I've enjoyed hanging out with them because they're fun; they make me laugh. But they're... not like my usual friends."

I was doing well. If you forgave my inaccurate use of the plural, it was almost all true. Which was fortunate, because I was a whole lot better at white lies than bald-faced ones.

"And why not?" my mother inquired. "What's so terrible about them that you felt like you couldn't tell us?"

A tougher question.

I bit my lip.

*Sweet inspiration.* "Some of the things they do are... well... dangerous," I explained, picturing in my mind

Zane's balancing act on the tail of the glider. I felt a strong urge to smile, but squelched it. "Not that I ever did anything dangerous—you know me, I'm a total wuss around the water."

Whoops. A partial lie. Zane did send me in the ocean after that toddler...

"What are we talking about, Kali?" my mother interrupted. "Drinking? Drugs? Something else illegal?"

"No," I said, immediately wishing I hadn't. If I had any sense I would let her make up her own story. "I mean, nothing like that around me. But they're just not the type of people..."

My heart suddenly skipped a beat. Zane was on the deck, standing behind my mother. He was filmy and only partially solid, but he was *here*.

"Let's just say if I had a daughter my age, I wouldn't want her hanging around with them," I finished, releasing a pent-up breath with a whoosh. I wanted to throw a Zane secret *I don't mean you* look, but couldn't take the risk.

"Then maybe you shouldn't be hanging out with them," my mother suggested mildly.

"Probably not," I agreed. "But it's really not an issue anymore. They're leaving tomorrow."

The words passed my lips on a wave of sadness so fierce it nearly caused my knees to buckle. *Please, no. I didn't mean that about you, either.*

My mother stood up. "Well, that's good to hear, I guess," she said, sounding anything but settled. "It seemed to me like you and Matt were getting along well tonight. Wouldn't it make more sense to hang out with him and his friends, who you might actually go to school with next year?"

"Of course," I agreed, relief setting in. I was going to get out of this mess after all. Amazing. "I told you, Matt and I are going out again tomorrow."

"Yes, I know," she said, still looking at me somewhat suspiciously. She took a step toward the doors, then turned. "Do you like him, Kali?" she asked, her emphasis on the word "like" making her meaning clear.

My eyes caught hers, and it occurred to me that up to now, I hadn't really looked straight at her. I wondered if she had noticed that. I wondered if I was really getting away with everything I thought I was.

"I'm not sure, Mom," I said honestly. "Right now, I really just don't know."

My mother smiled. But it was a smallish, sad little smile. "Okay, Kali," she said heavily. "We can talk more later, if you want. Goodnight."

"Goodnight, Mom."

She walked into the condo and closed the doors after her, and I sunk down into one of the patio chairs.

Quite suddenly, I was exhausted.

"An Oscar-worthy performance," Zane said without humor, slipping into the chair opposite me. His expression was grave.

"What do you mean?" I said, irritated by his downer tone even as I was, in fact, deliriously happy to see him again. "I didn't really even have to lie... much."

"You shouldn't have to lie at all," he stated.

I took a good look at him. He looked terrible. Aside from the fact that he was so translucent I could make out the features of his chair through the majority of his torso, his hair was an unruly mess and he was wearing slacker clothes again—a gray hoody and baggy sweats. On another guy the look might be grungy and unattractive, but Zane could look good wearing trash bags. What bothered me far more was the morose expression on his flickering-solid face.

"What's wrong with you?" I demanded, my heart beginning to race again. "Did something happen?"

"Nothing happened. Nothing earth-shattering, anyway. I remembered some more, but I wasn't really trying."

He looked up at me, catching my gaze firmly with his. "Kali, there's something I'd like you to do for me. After... well, after I'm gone."

I didn't want to think about that. I couldn't.

"What's that?" I asked, trying to lighten my own tone. Knowing, even as I asked, that I would do anything for him.

He continued to hold my gaze. "I want you to tell your parents the truth. About your gift."

My eyes widened. "About my *gift*?" I sputtered. "Are you crazy? I told you, I could never do that! It would kill them. It would kill me!"

He leaned forward. "I understand what happened before," he said earnestly. "You were a child, and your parents were frightened. But can't you see that things are different now? You're practically an adult. You're well adjusted in every way. Do you really think that if you told your parents the truth, they would believe that you were mentally ill? Please, Kali. Give them some credit. If you explain *everything*, including how you lied on purpose back then just to make everyone stop worrying about you, they'll believe you now. How could they not? They know you're smart, they know you're sane. But they've seen for themselves how you react when you're in a place with strong emotions attached. They'll put it all together, and they'll know you're telling the truth. They may not understand it any better than you do, but they'll *believe* you, Kali. And they can help you."

I pushed back my chair and stood up. I couldn't believe he was laying all this on me now. How dare he try to fix *me!*

"Help me?" I repeated angrily. "How can anyone help me?"

Zane stood up with me, bending down to make his face level with mine—still holding my gaze, not giving an inch.

"By listening to you!" he thundered. "By being there for you to talk to. By letting you know that you're not crazy, and you're not alone. By stopping you from having to lie to everyone you love every day for the rest of your life!"

I started to open my mouth. Then I closed it again.

I looked into what I could make out of Zane's once-beautiful green eyes, and my anger melted instantly.

He was doing this for me.

He could see how much I hated lying to my parents. He could see how much it meant to me, the last few days, to be able to share everything that was in my heart. He knew he would be gone soon—we both knew that. He didn't even know where he would be going, but right now, he was worried about *me.*

"I'm worried about you, Kali."

My eyes teared. I sniffed out a laugh. "Yeah," I said, stammering like a fool. "I can see that."

His brow furrowed, but some of the darkness in his expression lifted. "Well, then? Will you promise me?"

Promise you what? A cruise to Aruba? Ten kids? Name it.

"I… um…" I backpedaled. The ten kids would be easier, actually. "I don't know, Zane. I'll need to think about it."

"Don't think about it," he pressed, "Just promise me. Promise me you'll tell someone the truth. Someone besides me. Someone you trust. *Please,* Kali."

His form, which had become more solid as we talked, blurred suddenly; within a fraction of a second he had changed from the gray sweats into the hottest outfit I'd ever seen—a soft, skintight muscle shirt and workout shorts, with his feet bare and his blond curls framing his face like he was posed for a movie poster.

I pitched back a step and laughed out loud. "Oh, that is SO unfair!"

He flashed a killer smile. "*Promise*, Kali."

"All right! All right!" I conceded, all but forgetting whatever it was I was promising. "Just put the freakin' sweats back on, okay?"

He smirked in victory. "How's this for a compromise?" In a blink, he was back in his favorite board shorts. His curls were damp.

"Put a shirt on," I ordered.

His smirk widened. "Fine."

A white tee shirt appeared, and I nodded in approval.

"You promised," he reminded.

"I know." What had I done?

Bright lights were on inside the condo; I could see my parents inside, and my mother glancing my way. The porch light was dim, but she could still see me. I seated myself at the table again, facing away from the house and toward the ocean. The waves pounded on the shore in the distance, and a light breeze ruffled my hair.

"It would be nice not to have to pretend anymore, wouldn't it?" Zane commented, slipping into the opposite chair.

"Enough about me," I responded, even as I had been thinking the very same thing. "I want to know how you're feeling. You're..." I tried hard to sound positive. "You're getting fainter every time I see you. Do you feel different?"

He paused a moment, then nodded, his gaze trained on

his own, ill-defined hands. "I can feel something happening, yes. At first, I just felt disconnected somehow, like part of me was somewhere else. But more and more, I feel..."

I leaned forward, wanting desperately to understand, even as I feared what he would say.

"I feel like something's pulling at me," he finished. "Like part of me *is* in another place, and the part that's here—." He broke off. His expression seemed pained. "The part that's here isn't supposed to be."

I swallowed. I would be optimistic about this, for his sake. I *would*.

"Well, we knew that," I said, as lightly as I could manage. "Your being here at all—like you are—had to be a mistake of some kind. But now that you're connecting with your memories... you can be whole again. You can move on."

He raised his head and looked at me. "Right. Move on."

He didn't want to go.

My breath caught in my throat. This wasn't right. Any of it. And it was my fault. I wanted him to stay because I would miss him—but that wasn't fair.

Who was I kidding? It was his *dying* that wasn't fair!

Maybe he shouldn't be with me, but he didn't belong in some perpetual... *whatever,* either. He deserved to be alive, to be young, with his whole life still ahead of him!

"I can answer your question now," he said, intruding on my thoughts, and mercifully so.

"What question?" I asked, my voice ragged.

He leaned forward and smiled at me. My knees wobbled again, but it was okay this time... I was sitting.

"You asked if I ever had a serious girlfriend. I remember now—or at least I think I do. The answer is no.

Not unless I met someone particularly outstanding right around the time I died, which would be doubly tragic, I suppose."

His tone was pleasant, despite the gravity of his words.

"I don't believe it," I said without thinking.

He smiled at me again. "Oh, no? Why not?"

"Because!"

"Because why? You think I'm not selective?"

"No, you idiot," I teased, grateful for the return to a frivolous topic. "Because you're ridiculously hot and I know for a fact you wouldn't last ten minutes in any high school without half the population fighting to be your girlfriend."

His eyes narrowed. "I repeat: you think I'm not selective?"

"Even if you are," I protested, "you could have anybody."

He leaned back in his chair. "I wish," he said solemnly.

His mood turned gray again. Wishing like crap I hadn't used the present tense, I hastened to brighten it. "You're seriously telling me that in your high school in Hackensack, there wasn't a single girl who interested you enough to go out with more than twice?"

He drummed his fingers on the table. At first, the tips went through the metal, but after a few tries, he mastered the illusion perfectly. "You're making it sound like I was an operator," he answered. "But you're wrong. I never had any trouble getting dates, that's true. And to answer your other question, yes, I did really dance at the dances, when I could go to them. But once I started having to work all the time, I never could. I couldn't do much of anything."

He was quiet for a while. I knew he was remembering more, because his form grew fainter as I watched.

I interrupted him before I could stop myself. All good

intentions aside, I just couldn't stand the sight of it. "Okay, *that* I understand. Maintaining a girlfriend would take some time."

"It wasn't only that, Kali," he said seriously. His gaze moved over my shoulder to the inside of the condo, and he gestured in the direction of the window. "You see that?"

I turned and looked in. My parents had their arms around each other. My father was holding some sheet of paper—it looked like a real estate flier—and they were laughing together, canoodling like newlyweds.

I whirled back around. "Yeah, I know. Embarrassing, aren't they?"

Zane looked at me incredulously. "Are you kidding me? What they are is *happy*." He stood up from the table with a jerk and began to pace. "Not that it matters anymore, seeing as how I'm dead," he said ruefully. "But if you want to know why I wasted what little dating life I had being 'selective,' it's because I was determined not to wind up like my parents.

"Neither of my parents were ever happy. They were both good-looking and successful and had plenty of opportunities for companionship and sex, but I don't think either of them was ever in love. My dad had no concept of it; he was completely self-absorbed. My mother got infatuated with a different guy every five minutes, but she never really cared about any of them. Both my parents claimed they were happy, but even as a little kid, I could see they weren't *content*. They spent their whole lives feeling restless, always looking for something else, having no idea what that even was."

He dropped down in his chair, and his gaze floated back over my shoulder. "But I knew what I wanted. I wanted what your parents have, Kali. I wanted *that*."

Warily, I cast just enough of a glance over my own shoulder to see that my parents were now, as expected, making out in front of God and everybody.

I turned my head back around and groaned.

Zane glared at me again.

"I'm sorry," I apologized. "I don't mean to sound ungrateful. You're right, my parents are happy. They've been married forever and they're still happy. It's great."

"No," he said after a moment, his voice more upbeat. "I'm sorry. I didn't mean to unload all my childhood baggage on you. It doesn't matter now, anyway."

He stood up again. He walked to the opposite edge of the deck and leaned his arms on the railing, looking out toward the ocean.

Wordlessly, I joined him. I knew I was doing a lousy job of this. I wanted to give him what he needed—whatever that was—to feel good about what was happening. I wanted him to have hope for his future. But I was failing. I was too damn depressed about what he had already lost. And, yes... I'll admit it. What *I* was losing.

"Zane," I asked quietly. "You said you felt like something was pulling you. I can't tell... I mean... is it a good feeling?"

He didn't answer for a moment. "It doesn't feel like anything at all," he said finally. "I think about my past, and I get gloomy. I try not to—I really do. I try to remember the good times. But the bad things that happened at the end... they're stronger. They still weigh on me, if that makes any sense. While I've been here, I've been free of them. I've laughed. I've played. I've had fun. You have no idea how long it's been since—"

He broke off. He gave his head a shake. "It's been like a dream, you know? I can see now that none of this was real. The only real thing is this force that's pulling me away. It's like someone is telling me, 'Enough. The party's over. Come on to the endgame.'"

"The endgame," I repeated thoughtfully. "That's what I'm asking. Please tell me you have some positive feelings about that."

"I wish I could, Kali. But I don't feel anything at all." He exhaled slowly. "Backwards is sadness, loneliness, guilt. Forwards is just... nothing."

He turned to me and smiled weakly. "Looks like the fun's all here. But my ticket's expiring. I can't stay any more."

My accursed eyes began to water again. "I'm so sorry," I said helplessly. "I really thought... I mean... I wanted to make things better for you."

"I know you did," he said softly. His eyes locked on mine, and I leaned on the railing to steady my jelly legs. "I wouldn't trade getting to know you for the world, Kalia Thompson."

My heart beat like a jackhammer. I stood breathlessly, unable to move, as he stretched out one faint, flickering hand and gently traced the line of my cheekbone.

I felt nothing. Nothing physical, at least. Inside, my heart was shattering.

"Zane," I whispered breathlessly, knowing it was wrong, but powerless to stop myself. "If things were different... if you were alive... and I was alive—"

"Yes," he said immediately, interrupting me. He leaned in closer. His voice was no more than a whisper. "Absolutely, yes. Don't ever doubt it, Kali."

I stood, frozen, while his head slowly lowered. Our noses touched. His lips grazed over mine.

But there was nothing to feel. No sensation. No warmth. Not even the faintest buzz of vibration I had seemed to feel before. His face was no more than a mist...

a vapor.

He drew away again.

A tear rolled down my cheek.

# chapter twenty-one

"Kali?" my mother called. "Come on in, will you? It's getting late."

I wiped my eyes hastily with a fist. "Yeah, I know. I'm coming."

"Lock the doors behind you."

"Sure."

Zane's form began to drift away.

"Don't you dare!" I ordered.

He stopped, but wouldn't look at me. "I'm sorry. I shouldn't have—"

"Yes, you should," I said shortly. "And I'm not sorry." My voice began to crack, but I steadied it. "You haven't got much time. We both know that. And I don't want to spend whatever time you have left with the both of us feeling sorry for ourselves."

The words coming out of my mouth surprised even me. "I know. Come to my room. We'll have a slumber party."

Zane's faint eyes danced. He laughed out loud. "A *slumber* party?"

"Yes," I said with authority. "A slumber party. Ever been to one?"

He smirked. "Not likely."

"Well, I don't have any popcorn," I admitted. "And the usual procedure is to giggle and talk about boys all night. But we can modify."

His eyebrows rose.

"I'll sleep on the bed; you can float around in mid air. We'll talk about whatever makes us laugh. And we'll keep each other company till the wild chickens crow. What do you say?"

He grinned at me a moment. Then he answered with a mirage. The tee shirt and board shorts disappeared; in their place were SpongeBob Squarepants pajamas.

I laughed so hard my stomach hurt.

I opened the doors and led him inside.

—⟨⟨⟩⟩—

I don't know when I fell asleep. I didn't think I would sleep at all. But at some point I closed my eyes, and time skipped cruelly forward.

"Kali?"

The urgency in Zane's whispered call brought me back to consciousness immediately. Morning sunlight peeked through my shutters; the drone of the ocean was calm and distant.

"What? What is it?"

His voice was feeble, indistinct. "Sorry to wake you. But... I don't think I can do this much longer. And I didn't want you to think I'd just left you."

He was leaning against the side of my bed, his legs stretched out across the floor, his head close to mine. No part of him was solid.

"The pull is really strong now," he continued. "I've been trying to fight it. But I just keep feeling... well, weaker, I guess."

I slid off the bed and down onto the floor beside him. My arm overlapped visibly with his, but still, I couldn't feel a thing. "You'll be all right, Zane," I assured helplessly.

"I know I will," he responded confidently. "You were right about me, you know that? I didn't give up."

My eyes widened. "You remember about that?"

We had talked and laughed for hours last night—but

mainly about nonsense. We had steered clear of his
unpleasant memories, focusing only on the good times.
That had left precious little to discuss of the recent past.

He nodded. "I know how I died, Kali."

My heartbeat quickened. Just hearing those words on
his lips struck daggers through my gut.

You should never have died at all.

"How?" I murmured.

"When I turned eighteen," he began, not looking at
me, "I was released from the foster care system. Or at
least, I released myself. I called my father's lawyer in
California, the executor of his estate, and he wired me the
money I was expecting—a decent lump sum my dad
wanted me to have as a birthday present. I bought a cheap
used car and a tank of gas, and I hit the road."

I swallowed. "Hit the road to where?"

Zane didn't answer for a moment. Even talking
seemed to be getting more difficult for him.

"I don't want you to think I was running away, Kali,"
he said defensively. "That's never been me. I had nothing
left to run away *from*. My mother was dead. I'd been in
three different foster placements in less than a year; there
were no bonds there. I'd been in four different high
schools in the last eighteen months and my transcripts
were all messed up; there was no way I was going to
graduate on time. I didn't even have any friends left."

"I don't believe that," I interrupted. "You must have
had friends—anyone who knew you would care about
you!"

He smiled sadly. "I did have friends, Kali. At my
regular school. Good friends. But when my mother started
using... well, you can imagine. I didn't want anyone to
know how bad things were. I was embarrassed by what
she'd become; and I was mad at myself for letting it

happen. So I pulled away from them. It wasn't difficult; I was working all the time anyway. Then when we moved and I had to switch schools; they couldn't have kept up with me if they'd tried. I didn't want to be found."

I fought hard to keep my voice steady. "So, after your mother died... there was no one?"

He shook his head. "It was my fault, not theirs. But no... at that point, there was no one." He stopped and looked at me. "I was okay with that, though. I really was. I was depressed as hell about my mother and the whole situation, but I never gave up on *me*. On the life I still wanted to have. I just made plans. The whole time I was waiting for my birthday to roll around, I sketched everything out. I was going to start over... make a brand new life for myself."

The slightest splash of color flickered in his cheeks. The sight of it warmed me.

"I wanted to drive across the country," he continued, his voice stronger. "Solo trip, you know. Seeing what there is to see. As many times as I'd flown to California to visit my dad, I'd never once seen the country in between. I wanted so badly to have that freedom... to be on my own... just driving wherever the road took me. I figured I would eventually get to California and settle things with my father's lawyer—finances, plans for college. And I wanted to go back to the place in Malibu where I took my first surfing lesson. After that..."

He turned and smiled at me. "Before I started college, I was determined to do something I'd wanted desperately to do ever since I was nine years old. Can you guess?"

His smile was contagious, and my own grew broad. I didn't have to guess; I knew. "You wanted to surf the North Shore."

His wispy eyes danced with light. "Oh, yeah."

I chuckled, even as the irony of it all was so tragic I could have cried. "Well," I said as brightly as I could fake, "you got your last wish then, didn't you?"

His expression turned suddenly sober. "No, actually I didn't. I'm pretty sure I never even got to California. The last thing I remember is driving down an interstate at night and seeing a car with no headlights right in front of me— going the wrong way."

"No!" The word escaped my lips before I could sensor it; my body turned suddenly cold. "That can't be right!" I continued to blather. "You're here now; you *must* have made it!"

I knew it was a stupid point to obsess on. Zane had died at the age of eighteen, and nothing about that was just. He had lost years. Decades. Did it really matter where he had spent his last few days?

Yet I couldn't stand the thought of it. Couldn't stand that he had withstood so much, taken it all so well, turned his life around—only to have it snuffed away on some stupid interstate by some idiot drunk!

"It's so unfair!" I cried helplessly, my own frustration and anger spilling over. "*Why* do people have to drink and drive?!"

Zane looked at me fondly. Perhaps it did help, a little, for him to see me express what were, almost certainly, some of his own feelings.

"She wasn't drunk," he said quietly. "She was just old."

I blinked at him. "How do you know?"

He took a breath. "I saw her face. Only for a second, as I swerved to miss her, but she had the dome light on in her car. She looked terrified."

I studied his face in amazement. There was no malice there. No blame. Only regret.

"It was a split second, really," he continued

WRAITH                                                    243

thoughtfully. "I don't know if I hit her or not. I don't remember the actual crash. But I can see her face so clearly, Kali. I can't imagine why she had the inside light on and her headlights off. She must have had trouble with the controls; I don't know how she could see well enough to get on the interstate in the first place."

He paused. I looked down; the arm that had been overlapping with mine was no longer visible. His torso was a floating wisp. His legs were gone. He seemed to be talking loud—but what I heard was faint as a whisper.

"I hope I didn't hit her."

His face wavered into nothingness.

"Zane," I cried, "I can barely see you!"

I saw an outline of his head as he turned his face back to me. "I can't fight it anymore, Kali. I'm sorry."

I struggled to get closer to him, struggled to hear the rest of his words. A wave of crippling heat welled up within me—tears that wanted to fall, screams of frustration threatening to erupt—but I fought them down. There would be time enough to fall apart... later.

"Don't apologize to me, Zane," I said firmly. "I've loved every minute we've been together. And you *did* get to surf the North Shore; you did! You made it happen through sheer force of will!"

I think he smiled then; but I wasn't sure. He was no more than stray wisps of color.

"Remember what you promised me, Kali," I heard faintly.

"I won't forget."

He was saying something else, but I couldn't hear it. He was thanking me for something. Telling me...

I stopped my own breath. It made too much noise; I needed to hear!

There was nothing. The sound had stopped.

I let out the breath with a cry. "Zane!"

I couldn't see him. I couldn't see anything.

I passed my hand over the place where he had been, but felt only a bedspread and a carpet gritty with sand.

He was gone.

# chapter twenty-two

"Kali," my mother asked with concern, pouring me a cup of orange juice. "Are you all right? You don't look like you slept well."

I thought about answering her, but my jaw seemed too heavy to move. It had been all I could do to force myself to get dressed; to come out where people could see me.

I had sat on the floor forever after Zane left, trying to find a way to make peace. Trying to reason out in my head somehow, some way, an explanation that made me feel good about everything that had happened—and the part that I had played in it. Some scenario whereby I had not taken a strong, carefree surfer guy who spent all day every day in the sun, doing what he loved to do, and convinced him to remember himself into weakness and oblivion.

I couldn't think of a thing.

It would be different if he'd been happy to go. If he'd felt some warmth in the pull that was calling him. That's what it was supposed to be like, wasn't it? *Walking into the light.* But he had said he felt nothing. Nothing... and nothingness.

I had yet to cry. I knew that I needed to. There wasn't a doubt in my mind that if I didn't, and soon, something inside me was going to explode. But somehow, as long as I was sitting on that floor where Zane had last sat, I couldn't give up the idea that he could still see me. That maybe some part of him was still there, watching. And I could not let him see me cry.

I had tried to make him believe it was for the best. I'd darn well better act like it.

"Kali?" My mother asked again.

"I'm okay, mom," I lied. "But I didn't sleep well."

"Oh?" she pressed. "Why not?"

I had to get out. I had to get away—away from her, away from everyone. I had to find a private place where I could cry and scream my guts out. And I had to find it fast.

"Mom," I began, ignoring her question, "do you think I could take the car out this morning? Just for a little bit?"

She frowned. "I thought you said those kids were leaving today."

*Kids?* Oh right, the cover story. White lie #746.

"I'm not going to see them," I said earnestly, looking her in the eyes. "Actually, I just want to be alone for a while. I thought I'd drive up to La'ie point—where Matt and I saw the humpback."

My mother's brow continued to crease. "I'm not sure that's such a good idea. Your father and I need the car at eleven thirty; we've got a lunch date with a couple from the base."

"I'll have it back by then," I promised. "I just need a little while. To clear my head."

My mother threw me a long, searching look. For one horrible moment, I was sure she would say no. But she surprised me. "All right, Kali," she agreed, sounding defeated.

"Thank you!" I said sincerely, jumping up and hugging her around the shoulders. To make her happy, I downed the orange juice, which promptly burned my gut like acid. I grabbed my bag from my room and the keys from the counter and swept outside and down the stairs.

—m—

I didn't make it to La'ie Point. I couldn't find the place.

I drove around the town in a daze, pulling into random parking lots, staring at the Mormon temple at the University, trying to remember where Matt had gotten off the main road and how many turns he had made. I would like to think that if I'd been in the proper frame of mind, I would eventually have managed to find my way to the beach from the edge of an island. But I was not in the proper frame of mind.

After way too much aimless wandering, I put some very expensive gas in the tank and resolved to head home. My parents were going out soon. I would fall apart then.

Impatient cars whizzed past me all along the Kamehameha Highway. They didn't understand the burden I was plagued with—how carefully I was obliged to creep on a highway clogged with restless shadows. This morning I moved even slower than usual, looking at every shadow with the vague, unspoken hope that it would suddenly sport blond curls and smile my way.

None of them did. The shadows just floated about their business, taunting me with their self-absorption, their complete and utter apathy toward me and anything else that was alive.

They were everywhere. And none of them was Zane.

I had driven past Turtle Bay and was nearing home when I realized I couldn't make it any farther. My body was cold; my head was hot, and the emotions bottled up inside me could be contained no longer. I turned off the road by a sign for a convalescent home, pulled partway down the drive and off into the grass, and killed the engine.

Then I exploded. Wracking sobs shook my body; hot tears coursed down my cheeks like lava spilling from a volcano. I wasn't just sad. I was angry. Angry at everything that had happened to make Zane's life so wretched, but more angry that his life had been cut so cruelly short. Could he not have lived another year? Another three weeks? Could he not, just once, have ripped a set at Sunset Beach?

A part of me tried to see the bright side. Perhaps Zane's unwillingness to accept death was a gift in itself. His body might have been lost to him, but his spirit had traveled to Oahu anyway—out of sheer, blind determination. He had had fun for a while, but it could not last forever.

I should be grateful for the time he did have, shouldn't I?

Perhaps I should. But I was not. Because it still wasn't fair. Any of it.

I knew that many people died too young. But I had always believed that they went to a better place. If only Zane had actually *seen* a light. If only he had felt the presence of his mother, or his father, calling him on... welcoming him.

He said he felt *nothing*.

The convulsive sobs continued, even as my tears slowed from dehydration. I could not seem to stop. I did not feel any better.

I wasn't sure I ever would.

"You there! Missy! What the devil do you think you're doing, driving all over my hibiscus!"

My head lifted. The voice screaming at me belonged to a haggard old man who was waving his arms frantically outside my car window.

I brushed a hand ineffectually over my cheeks, sat up, and rolled the window down. I started to apologize, but couldn't get a word out.

"Does this *look* like a parking lot to you? Can you not see the flowers growing right there? Do you have any idea how much hand pruning it takes to get hibiscus like that? Huh? Do you? Do you?"

I blinked, my vision still fuzzy with tears. The man was positively irate, and would have been downright scary, if he hadn't weighed less than me and looked about a hundred and ten years old. His skin was dark, as if he had some Polynesian blood, but he was covered with age spots and freckles as well. The fingers that pointed accusingly into my face were nothing but waxy skin and bone, and a thin hospital gown hung loosely over his gaunt frame. His head was topped off with a handful of wiry, snow-white hairs, and his eyes were dark and burning with irritation. Despite his bluster, he looked frail enough to collapse at any second—and given the state he had worked himself into, I was not at all sure he wouldn't.

"I'm sorry," I stammered, opening the car door and stepping out. I hadn't seen any flowers driving in, but I didn't doubt his word. I had hardly been paying attention.

"Just look at this!" he continued, leading me around the front bumper of the car, gesturing wildly toward the tires. "Look at them! Crushed to death!"

I looked, and he was right. I had taken out an entire bedful.

"I'm really sorry, sir," I said again. "I'll move the car."

"Well, it's a little too late for that now, wouldn't you say, Missy?" he fumed.

I started to apologize one more time. But the words never made it to my lips. As I looked into his face, a palm frond waggled in the wind through his right ear.

My body went rigid. I stared.

He was almost entirely solid. With a cursory glance or two, I would never have noticed. But now I was sure of it. A ripple of transparency flitted through one foot, even as his ear had become solid again. He was as indistinguishable from a living person as Zane had been when I first met him.

And like Zane, he could see *me*.

"You aren't alive," I murmured. "You're a ghost."

The man's tirade ceased abruptly. It was his turn to blink at me. "You can see me, can't you?" he asked suddenly, almost with embarrassment. "I guess I forgot to notice. How come you can see me and no one else can?"

The question of my life.

"I don't know," I answered, my voice still scratchy from crying. "I just can."

"Oh," he stammered, now completely put off guard. "I was so mad about the damn hibiscus, I didn't even think…"

"I'll move the car," I said agreeably, seeing an opportunity to ask a question of my own. "But I want to know something, if you don't mind. *Why* are you a ghost? Do you know? I mean, why haven't you… moved on?"

His eyebrows rose. He stared at me, long and hard. "Little lady," he said impatiently, though not without a hint of sympathy, "I don't know what the hell mumbo-jumbo you're talking about. All I know is, I'm ready and waiting to die, as is my right, and I'd have been gone days ago if it weren't for those interfering brats of mine in there!"

He gestured toward a window on the ground floor of the convalescent home. I looked back at him in confusion. "Who won't let you die?"

"The kids!" He railed, gesticulating with his bony, almost perfectly solid arms. "They're all on and on about the sanctity of life, and how if there's anything anybody can do to keep my heart beating, they've got to do it. Never mind what I told them! Never mind how many times I said, 'I don't want to live like a vegetable. Don't want no tubes, no machines. When it's my time, just let me go.' That's what I told them. Told them all!"

A quivering feeling arose in my legs. My feet froze to the ground.

It couldn't be.

Could it?

"They won't let you die," I repeated, my voice rough as gravel. "You mean, they won't let you cross over?"

Deep furrows knit his brow. "Don't you get it, girl? I want to *die*, period. My body's shot. Kaput. Worn out. I'll never walk or garden again, not after this last stroke—and they all know it. I've lived a good life, I'm ready to go. Got my wife waiting for me in heaven—I know that. Everybody else too. Why the bloody hell would I want to rot in that nursing home bed another damn day?"

I looked from where he stood over to the window.

My feet began to run.

"Now what are you doing?" he complained, floating awkwardly beside me.

I reached the window in seconds. I pressed my face against the glass and peered in.

Two middle-aged women and a man sat beside a bed, looking glum and miserable. Lights flashed on a IV machine. A single tube led from it to the motionless, closed-eyed man on the bed. The same man whose spitting image stood beside me.

My eyes fixed on the blankets that lay over the bedridden man's chest. I stared at the spot. I stared as hard as I had ever stared at anything in my entire life.

The blankets moved.

He was breathing.

He was alive.

My heart pounded. My breath flowed in and out with great, heaving gulps. "You're alive!" I shouted, turning to the ghost—or whatever he was—beside me. "You're

ALIVE!"

The old man looked irked enough to strangle me. "I *told* you that!" He shouted back. "I'm not dead yet, but I will be soon; I can feel it. Their begging can't keep me around forever."

"If that's what you want, I'm sure it will happen," I answered, the words forming and coming out of my mouth of their own accord. The majority of my brain was somewhere else.

Somewhere that the sun was shining again.

He was ALIVE!

"I'll move the car right now," I continued to babble. "I'm sorry to bother you. Good luck with everything—"

I was running again. I have no idea how I got to my car, much less how I drove it back onto the Kamehameha Highway and all the way back to the condo without wrapping the both of us around a palm tree. The thoughts, the images, consumed my brain so fully it was a miracle I remembered to breathe.

They could *talk* to me. Both of them. None of the other shadows could. The old man was alive...

I had seen both the old man's body and his spirit. But I could see nothing, anymore, of Zane. If *he* had... if he was...

I pulled the car into the condo lot. My arms shook visibly on the steering wheel. I turned off the engine and sat quaking in my seat.

But where?

Zane couldn't be in Oahu—he said he had never even made it to California. He must still be wherever the accident happened. On the mainland.

I jumped out of the car.

Images flashed before me. Zane's physical body, the body I had never seen. Chest moving, lungs breathing...

yet horribly, dreadfully broken. Bruised and bleeding, struggling with the specter of death...

The thought chilled me to the marrow. How would Zane feel to see himself like that? No way was *he* ready to die. But unlike the old man, Zane had no one to sit beside him. No one to hold his hand, to whisper encouragement. No one to tell him they loved him.

No one to wish him back.

I flew up the stairs and into the condo.

My parents were waiting for me in the kitchen, looking perturbed. "About time," my father snapped, wresting the car keys from my trembling hand. "Two days in a row, Kali? I don't know what's gotten into you!" He turned toward the door. "Come on, Diane. We're late enough as it is. Kali—we'll discuss this later."

My mother stood still, studying me. I had no chance in a million of convincing her I was all right, even I wanted to, which I did not. My eyes were puffy as grapefruits. My every limb shook. There was no telling what my facial expression was conveying. My father might be capable of missing all those clues, but my mother took in every pathetic inch of me without missing a beat.

"You'll have to go without me, Mitch," she said calmly.

"What?" he whirled around. "Why?"

"Tell them that Kali isn't feeling well."

My father did look at me, then. And when he did, his expression changed instantly from exasperation to concern. "Well, I guess—. I mean, should I—"

"You go," my mother said authoritatively. "We'll be all right."

My father looked hesitantly from my mother to me. Then he gave us both a quick kiss on the cheek and departed.

I swallowed. My mother merely stood and looked at

me, waiting for me to begin.

I couldn't imagine how.

"Let's sit down," she suggested, gesturing toward the sofa.

My legs wouldn't move. "I can't," I protested, my voice little more than a squeak. "I don't have time."

My mother's eyebrows rose. "Time?"

I nodded.

They'll believe you, Kali, Zane's words echoed in my mind. And they can help you.

"You were right, Mom," I began in a rush, hardly censoring the words as they spilled out. I didn't think I could tell her everything—not yet. But I could do a whole lot better than I had been.

"I met someone here on the beach. We've been spending a lot of time together, and I know it hasn't been long, but I—I've come to really care about him."

My mother's face remained expressionless. "Go on."

"He's the one I was hanging out with at Turtle Bay, the only other tourist I've met. He's not dangerous—there's nothing wrong with him at all. In fact, I think you and dad would both really like him."

"Kali," my mother broke in, her calm demeanor breaking at last. "*Why* were you keeping him a secret?"

Another image flashed suddenly through my mind. On the way back from Turtle Bay yesterday, when his mind was idle, Zane had been wearing a hospital gown...

"Mom," I said, my voice choking. "He's gone now. He left, but... he's been in a car accident—back on the mainland."

Her eyes widened. *"Already?"*

"I know it doesn't make sense!" I blurted, tears spurting from my eyes again. "You couldn't possibly understand unless I told you the whole story, and I will; I promise I will. He *wanted* me to tell you. But I can't tell you everything now, because I have to get back home. As soon as I can. I have to be with him. He's dying, Mom!"

My mother's face contorted with a series of emotions, not least of which was annoyance. "Kali," she said finally, her voice poorly controlled. "You can't possibly go back to Cheyenne now, all by yourself. I thought you were enjoying Oahu!"

"I love everything about Oahu!" I nearly shouted. "Because of him! And if I don't get back to the mainland soon, and help him, he may never see it again himself!"

She exhaled. Long and slow. "You are telling me that you met a guy... wait, how old is he?"

"Eighteen," I answered quickly.

"A teenager," she continued, "and you kept him a secret from us, for reasons you still can't explain, but in a few short days you've come to care about him so much that you're willing to give up the rest of your time in Oahu so you can fly back home and hold his hand in the hospital?"

"*Yes*," I said heavily. "I'm not making this up, Mom. I swear. For a while I thought he had died in the accident—that's why I've been falling apart. But he didn't... he's still alive. At least he was. I mean... I don't know! Don't you see, he could die at any moment! That's why I have to fly back now!"

I flung out my last words, exhausted. There was nothing left to say. If I tried to explain the shadows to her now, in the state I was in, I knew I would never make it back to him. She wouldn't put me on a plane—she would probably drug me and put me to bed. Getting a grasp on that whole realm of surreality was something that would take time I simply didn't have. And I couldn't do without my parents' help; it wasn't possible. I had no money for a plane ticket; I didn't even have a credit card.

"Please, mom," I begged. "I'm telling you the truth. Just help me switch my ticket to today—I'll take the first flight out."

My next words were barely audible. They came out as a breathy rasp. "He *needs* me."

Looking in my mother's eyes then, I knew what odds I was facing. She had little reason to believe me, and a hundred thousand good-parenting reasons for forbidding me to fly across an ocean by myself.

"What's his name?" she said flatly, unexpectedly.

"Zane," I answered, enjoying the sound of the word even as it reached my ears, reveling in how nice it felt to voice it to someone real, out loud.

Her eyes searched mine again, and I knew that she was looking far deeper than the past few days. Covering up the shadows was an unfortunate art form I'd been forced to adopt, but other than that, I had always been honest with her. Lying was not in my nature. And as I stood there, awaiting her verdict, I realized how very much that mattered. When every other girl in the ninth grade had told her parents she was going to a sleepover, I had admitted we had tickets to a concert in Denver. When I was ten and spilled root beer on my best friend's father's laptop, I had confessed—even though he had blamed their cat. And when I had promised my dad last New Years that I would leave a friend's party if any booze or drugs showed up, and both did, I had left.

Miserable experiences, all. The concert didn't happen; my friends were furious. I lost my allowance for months. My New Years sucked. I wasn't so sure I had made the right calls then, but I did not regret my honesty now.

What mattered to me most in the world was riding on it.

My mother's gaze didn't waver. I held my breath.
She let out a long, resigned sounding sigh.
"All right, Kali. I'll change your ticket. You can fly back
home."

# chapter twenty-three

My mother pulled out her cell phone. I went into my room to pack. When I came back out with my suitcase she was just finishing a call.

"We can get you on a midafternoon flight," she said uncertainly. "But it would get into Denver in the middle of the night."

"That's fine," I said quickly. "Did you book it?"

My mother leaned heavily against the counter. "We have to think this through, Kali. You do remember that we have no car at the airport?"

Crap.

How could I forget? My dad had a thing about paying for parking. He never drove to the airport if he could hitch a ride, which he always managed to do. We had ridden all the way down to Denver on the trip out by cramming into the back of an SUV driven by a buddy of his who happened to be a traveling dog food salesman. My suitcase still reeked of kibble.

"I can get a ride," I said confidently.

"From who?"

"Kylee."

My mother frowned. "All the way from Cheyenne to Denver and back? At that hour?"

I drew in a breath, sharply. Kylee had her own car. She liked to drive; she was good at it. Unfortunately, she was *not* a morning person.

With luck, we could be home by morning.

"That's an awful lot to ask, Kali," my mother pointed out. "You'd need to call her, right now. I'm not booking a ticket unless I know you can get back to Cheyenne safely.

You're going to be exhausted after the flight—you shouldn't be driving yourself anyway. Which brings us to our next—"

I was already dialing. Kylee's ever-cheerful soprano picked up on the second ring.

"Girlfriend!!! What's up?!"

"Hi Kylee," I began, trying hard to slow my breathing. "Listen, I don't have a lot of time to explain, but I need a favor."

"Name it!"

I love you.

"I'm flying back to Denver this afternoon—I'll get there late tonight."

There was a momentary silence.

"You're leaving early?" she asked incredulously. "What happened? Is something wrong?"

I took a deep breath. "A friend of mine was in a car accident—a bad one. I have to get to him as soon as possible."

Another span of silence followed. I could picture Kylee easily; eyes wide, mouth open. "*Him?* Who are you talking about? Somebody I know?"

"No," I said quickly. "I met him here in Oahu. Listen Kylee, I can explain later—but the thing is, I don't have a ride home from the airport. I know it's a lot to ask, but is there any way your parents would let you drive to Denver to get me?"

"Where is he?"

I blinked. "What?"

"I said, 'where is he?' This guy—if you met him in Oahu, what's he doing in Cheyenne?"

A wave of cold, fringed with nausea, swept viciously from my head to my toes.

Holy crap.

I had no idea. I could only think one step at a time—
getting back to the mainland was as far as I'd gotten.

"Where is he?" I repeated dumbly.

From her position by the counter, my mother let out a
frustrated sigh. "That was my next question."

My brain searched desperately for an answer. "He's...
I..."

Think, Kali!

"I don't know the exact hospital. I just know he was in
an accident. But I'll find him."

Kylee responded patiently. "Are we talking... say...
Wyoming?"

"I don't *know!*" I cried, my voice close to breaking
again. "Please Kylee, can you pick me up at the airport or
not?"

She wouldn't answer. "This isn't the jock, is it?"

"No!" I said, giving my foot a useless stamp on the
condo carpet. "It's the surfer guy—" I paused a second.
Even saying the words brought heat to my stinging eyes.
"The one with the curly hair."

I moved the phone away from my ear.

Kylee shrieked profanity across the Pacific.

"Will you pick me up?" I pressed.

"Are you kidding? You know I will," Kylee affirmed,
her voice charged with determined energy. "Don't worry,
Kali. We'll find him. How bad was the accident?"

"It was bad," I murmured, "Really bad."

My beloved pal didn't miss a beat.

"Text me before you take off; give me the arrival time.
I'll be there. And Kali?"

I let out a sniffle.

"Call Tara. She can figure out what hospital he's in."

*Tara!* Of course.

I found my voice and thanked Kylee profusely.

We hung up.

I looked at my mother with something resembling a smile. "All set. Can we book it now? Don't I have to leave soon?"

Her lips twisted. "That's another issue, I'm afraid. Your father won't be back with the car for at least another hour. I'm not sure we can get you to Honolulu in time—it would be really close. It would be safer to book the next flight."

"When does that one leave?"

"Ten-thirty tonight."

"No!" I ran my hands through my curls—or tried to. I hadn't brushed them in so long my fingers hardly moved. "Mom," I begged, "I can't lose that much time!"

The front doorbell rang. We both ignored it.

"I don't see that you have much choice, Kali," my mother said quietly. "I'm sorry, but a cab from here would be way too expensive, and even if we reached your father at the restaurant and begged him to start out now, you'd still be cutting it close. Particularly when you can never tell about the traffic."

A shadow drifted through my mother and across the room, and I fought down an irrational urge to scream at her. She was a pretty young woman wearing a yellow peignoir, and she radiated romantic notions like living women smelled of perfume. She had amused me in the past, but now her presence was irritating in the extreme.

"Can't we try, mom?" I begged. "Please?"

The doorbell rang again.

A niggling memory shot through my flustered brain.

"What time is it?" I asked.

"Noon," my mother answered.

I flew into the hallway and swung open the door.

I had never been so simultaneously excited—and

painfully sorry—to see anyone in my entire life.

—ɯ—

We stopped for fast food in Haleiwa. It was not the lunch Matt had hoped for, but his determination not to show it tugged my heartstrings like lead.

"I'm really sorry about the change in plans," I said again, looking at my fries without appetite. "I feel terrible about asking you for a ride, but you have no idea how important—"

"Will you stop apologizing?" he said lightly, in between bites of the burger he balanced on his lap as he drove. "I was taking you to Honolulu anyway. I'm just sorry you're leaving."

"I'm not leaving forever," I said quickly. "I really love it here. I can't wait to get back."

He smiled. "Really?"

"Really," I said sincerely.

His brow creased slightly. "This friend of yours... you didn't mention him before."

My heartbeat quickened. I hated this. I had never intended to be dishonest with Matt about Zane. I had never thought Zane was alive.

"No," I said vaguely.

"Well," Matt asked simply, "Is he your boyfriend?"

An uncomfortable lump rose in my throat, and my stomach churned. I could not finish the fries in my lap if my life depended on it.

"No," I answered. The words were perfectly honest, even if I did stammer in saying them. "I would have told you if... I mean, when you and I went out, he and I were just friends."

I was splitting hairs on the timing and the verb tenses,

but I hoped he wouldn't notice. He had assumed that my "friend on the mainland" was someone from Cheyenne, and neither I nor my mother had corrected him. What else could he think, when the truth was too ridiculous for words? That just last night, I had *sort of* kissed this other guy, but that it didn't count, because I thought he was dead?

I could not tell if Matt was bothered by my verb tenses or not. He looked thoughtful for a moment, but made no comment. All he did was take another bite of burger.

I fidgeted in the seat. My cell phone was burning a hole in my pocket—I *had* to talk to Tara. I hadn't gotten a chance since Matt arrived, and every second counted. But how could I say what I needed to say in front of him?

Texting everything would take forever, but I had no choice. Once I got on the plane, I'd be out of touch for the rest of the day.

"Do you mind if I text someone?" I asked Matt, still feeling guilty every time I looked at him. "I don't know what hospital he's in yet—but I'm hoping my friend Tara can find out for me."

He shrugged. "Sure, go ahead."

My fingers flew across the keys.

> **NEED HELP FAST! Friend in hospital. Don't know where. Was in car accident recently. Name Zane Svenson.**

Mercifully, I had to wait only seconds.

> **Kylee told me. How recently? You have a state?**

I let out a long, relieved breath. God bless Tara. Not only was she at whiz at researching just about anything on the internet, but her father was an assistant police chief and her mother was a state trooper. The girl had connections.

She would find him. She *would*.

Even if it might be a little harder than she expected.

> Don't know how long. Location probably on interstate, somewhere between Hackensack NJ and Malibu CA. THANKS!!!

Less than a minute later, my phone rang. I threw a weak, apologetic look at Matt and picked it up.

"Hello?"

"Are you *insane*?" Tara's gruff alto bellowed. "Between *Hackensack* and *Malibu*? With no date?"

"I'm sorry, Tara," I said as softly as I could manage, knowing it was pointless. I couldn't possibly talk low enough for her to hear me without Matt overhearing also. "That's all I know."

"You must know something else!" she insisted. "Think hard. Anything. How old is he? What are his parents' names? What kind of car was he driving?"

I thought. "He's eighteen. His dad's last name was Svenson too—I don't know his first name. His mother was Alisha Bayne. She was an actress. But they're both dead now. I have no idea about the car. Does any of that help?"

There was a pause. I could hear the clicking of a keyboard in the background. "A famous actress? Like, a professional?"

"Yes. He said she was on a soap opera."

Matt cast a glance sideways and looked at me oddly.

What little lunch I had consumed curdled in my gut. Could this get any more awkward?

"Tara," I said desperately, "I don't even know if he's... I mean, I don't know his condition. I have to get there soon... it's important."

The keyboard clicking continued. Her voice softened. "I know that, Kal. I'll text you as soon as I have something."

My eyes grew moist again. I didn't think I had any moisture left. "Thank you."

We hung up.

Matt and I spoke very little on the rest of the journey. Whether he was trying to be sensitive to the fact that I was falling apart, or whether he just had no idea what to say to me, I wasn't sure.

I only knew that, when at last we pulled up at the airport and he lifted my suitcase wordlessly out of his trunk, I wanted to hug him.

So I did.

And more accursed tears started falling out of nowhere.

"You've been so great, Matt," I said genuinely, as soon as I could talk. "Tour guide, dance date... now chauffeur. I have no idea how to thank you."

He stood with his arms still around my waist, not quite willing to let me go.

"So don't," he said casually, his blue eyes twinkling again. "I've had fun, too, you know."

I swallowed. "I'm glad."

I was enjoying his strong arms around me—I couldn't deny it. But if I stood there, basking in his affectionate comfort for one more second, there wasn't a doubt in my mind that he would kiss me.

I couldn't do that.

Instead I stood on tiptoe, wrapped my arms around his neck, and hugged him tightly for one last second. Then I kissed him on the cheek and pulled away.

"I'll see you in June," I said unevenly, picking up the

handle of my bag and starting to step away. "And I expect
to hear that Frederick's water polo team totally destroyed
Saint Anthony's in the semifinals."

I looked over my shoulder and grinned at him. "Or I'm
not enrolling."

He grinned back broadly. He offered a crisp salute.
"Count on it."

—〰—

My phone buzzed with another text just as I sat down
at the gate. The flight was right on time.

**Is his real name Zachary?**

I bit my lip, even as my heartbeat quickened. How
could I forget to tell her that? My brain was mush. I would
have to try to sleep on the plane. I would never be able to
get where I needed to go if I didn't.

**Yes. Sorry. Zachary Bayne Svenson. Did you find
anything?**

I waited restlessly. The airport was crawling with
shadows, but the vast majority of them were in the wrong
places—too high, too low, moving through walls. That
always happened with remodeling.

The ringing of the phone startled me so much I nearly
dropped it.

"Yes? Tara?"

"I'm not there yet, Kali, but it's too much to text," she
responded, her tone all business. "It's a good thing his
mother was a celebrity, or I couldn't have found half of
this." She cleared her throat. "About his mother... do you
know how she died?"

I winced. The reports in the media of her last years were sure to be less than flattering. "I know she overdosed, yes."

"Okay," Tara said tentatively. "Unfortunately, that's also where Zane drops out of sight. Before that, I did find some stuff about him, from his first couple years in high school. Not much—either he wasn't into social networking or he kept it private, but I did find one picture of him—from the swim team. Damn, he's hot."

My chuckle was bittersweet. *Tell me about it.*

"But I can't find an address for him after his mother died. I can't find any hits on him after that."

"He went into foster care," I explained.

Tara was quiet a moment. "That explains it. But we should still be able to find him in the accident reports. The thing is, Kali, I need my mom for that, and I can't ask her for a couple hours yet. Not just anyone has the right kind of access; I think she does, but I'm not sure. Especially if it happened out of state. I was hoping there would be an online news story about the accident that listed his name, but I couldn't find one. Are you sure he was over eighteen when it happened?"

"Positive."

"Then if there was an article, it didn't identify him," she pronounced. "Probably because there was a delay in notifying next of kin."

Which of course there would have been. A long delay.

"I might be able to find it anyway if we had the general location," she continued. "Can't you ask whoever told you about the accident? And you must know the date. Was it yesterday? The day before?"

My shoulders sagged. I had been kidding myself. Even if I hadn't made that promise to Zane, there was no possible way I could get to him now without sacrificing my darkest secret. It was a miracle my mother had let me go with only the agreement of more explanation later; Tara would be even harder to put off. If I expected her to find out what hospital he was in, she would have to know—or would inevitably find out—the date of the crash. And she would know that Zane couldn't possibly have been with me in Oahu.

I faced the same problem with her as with my mother. If I freaked her out to the point where she really thought I was losing it, she would stop legitimately searching for Zane. I couldn't let that happen. For now, I had to avoid the whole truth... however I could.

"Listen, Tara," I said firmly. "I know that this won't make any sense to you, and I'm sorry. I can't explain until I get home. But the accident didn't happen yesterday. I'm thinking it happened about a week ago, but it could have been longer."

"A *week*—"

"I know Kylee told you I met him here," I insisted. "In a way I did. But the accident happened before I left Cheyenne, and... the person who told me about it is someone I can't contact anymore. They didn't give me a location. But they did describe the accident, a little bit..."

In halting phrases, I told her everything I could remember of Zane's description of the crash. She didn't utter a word, and finally I stopped talking and listened to the stony silence on the other end with a steadily increasing fear.

"Tara? Are you still there?"

"In theory," she said dryly. There was another long pause. "Kali, will you answer two questions for me? No, wait... make that three."

I swallowed. "I'll try."

"This guy is real, right? I mean, I can see online that he

exists, so I guess I can assume that—"

"He's real."

"And you have actually met him... at some point? You haven't gone loopy over a poster in some surfing magazine—"

"No, I swear. I..." My voice broke. "I know him really well."

"Are you in love with him?"

The question stopped my breath in its tracks. I started to think about it. Then I decided not to.

"Yes," I answered.

I heard nothing for a moment. Then Tara exhaled loudly. "Apparently, I am as insane as you are, Kali. I'll talk to my mother as soon as I can. Call me back when you get to Denver and I'll tell you what I know."

"It will be in the middle of—"

"Yeah, I know. You can wake me up. What else have I got to do? Sheesh."

I love you, too.

My eyes clouded over again just as the gate agent announced the flight was boarding. I mumbled some unintelligible, sob-choked words of gratitude, grabbed my bag and my ticket, and headed for the jetway.

# chapter twenty-four

I was out on the waves, floating on a surfboard. The sun was warm, and I wasn't scared of the water. I just couldn't remember how I had gotten here. The waves were tall, wide swells, but my board lifted me up and over them as if it were rocking a baby. Out to sea, a humpback emerged, twisting its massive frame in a half spin and splashing back down into the water. The beach was a long way away, but I could see that there were people on it, strolling and playing in the sand. Palm trees swayed in the breeze. Sharp green mountain peaks stood tall on the distant horizon.

I heard a noise near me on the ocean, and turned. It was the loud, obnoxious motor of a jet ski. I frowned and would have yelled for it to stay away, but I knew the driver couldn't hear me. He kept coming closer, spraying unnatural plumes of water to either side, oblivious to my proximity. He was within ten yards when he suddenly killed the engine and stared at me, his face shining with glee.

It was the old man from the convalescent home. He was still wearing his hospital gown, but the back was only half tied, and the wind whipped it up so that he mooned half the beach. He looked at me and cackled with laughter. "Are you still here?" he mocked. "You'll never get anywhere on that thing. I told you, honey, you're too damn slow. Sun's going down now. It'll be too late for him."

The man tossed his head in the direction of the beach, and my eyes followed with apprehension. The people on the beach had stopped moving. They were gathered in a circle, looking down at something on the ground. The warmth of the sun was gone. Both sky and water were gray. The winds picked up. I shivered.

"Just paddle, idiot!" the old man ordered. "It's the only shot you've got!" I looked back at him, and saw that he was no longer on a jet ski but was balanced precariously on a regular shortboard, which was cutting through the waves and out into open water propelled by no visible force. "Gonna die if you don't!" he shouted, his speed only increasing as he streaked out of sight.

I looked frantically back toward the beach. The crowd of people obligingly parted, leaving me a clear view of someone else in a hospital gown. It was Zane, pale and thin, lying flat on his back on the wet sand.

Motionless.

"No!" I paddled my arms in the water and kicked my legs, trying desperately to move the awkward board in the water. The waves should have helped me—they should have pushed me toward shore—but all they seemed to do was suck me backward. I flailed like a mad woman, but could get no closer. A white van drove toward the crowd on the beach; some medical types jumped out.

I ditched the unhelpful board and plunged headlong into the water. I could see fish swimming beneath me, and I wasn't afraid. I could swim as well as anyone. I freestyled like an Olympian, and the beach drew closer. A shark fin rose out of the water beside me, and I smacked at it and told it to go away. I was getting to the beach, dammit, and nothing was going to stop me.

My feet hit sand. I stood up. I started walking.

The men from the truck had reached Zane. They stretched out a white sheet. They pulled it over his head.

"NO!!!"

"Take it easy!" a man's voice beside me bellowed.

My eyes flew open.

I was on a plane.

"I'm sorry," I apologized, realizing that in jolting awake, I had inadvertently knocked the middle-seat man's laptop into the aisle-seat woman's lap. "I didn't... I'm sorry."

I curled back into a ball within my window-seat sanctuary and tried to calm my pounding heart. The nightmare shouldn't be surprising. It was more surprising that I had slept at all, even given the antihistamine I had popped upon boarding seven hours ago. But I was glad that I did. I would need to be alert—and stay alert—very soon.

The pilot announced our descent into Denver, and my legs itched to move, to run. I knew the dream meant nothing. I might be "gifted" at seeing dead people, but my dreams had never been prophetic.

Regardless, the closing image replayed itself mercilessly before my eyes.

It'll be too late for him.

*No,* I fought back stubbornly. It will *not.*

The plane landed in the dead of night with stray snowflakes melting against the windows, and before the flight attendant could finish her announcement about electronic devices I had Tara on the other end of the line. "Did you find him?" I begged.

I had no plan. I knew that I needed to get back to Cheyenne, to the family's spare car, and to the cash I had accumulated from years of babysitting and two summers working the snack shack at the community pool. If Zane were anywhere within a three-state radius of Wyoming I would drive until I found him. But if he were still out East...

"I have some good news, Kali," Tara said smoothly.

My heart filled near to bursting. "Is he alive?"

"I…" Her pause was maddening. "I can't tell you that for sure. I'm sorry. But I don't know otherwise, either. My mother found an accident report, and it fits your description exactly."

I couldn't breathe.

"It's good news," she repeated mercifully. "He's not that far. The accident happened on Interstate 80, smack dab in the middle of Nebraska. Near a town called Lexington. I don't have confirmation on the hospital, but my mother says he'd almost certainly be taken to the ER in Kearney. That's the nearest level II trauma center."

I let out my breath with a whoosh. My heart pounded against my ribs. "Interstate 80?" I repeated, hardly able to believe what was—for once—an amazing stroke of good luck. "In Nebraska? That shouldn't take—"

"It's about a five hour drive from Cheyenne," Tara interrupted. "You shouldn't have any problem finding the place. Just get off at the Kearney exit and head into town. The hospital's only, like, two blocks off the main drag— I'm sure there'll be signs to follow. But Kali, I have to tell you…"

I couldn't take anymore. I really couldn't.

Tara drew in a breath. "The accident happened over a week ago. And it was really bad. When he swerved to miss the other car he crashed into one the concrete supports for the overpass. His car was totaled. And the report said… well, it said that his condition was critical."

That means nothing, I told myself. You knew that.

"Kali," she continued, "I wish I could go with you, but I can't. Both my parents are working and I'm on demon watch. Sorry."

A reluctant smile turned up the corners of my mouth. Tara was the second oldest of six kids, and the only girl. Her little brothers deserved their nickname.

"You've done more than enough," I answered, gathering my stuff. In another century, the people in front of me would finish getting their infernal baggage from the overhead bins and I could get out of this plane and on my way.

On my way to Zane.

The nightmare image of the rising sheet forced its way into my brain again, but I fought it back with a vengeance.

"I'll make it just fine, Tara," I answered.

—⟞⟝—

"Kali? Are you awake?"

For the life of me, I didn't know the answer.

"I think so," I mumbled.

"I think not very," Kylee said with a chuckle. "That's okay. You needed it. You couldn't have gotten much quality sleep on the plane. And were you really up most of the night before, too?"

I thought about it a moment. I vaguely remembered explaining that to Kylee before asking permission to snooze. The truth was, I had hardly slept at all in two days, and wouldn't be sleeping now if I didn't have important driving to do. Hard as it was to still my tortured mind, I had forced myself to give in to the fatigue as soon as I had slipped into Kylee's car and buckled my seat belt. I figured even an hour would refresh me, and it was a two-hour drive back to Cheyenne.

I had been right. I sat up, and the cobwebs scattered instantly. We were nearing home.

Just five more hours, Zane. I thought helplessly. Please hang on.

"Are you sure you're going to be okay to drive?" Kylee asked. "If you can wait till midmorning, I can go with you.

Then you could get a little more sleep—"

"I can't wait, Kylee," I said brusquely. "I couldn't sleep any more now if I had to. I'm going home just long enough to have a two-minute shower, grab my money and a sandwich, and start on the first of about a million cups of coffee."

"Since when do you drink coffee?"

"Since now."

Kylee turned off onto the road that led to my house, and I realized I was pressing my feet against the floorboard, willing us on.

"Kali?" she asked seriously.

I turned my head to look at her. Kylee was hardly ever serious about anything. Such was her reputation—cheery, fun, spontaneous. She was slightly on the plump side, with a smile that lit up a room and dark eyes that sparkled with mischievous humor. People who saw her with her parents often assumed she was a Chinese adoptee, but neither was true. Kylee lived with her biological mother and stepfather; her birth father was Vietnamese. He was also—to put it mildly—a total jerk, having abandoned Kylee's mother when she was pregnant. But Kylee had always been very close to her Vietnamese-American grandparents, who—despite having long ago washed their hands of their self-absorbed son—adored both their granddaughter and her mother.

"What?" I asked, alarmed by her tone.

"This guy you're going to see… is he really the surfer you met on the beach?"

The wheels in my brain chugged slowly, painfully. I could no longer keep track of whom I had told what—and what part of the truth made sense with it.

"Yes," I answered tiredly. "But I can't explain now. I will later, though. I promise. To you and Tara." I looked at her beseechingly. "But nobody else, okay? I'm afraid it's going to be... really hard for you to understand."

To my surprise, Kylee smiled at me—an odd, crooked little smile. Her car rounded a bend and I could see my house in the glow of the streetlights ahead.

I was home.

"You might be surprised about that," she returned.

—m—

I had been driving for two hours already before the sun rose.

The faint orange light that broke over the horizon ahead of me could be beautiful or eerie, depending on one's perspective. I had not seen a whole lot of sunrises in my life, until I went to Oahu and the time change made me think dawn happened in the middle of the morning. Those sunrises had been spectacular. Full of color, warmth, and promise.

This one, stretching out over the rolling plains of western Nebraska, held more promise than I could ever have imagined... but it also held more anxiety. Every minute that ticked away was a minute I had lost forever.

I told you, honey, you're too damn slow.

I gritted my teeth and concentrated on my driving. I was going as fast as I could—I would not be stupid enough to waste forty-five minutes getting stopped for a ticket. Or worse—to cause another accident. Neither would help Zane.

The sky continued to brighten; the largely barren landscape came to life. I was thankful for the relatively sparse population. Ordinarily I would see few shadows in a place like this, but lately I'd been seeing ten times as many shadows as usual, and the barren fields of Nebraska proved no different. Native Americans, pioneers, farmers, bikers, rednecks... all were represented. All were ignored.

The lingering specter of the old man, however, I could not get out of my mind. He and Zane had looked and acted so much alike... never mind that the old man seemed to know what was happening to him, while Zane did not. If Zane could have seen his physical body, wouldn't he, too, have understood?

What troubled me far more was what had happened to Zane after I met him.

My mind kept coming back to the question; my heart kept shoving it away. Yes, Zane had grown less solid every day that we had spent together. Yes, his spirit had ultimately ceased to be visible. But I had no way of knowing what that meant. I could not and would not assume the worst.

I just had to get to him. Period.

I cast a glance at the speedometer, groaned with frustration, and eased up on the accelerator. I had to be more careful, or I *would* get a ticket.

The sun rose rapidly in the sky; the miles ground away slowly beneath my wheels. I turned on the radio to soothe my mind with other thoughts.

It was pointless.

My brain replayed every moment Zane and I had spent together, analyzing everything he had said and wondering about what he hadn't. He hadn't wanted to go back to the past, but he had never wanted to die, either. All he had wanted was a second chance.

And he had *had* it.

Did he still?

I was speeding again. I took another gulp of the vile energy drink I'd picked up at the gas station and breathed deeply. My dad had to be the only person in Wyoming who would buy a used car without cruise control. Probably because he himself speeded like a maniac whenever he could get away with it.

The hours ticked by with excruciating slowness. I was so focused on measuring the miles until Kearney that the significance of Lexington didn't register until I found myself upon it.

The exit loomed ahead; I could see the overpass at the interchange.

I found myself slowing the car. A cold chill coursed through my veins.

It had happened here.

To other eyes, the scene ahead was unremarkable. Solid walls of concrete patterned with giant hexagonal shapes rose up on either side of the road, while the bridge above cast a broad shadow over the otherwise sunwashed interstate. To most travelers the overpass meant no more than a second's worth of relative darkness. To me, it seemed the center of the earth. The sunless space seemed ominous; uncanny. I allowed my car to drift through even as my brain screamed for release—the concrete walls seemed clammy and suffocatingly close; the darkness absolute. The concrete supports in the center of the overpass were not simple pillars, but massive gothic arches, and for all the protection the metal guard rails offered a skidding car, they might as well be solid walls of stone.

Bile rose in my throat as I glanced across the median and glimpsed what was left of the westbound guardrail: strips of mangled iron.

A tortured cry escaped my lips. My foot hit the accelerator, heedless of the consequences.

"He did *not* die!" I shouted out loud, needing to hear the words as much as say them. "He wanted to live, and he fought it, and he *won!*"

My eyes misted, but with a mighty effort I forced the tears back. Under no circumstances could I fall apart now. I had come too far; I was too close.

Zane's fading away from me in Oahu did *not* mean he was dying. It did not have to mean anything. How could it, when in so many ways, he had been coming more alive every day? We had so little time together, and yet he had come to know me so well... better than friends I'd had for years. He could look at me and guess what I was feeling— he could read my every mood. He asked me about myself; he was in interested in me, for me.

And what other option did he have, exactly?

I bit my already sore lip. The realization was not a new one, but I hardly wished to dwell on it now. I had known all along that Zane's appearing to care for me when I was, in absolute fact, the *only* woman in his world was hardly a fair test of his attraction. If we had met under different circumstances, would he still feel the same? Among a crowd of other admirers on a level playing field... would he ever even have noticed me?

Don't ever doubt it, Kali.

His words seared forward in my mind with the force of a freight train, and the tears I'd been fighting spilled over.

It didn't matter.

All that mattered was my getting to him.

The stretch of road ahead seemed endless, even as the numbers continued to chip away. Thirty miles to Kearney. Twenty miles. Ten. Five.

Exit 272.

I was here.

I turned off and headed north into town, staying on the main drag, as Tara had instructed. The town was classic heartland generica—perfectly flat, laid out in a grid, and chock full of franchises. But I could see no signs for a hospital. Six billion stoplights choked the road, and every red made me pound the steering wheel in frustration. The town was a little more sprawling than I had hoped, and when it seemed I had been starting and stopping forever, I tried desperately to remember Tara's directions. She had said it was only a couple blocks from the main road, and I hadn't turned off...

At long last, I saw one. A blue sign with a big fat H on it. It was one of the most beautiful sights I had ever seen—and the arrow pointed straight ahead.

Within five more minutes, I was in the parking lot. Twenty seconds after that, I was standing at the information desk.

"Can I help you?" greeted a short, stout woman of late middle age.

"Yes," I said, gulping air into my oxygen-starved lungs. "I'm here to see a patient. He was in a car accident. Zane—I mean Zachary—Svenson."

The woman made no response, but set herself to typing on a keyboard, lifting her nose to train her bifocals to the appropriate spot on the monitor. The hospital lobby was busy, and probably noisy, but all I could hear was the clicking of her keys and the heavy whooshing of my own labored breaths.

"Birthdate?" she said mechanically.

I swallowed. "I don't know the exact day. He just turned eighteen recently."

The woman clicked more keys. She stopped for a while and stared at a screen. Then she clicked some more.

I braced myself to keep from exploding.

She stared at another screen. She clicked a little more. Then she turned away from the monitor and faced me. "I'm sorry," she said brusquely. "But I can't give you any information about that patient. He's no longer in our computer."

My breath stopped. Everything about me stopped. My body went cold. My feet froze into the floor tiles. The lobby swam.

I don't know how long it took me to respond. But my stupor did not go unnoticed.

"What do you mean, 'not in your computer?'" I said at last, my voice so low it hardly reached my own ears. "He was here; I know he was. He obviously *is* in your computer. *What happened to him?!*"

The woman stood up from the stool on which she'd been sitting. The action made little difference to her height, but I could tell from her posture that she feared I would collapse before her eyes. Her countenance softened, her voice became mild.

"All I can tell you is that the patient is no longer registered in this hospital," she said evenly. "Because of privacy laws, I can't give out any more information than that. Are you a relative?"

I shook my head weakly, but I had a feeling she knew the answer even as she asked.

"I'm sorry, honey," she repeated. "I really can't help you."

No more information?

No. Freakin'. Way.

I looked back into the woman's small, bluish-gray eyes. She might be a lover of rules, but she was not inhuman. And I would not give up now. I would *not*.

"Marsha," I said softly, reading her nametag, "My name is Kali. I have just spent seven hours on a plane flying over the Pacific Ocean from Oahu, and another seven hours in cars driving across three states, to reach 'the patient' before he dies thinking that no one on the entire planet gives a damn. He was in a horrific accident, he was brought here in critical condition, both his parents are dead and he doesn't have a single living family member. I am the only friend of his on the face of this earth that even knows he's here—and I am *going* to do absolutely everything in my power to make sure that he does *not* die alone. Do you understand me?"

The woman blinked. Patches of red had risen in her cheeks. Her eyes were wide. I was getting to her. "It's not my decision. The privacy laws—"

"What kind of privacy law protects a patient from being cared for by somebody who actually loves him?" I argued, my voice choking up. "Can't you at *least* tell me if he's still alive?"

The woman stared at me.

I stared back. My cheeks were wet again. My strangled voice could choke out no more.

I could see the scene on the beach again, plain as day. The scene in my nightmare.

The sheet was lifting.

It was covering Zane's chin, his cheeks, his eyes...

"Telling you anything about a particular patient could cost me my job," Marsha's voice continued from somewhere far away. My eyes were closed. My body swayed.

"But I can tell you this," she continued, her voice suddenly sharper.

My heart thudded. I concentrated on staying upright.

"When patients are medically stable, but in a coma, they're often transferred to long-term care facilities. There's one not far from here, in fact. Just four blocks west, on Thirty-First and Fourth."

My eyes wrenched open. The meaning of her words sank slowly in. When the process was complete, it was all I could do not to vault over the desktop and kiss her.

Zane *was* still alive.

He really was.

He was alive!

I did vault over the desk and kiss her. It couldn't be helped, really. One has to do what one has to do.

I whirled away toward the door, leaving behind me in the lobby a trail of far-flung tears, a few confused bystanders, and one very red-faced information desk clerk.

Zane was in a coma, but he was alive.

Absolutely nothing could keep me from him now.

# chapter twenty-five

"You're here for Zachary?" the tall, buxom nurse loitering in the front lobby interrupted as soon as she heard my words to the receptionist. "Seriously? Well, it's about damn time. That boy needs some visitors!"

My heart nearly leapt from my chest.

"Can I send her on back then?" the receptionist asked timidly. "I know the doctor's supposed to be in this morning—"

"Bah!" The nurse waved a hand dismissively. "Doc'll get here when he gets here. He'll be happy to see her, too. Said all along that boy needed somebody to talk to him, and here she is!"

The woman's broad mouth smiled, revealing surprisingly white teeth. She was an immense figure, nearly six feet of mostly muscle, and her deep voice boomed like a cannon. In another life, she could have been a drill sergeant. But perhaps not a very effective one; her eyes were open windows to what I could see was an exceptionally warm heart.

"Can I... see him now?" I asked, hardly daring to believe that no more obstacles stood in my way.

"Right now," the nurse agreed cheerfully, turning to lead me down a blue-paneled corridor. I noticed that she walked with a limp. "No offense, honey," she chatted, "but you look like you walked through fire to get here. Where'd you come from, anyway?"

"Oahu," I mumbled, casting glances into the rooms left and right along the hallway. A prickle of fear coursed painfully up my spine. This was not a rehab hospital, much less assisted living. The patients here were elderly, bedridden, frail. The kind of patients no one expected to check out again.

Zane couldn't be here, with them. He just couldn't. Unless...

It didn't matter. It didn't matter what shape his body was in.

He was alive.

"*Oahu?!*" my escort exclaimed. "You're kidding. When did you get here?"

"I came straight from the airport," I answered. As much as I appreciated the woman's optimistic gaiety, my own anxiety continued to climb. Now that I was so close, at last... I was afraid.

"How is he?" I asked as we walked. "In a coma, still?"

The nurse nodded solemnly. "Yep. Still in a coma. But it's a miracle he's alive at all—you know that?"

I nodded.

You don't know the half of it.

"He's been through hell and back—that boy. Crash like that could have killed a buffalo. But he hung in there. Only problem now is bringing him back." She stopped at a half-closed door, then turned and looked at me. "You can ask the doc more about his condition when he gets here. In the meantime, don't be afraid to talk to the boy out loud, even if you feel like an idiot. It's good therapy."

The nurse pushed the door the rest of the way open. Then she stood back and waved me in.

My heart beat violently against my rib cage.

My feet wouldn't move.

I called up a vision to memory—a vision of Zane on his beloved waves, his curls wet, his eyes bright, his suntanned face lit up with joy.

I inhaled a sharp breath and stepped forward.

Only one of the two beds was occupied. On it lay a

pale figure, stiff and still. He was covered to the neck with sheets and a blanket. One arm rested outside the linens, the wrist hosting an IV tube attached to a pole.

I took a step closer.

Scruffy curls spread out over the thin pillow. The face within them was wan, the chin and neck covered with blondish stubble. The eyes were closed.

The room around me spun.

It was Zane.

"Yo there, Zachary!" the nurse boomed, stepping in around me and leaning down to pinch a toe through the covers. "Got a little surprise for you. And she's a looker, too," she added with a wink.

"Zane," I corrected automatically, my voice ragged.

"What'd you say?"

I cleared my throat. "His name is Zane. That's what he goes by."

The nurse smiled. "Well, hell! No wonder he's been ignoring us. Ha!" She turned towards the door to leave. "You just keep talking honey. Doc'll be in soon."

She walked out and shut the door behind her.

We were alone.

My eyes remained riveted on the figure in the bed. I couldn't seem to move.

Staring at the blankets that covered his chest, I held my breath, waiting for the movement that would confirm his own.

The blankets lifted slightly, then fell.

A rush of heat spurred my frozen limbs to motion; tears welled up behind my eyes. I crossed the distance to the bed in a heartbeat. "Zane," I said unevenly. "It's Kali. I'm here now. I found you."

I leaned in closer, reached out a trembling hand.

"You *didn't* die, Zane," I sputtered. "You wanted to

live, and you *did*. You have a second chance!" My vision blurred with moisture. He looked so weak, so fragile. So terribly, terribly... tenuous.

My fingers were inches from his, and I ached to touch him. My body trembled with the need—to actually *feel* him, warm and solid. And yet I was terrified. Terrified that if I asked for too much, if I pushed for one more miracle, he would simply crumple away and disappear. His being alive at all was too fantastic to be true; my finding him and reaching him in this bed in this hospital in the middle of this vast stretch of country was too much for anyone to ask for.

Surely, at any moment, I would wake up alone again.

I blinked.

He was still there.

I stretched out my fingers. Slowly, shakily.

Their tips grazed the back of his hand.

My breath halted again. He was solid. He was warm.

He was real.

Sheer joy flooded through me, and with a strangled sob, I reached out and folded the limp, unresisting hand into both of mine. I held it tightly for a minute, reveling in its solidness, then slipped my fingers forward to his wrist.

He had a pulse.

My knees caved in on me, and I dropped down on the edge of the mattress. I raised his hand unashamedly to my face, feeling the warmth of his beautiful skin against my cheek, my lips. My tears dripped over both of us.

"It's going to be okay, Zane," I promised, unable to keep from smiling, even as I looked into eyes that were closed and unseeing. "It's all real, believe it or not. And I'm here now. You're *not* alone."

"I sure am glad to hear that!" a man's voice rang out from the doorway. I glanced back—briefly—to acknowledge the arrival of the physician.

The doctor stepped to the opposite side of the bed, laid a chart down on the end table, and extended a hand to me. "Phil Caldwell," he introduced.

I withdrew one hand reluctantly from Zane's. The doctor's shake was so hearty it was painful. "Kali Thompson," I returned.

"Can't tell you how glad I am to see you," he continued, performing a cursory examination of Zane as he talked. He felt the patient's pulse, his neck, checked his feet. "I have a feeling you're exactly what our boy here needs."

I swallowed. "Really?"

"Absolutely. Coma patients hear and take in a lot more than people used to think. He may not look responsive, but trust me—there's a part of him that knows exactly what's going on."

The doctor lifted one of Zane's eyelids with a thumb and shone in a penlight. I rose slightly, eager for any glimpse of the twinkle that meant so much to me—but it was not to be. The exquisite sea-green eye was perfectly, frighteningly blank.

I looked up at the doctor, my heart pounding again. "What makes you so sure?"

He studied me a moment, then pocketed his instrument and stood with hands folded. "You know about the accident?" he asked mildly.

I nodded. "A little. I know he swerved to miss another car and"—my voice wavered at the sudden, ghastly memory of the mangled guard rail—"his car crashed into the concrete."

"That's the nuts and bolts of it," he agreed. "It wasn't his fault, that's for sure. The other car was driven by an 85-year-old woman with early-stage dementia whose son had taken away her car keys three times already. She drove down the entrance ramp to I-80, took a left, and headed East straight into oncoming traffic."

I gulped. "Was she... I mean, did he hit her?"

The doctor smiled crookedly. He cocked his head in the direction of a small flower arrangement which sat near the window. "No, he didn't. Though the poor woman feels so guilty I imagine she wishes he had. She sent those flowers herself. She's been calling almost every day to check up on him."

*At least someone has*, I thought. But I was glad the woman was all right. Zane had worried about her; he would be happy to hear it.

I would be happy to tell him.

"What kind of injuries—" I asked haltingly, unable to talk coherently, for all my racing thoughts. "I mean, besides the coma, does he have... broken bones? "

"Surprisingly few, for a crash so violent," the doctor answered. "What could have proved fatal—and would have, in nearly anybody else—were his internal injuries. He lost a tremendous amount of blood at the scene, before he could be removed from the car."

I winced. Unwelcome images shot through my mind, an involuntary moan escaped my lips. I squeezed the limp hand firmly in mine.

"He suffered head injuries as well," the doctor continued, "which is why none us were surprised by the coma—at least at first."

The doctor cleared his throat. "The truth is, Miss Thompson, that almost no one on that trauma team expected this young man to come out of the ER alive. The fact that he kept on breathing... well... it says a lot about him."

I allowed myself a smile. Anyone could tell how much

Zane loved life. I had always believed that. No matter how bad things got.

"But what happened next was a bit of mystery," the doctor added, invading my reverie.

I looked up at him questioningly.

"Once he survived the initial assault, all that remained was to keep on healing," the doctor explained. "All signs were that his body was doing great. But when he should have regained consciousness, he didn't, and none of us could figure out why. This boy fought like a tiger to live— but then he wouldn't come back to us."

The doctor sighed. "Some of my colleagues would laugh at me for saying this, but I don't believe his failure to thrive had anything to do with our medicine—or lack thereof. Never in my life have I dealt with a patient this young who didn't have a single person at his bedside. We found out he had no family, but still, a kid like this—I figured he had to have friends. There had to be somebody who cared about him. But we couldn't find a soul. And I think that matters.

"So I had the staff talk to him. Put it in the orders and everything. I wanted them to encourage him, tell him he was missed and wanted, urge him to wake up."

The doctor chuckled a little. "Of course, I found out just now we were all calling him by the wrong name, weren't we? I'm sure that didn't help. But maybe it wouldn't have mattered anyway. What patients who survive coma tell us is that what did matter was their loved ones. They hear their voices; they know they're there. They feel loved, and it gives them something to live for."

A strangled sob rose in my throat. *I'm so sorry, Zane,* I pleaded, clutching his hand tighter still. *I didn't know...*

"At the worst of it, his brain activity was nearly stagnant," the doctor continued, leaning over to extract a tissue from the bedside, then extending it to me. "He just wasn't with us at all, and I was beginning to believe he didn't want to be. But then something happened."

I blew my nose. The doctor's tone had changed. "What happened?" I asked.

He shrugged. "I haven't the faintest idea. We weren't doing a thing differently on our end. He got moved to long-term, but his treatment was the same. He still didn't have a single visitor. But the nurses thought they saw something. They couldn't quantify it—maybe his color was a little better, or his hands felt warmer. But they seemed sure he was improving, and so yesterday I ran some more tests. Sure enough, they were right. Over just the past couple days, his brain activity's got back to near normal. About as near to normal as you can get and still be in a coma. Which I'm not entirely sure he still is."

My heart began to race again. "The last... few days?" I repeated.

The days when he was fading...

The doctor nodded. "Yesterday seemed to be the turning point. I've been expecting those green eyes of his to pop open any minute ever since. And now that you're here, holding his hand, looking at him like that"—he smiled at me broadly—"I believe I'd put money on it."

I stared at the still face on the pillow. I moved my hand to feel his pulse again.

He was coming back. All the time he had been fading away from me in Oahu, all the time that both of us had thought he was dying... he was actually growing stronger. His memories were reconnecting him—the pull he had felt was his own body, calling his spirit back into itself, trying to be whole again.

Of course.

The day I had met Zane on the beach, when he had

seemed so solid—it was *then* that he was closest to death. Just like the old man, who I was sure now would get exactly what he wanted—and might have already.

"I'll leave the two of you alone, Miss Thompson," the doctor said gently, retrieving his chart and turning away towards the door. I made no effort to hide my steadily dripping tears; he made no effort to call attention to them. "I'll tell the nurses to let you stay as long as you like."

Once his words sunk into my already overflowing mind, I opened my mouth to thank him. But he was gone.

I touched Zane's hand once more to my cheek. My other hand stretched out to his face, brushing a curl from his forehead, lightly tracing the strong curve of his cheekbone, his jaw.

I wanted desperately to kiss him. But the Sleeping Beauty imagery was just too much. Besides which, it seemed there was something vaguely wrong in taking liberties with an unconscious person.

I contented myself with a kiss on his hand.

I let go of him just long enough to pull up a chair, then sat where I could lean my head and shoulders on the mattress beside him, his hand cradled snug against my cheek.

"I want you to wake up, Zane," I ordered, even as the relatively comfortable position, combined with the overwhelming emotional relief—and unmitigated joy—I now felt to the tips of my toes made my own eyelids wonderfully, contentedly heavy. "You've been playing around in your precious waves long enough, you hear me? It's time to come back to the rest of us mortals. All those things you *think* you did? Surfing the pipe, jumping off airplanes, heck—even managing that arabesque on a shortboard—well, guess what, my friend? They weren't real. And if you want to do them for real, you have to get your act together. Now. You've got to go that last nine yards. You've got to come back to me."

I sniffled a little more. Then I laughed. "In fact, you *have* to come back to me, because I need you to teach me how to swim. You can fulfill that promise now, you know—and I'm holding you to it. In fact, I'm making you teach me how to *surf*."

I cuddled farther into his side; my words became stream of consciousness. I went over every day we'd spent in Oahu, reminding him of the fun we'd had, laughing at the antics he'd been so proud of. *A New Jersey boy!* I thought with near hysterical giggles. Had he ever even surfed a wave more than waist high?

I told him about my journey back—about the old man, my mother, and Tara and Kylee. I told him how much it meant to me that he'd cared enough to extract the promise—a promise I still intended to keep.

I told him everything I could possibly think of to tell him.

I even, I'm pretty sure, told him that I loved him.

Then I fell asleep.

# chapter twenty-six

I was vaguely aware that my back hurt. But I didn't particularly care. I knew that I was warm and safe, and that something fantastic had happened. Both the soul-wrenching sadness and the sickening fear that had weighed so heavily upon me were gone now—lifted, unshackled, flung to the winds. I toyed with the idea that I was dreaming, but my heart rejected that. Repeatedly. The warm, solid hand that I held against my cheek proved it, and I felt that hand again, for reassurance, every time my wandering, drifting brain tried to doubt.

He is too real. See? He's right here.

The cycle repeated itself, endlessly, for however long I dozed. I had no concept of the time. Time had ceased to have any meaning long ago, high over the waves of the Pacific.

What woke me was the feather touch on my hair.

My eyes opened. I pressed Zane's hand to my cheek for the three-thousandth time. *Still there. Good.*

I started to drift away again. I felt the sensation once more. It was as if someone was lightly stroking the top of my head.

I thought about that for a moment. Then I rose from the mattress with a jerk.

Zane's eyes were wide open. He was looking at me.

"Sorry," he tried to say, his voice gravelly with disuse. "Didn't mean to scare you."

Hoarse or not, it was the most wonderful sound I'd ever heard.

"You can go back to sleep," he insisted. "Don't let me stop you."

"Zane," I whispered, my own voice far from steady. "You're awake."

He looked at me for a moment, his gaze oddly studious. I found myself mildly disturbed. Something was... not quite right.

"I've been awake," he answered.

His gaze was piercing; his brow knitted into a frown.

I felt a sudden bolt of terror.

"Who are you?" he asked.

The terror turned to paralysis. I could see it in his eyes; had seen it from the beginning.

He didn't remember.

"Don't get upset," he said with an effort, trying to effect the same gentle, husky tone that never failed to weaken my knees. "I'm a little fuzzy in the head, that's all. I'm sure it'll come back to me. What's your name?"

I wasn't sure that I could speak. A part of me wanted to break down, right here, right now, pull out every hair from my head, and scream. *He didn't know me.* I had worried whether he truly cared or not... now I was no better than a stranger. He had come back—but not to me. *He didn't know me at all.*

"Kali," I squeaked, my voice nearly as raspy as his as I mechanically spelled it out for him.

"That's a beautiful name," he responded, smiling. "It sounds... Hawaiian."

His words filtered through my anguished brain, bringing with them a sudden, warm blast of sunshine.

Déjà vu, anyone?

My frozen heart started to beat again. I felt myself smiling back.

It was all right. Really, it was. He might have a bit of amnesia, but he was *alive*. Who was I to complain if he had not come back completely unscathed? He had survived;

his physical wounds would heal. That miracle alone was enough. He was still the same Zane. He would always be the same Zane.

Whether or not he was mine.

I realized, with sudden embarrassment, that I still held his hand captive in my own. Flustered, I returned it to his chest and released him.

To my surprise, he lifted it—albeit unsteadily—to my face, and brushed a stray shock of curls over my shoulder.

Bittersweet memory threatened to crush me.

He could do it, now. He had tried so many times—

"I'm sorry, Kali," he said slowly, arduously, turning the full force of his liquid eyes onto mine. "You do seem familiar. I just don't remember why."

"It's okay," I said immediately, my hopes brightening a bit.

"Why can't you swim?" he asked.

I blinked at him stupidly.

"Before you fell asleep," he explained, his voice still a croak. "You said I promised to teach you. Why didn't you ever learn?"

I put a hand to my mouth, stifling the half laugh, half cry that erupted from inside me.

He was the same Zane.

The same.

"You heard all that?" I stammered, disbelieving. "But I went on forever... and you didn't even know who I was!"

He grinned at me. "I had no idea what you were talking about, true," he interrupted. "But it sounded like fun."

In the depths of his eyes, I saw the twinkle. That same, indefinable spark of life-loving, carefree good nature that had made me love a dead guy so much it hurt.

With an effort, he collected both my hands into his own. He held them, somewhat awkwardly, as his green eyes looked questioningly into mine.

"Do-over?"

# author's note

*Wraith* is my first YA novel. If enough people enjoy it, I would love to follow it up with a sequel, so if you'd like to see another, please recommend it to your friends! I'd also love to have you visit my Wraith Facebook page (www.Facebook.com/EdieClaire/Wraith), where you can check out my pics of Kali's Oahu and tell me what you'd like to see happen in the next book!

In the meantime, you might also enjoy my classic romantic suspense novels: *Long Time Coming* (also a ghost story, about a girl who dies in a tragic car accident shortly after her senior prom), *Meant To Be* (about an adoptee rediscovering memories of her lost childhood), and *Borrowed Time* (wherein a woman is haunted by memories of what she did one horrific night when she was seventeen). If you like your mystery with a touch of humor, check out the Leigh Koslow mysteries, a series of six books beginning with *Never Buried*.

To find out more about my books, including my comedic stage plays for youth and adults, please visit my author website (www.edieclaire.com) or send me an email (edieclaire@juno.com). If you'd like to keep up with what I'm writing now and be the first to know when a sequel to *Wraith* is released, you can sign up for my newsletter on the site.

Thanks so much for reading!

*Edie*

# BOOKS & PLAYS BY EDIE CLAIRE

**Classic Romantic Suspense**

*Long Time Coming*

*Meant To Be*

*Borrowed Time*

**Leigh Koslow Mysteries**

*Never Buried*

*Never Sorry*

*Never Preach Past Noon*

*Never Kissed Goodnight*

*Never Tease a Siamese*

*Never Con a Corgi*

**Comedic Stage Plays**

*Scary Drama I*

*See You in Bells*

**YA Romance**

*Wraith*

4546594R00166

Printed in Great Britain
by Amazon.co.uk, Ltd.,
Marston Gate.